THE UNDOING

PART 1 OF THE UNDOING TRILOGY

By Desserae K Shepston

ISBN: 9781798111307

THE UNDOING

Copyright © Desserae K Shepston 2019

All rights reserved. No part of this publication may be reproduced in whole or in part, stored in a retrieval system, or transmitted, in any form or by any means, electronic, mechanical, photocopying, recording, or otherwise, without prior written permission from the author.

Printed in the USA. First printing 2019

For the next generations, whose hopes and ingenuity have the power to create a better world.

PROLOGUE

The white granite tower rose above her head hundreds of feet. Rebecca fought back the familiar dizziness and queasy sensation that overtook her any time she confronted high places. It didn't matter that she was on the bottom, looking up, and not on top, looking down. It was simply the idea of heights. The knowledge of the danger was enough to send her heart racing. Jonathan would not be afraid. He was never afraid of anything. He loved high places; he would head off at every opportunity to go climbing. If he were here, he would gently chide her, and then encourage her to overcome that voice telling her she couldn't. Jonathan would tell her she could. He would have her back. Literally. How many times did he try to talk her into going climbing with him? How many times did he try to convince her that he'd be right there with her, hand on her back if necessary, climbing a parallel route on the training wall. But she couldn't do it. She could face just about anything. But not that. If only he was here. If only she had taken him up on his offer. Now it was too late.

Shaking herself to shrug off those thoughts, she steeled herself against what she needed to do. It was up to her now. Jonathan was not here. She could hear his voice inside her head telling her she did not need him to do this. She was capable on her own. But he would be there, even if she couldn't see him, making sure she was alright. Just in case. Rebecca understood her strengths. Most things she had faced in life didn't really scare her that much. This fear of heights, however, had been with her for as long as she could remember. It had prevented her from venturing out with her friends when they all started learning how to climb, first on the nearby training wall, and then in the mountains at the edge of Quadrant 1. It kept her solidly on the ground or on the back of a horse. She was good there. Put a hiking trail in front of her, and she could go all day. As long as she stayed in the forest or far from any edges. She and Cedar could fly, without ever leaving the ground. There was nothing more freeing to Rebecca than to be sitting astride Cedar, hugging close to her neck, as Cedar let loose and raced across an open meadow. Rebecca wasn't afraid of much. As long as it did not involve heights. Even so, she had always counted on Jonathan. She had always taken for granted that he would look after her, even when she didn't need him to. But, now, he wasn't here, and it was up to her to get to the bottom of what was happening within her city, Montrose.

Tears had somehow slipped down her cheeks without her knowledge. She swiped the back of her hand across her face, gave a little laugh, and reached for that first rock hold above her head. She pulled herself up, her feet, one at a time, leaving the safety of the solid earth below.

****

It was hard to believe just a few months ago life had been normal. Less than a year ago, Rebecca was preparing to leave middle school behind, and Jonathan was getting ready to enter his final year of high school. They were three years apart and he was her rock. Her sometimes unwelcome protector. He always had been. From the time she was born, her older brother had looked after her, taking it upon himself to watch over her as she grew up. They were to have one year in high school together before he left for university. He had already been spending his spare time researching distant schools in faraway places. Even some as far away as Region 6. Rebecca did not understand why he couldn't stick around in Region 3.

Jonathan had big goals. He wanted to be a member of Council, to go higher up in government than their parents, even though that was a lofty goal, since future options were dictated by birth and what your parents' work assignments were. Only a few ever succeeded in going above their allocated station in the young, but rigid, hierarchy the government established twenty years ago. She was already dreading the day he would make his choice. He told her she was crazy. He told her he would be talking and messaging her so much, she would be telling him to leave her alone. He told her that wherever he landed, she would have a new place to come visit to feed that wanderlust spirit of hers because, with him there, she would be allowed to visit.

That day was never to arrive. In the months that followed her graduation from middle school, and in the midst of her family finalizing their summer camping trip on the fringes of Region 3 where her family lived, a strange illness started striking down people in their community. When they left for their trip in July, they had heard of a few incidents of a deadly virus taking the lives of people who lived among them. When they left for their trip, it had only hit a few people, and they did not know any of those stricken. When they returned, they found a different situation altogether. More and more people were getting hit. And now they knew some of these victims. They were friends of their parents. Grandparents of kids they went to school with. And even some of their own classmates. The symptoms came on rapidly, and there seemed little chance of survival once it struck.

It always started as something ordinary. A headache or a slight fever. These signs were easy to ignore. Easy to chalk up to a bad day. Within 24 hours, the illness blew up into the unbearable. The headache intensified to something worse than a migraine. The ringing in the ears was sharp and loud and inescapable. The body's heat would climb, the thermometer crawling upwards at a steady pace. And then the vomiting would start. Nothing would stay down. The worst was when stomach contents had been emptied, and yet the victim could not stop the contractions and lurching in his stomach. The dry heaves that brought no relief. It was then that most begged for their lives to end. But the illness would last three more days in the weakest and up to a week in the previously healthy before they were, by this time, mercifully released from the illness. So far, none had survived.

Her brother had been one of the previously healthy ones. One of the ones for whom the illness had lasted a full week. He had fought it, as some did. He had not begged for his life to end. Sometimes, after the delirium set in on day three, he would have moments of clarity. Moments when he would come back to a fully conscious state. It was then that he would tell Rebecca that she needed to find out what was going on.

She needed to find out the truth so that people would stop getting sick. Stop dying. He did not believe it was a virus as was the message being conveyed on the constant stream of news updates inundating the city. The government talking heads that came to the mic to speak all said the same thing. They all stuck to the message that this was a virus, in spite of the fact that this illness, from what they were told, was only striking her city. In spite of the fact that they could not name this virus. The citizens of Montrose had no way of knowing how far the virus really had spread.

Council had ultimate control over what was delivered on the "news." Each region had its own set of news outlets, with journalists who were restricted, generally, to their own city units or regions, depending on their level in their news organization. There were a select few who were designated as national journalists who were assigned to cover national level events when Council deemed it relevant. Only then would they assign the national journalists to cover a story outside of their region. Travel by ordinary citizens was also already limited. Once the virus hit, the restrictions became even tighter, with only those at the highest ranks in the government allowed to leave Region 3 under any circumstance, and leaving your residential quadrant required special permission. The city's occupants were told that it was a safety precaution. A quarantine imposed until they "got to the bottom of this."

The scientists were still, apparently, scratching their heads over the new illness, still trying to figure out its cause and identity, as officials continued to claim they would stop this supposed virus from spreading further. But they had not stopped it. They did not seem to be doing anything besides reassuring the city that they were doing everything in their power. No one mentioned what exactly they were doing. When asked in press conferences about vaccines or anti-virals, Talking Head, in his most reassuring voice, would simply say that the Health and Medicines Division was doing everything it could. That didn't exactly answer the question. But Talking Head would give a quick nod and move on to the next question. Rebecca watched these news casts in disbelief. She got it that the man up there was sent to the mic because he looked official and could think on his feet quickly when questions were thrown at him, when he really had no idea what was going on any more than anyone else. She expected this from the Council at any other time, but this was a crisis, and Rebecca could not understand why no one had any answers. Didn't the scientists work on this stuff all the time?

The city's citizens had grown quickly wary as well, and then moved on to outright panic. When the sickness started, those close to the sick, dying, and dead wanted answers. They were scared and felt hopeless in the face of an illness they could do nothing about. And they feared they were next, though the virus did not seem to be contagious by any of the normal means. Everyone else was interested. Curious, even, since it hadn't touched their lives yet. They had seen enough to think that the media was likely blowing it out of proportion, just as they did everything. This was something that had never changed. Doubtful it ever would. It served the media. It served Council. And it kept people feeling they had knowledge and even control. Of course, they did not. They didn't have either one. Not really.

After the first couple of weeks, though, as more people were lost and ever more were falling sick, and still no concern from Council, more people turned from an idle curiosity to an increasing anxiety. The panic set in around the end of the first month. Council could no longer stay silent and ignore the growing signs of impatience and desperation. Even they knew when they had to step up to tamper down the restlessness or anger or fear of the people. They did not want an out of control population. They worked too hard at their facade of a perfect society to ignore the signs of a mood that threatened to shatter the image should it grow too strong. Sometimes, individual people even disappeared if they said too much, asked too many questions, tried to rally a call of discontent. You learned to keep your head down and play the game. You learned to keep your thoughts to yourself. Rebecca knew this and had always played along. But this was different. They couldn't make a whole city disappear. So, they had to say something to get things back to normal. And they said it many times every, single day. It was not even worth the time or the effort to turn on the TV anymore.

****

Anyone alive more than twenty years ago, before The Reckoning, if asked, would say that the world seemed much the same today on the surface, but it didn't take much digging at all to find out how different life in Anecor really was. Kids still went to school every day. People still went shopping and to the movies—though the number of movies shown were few and far between, as scripts had to be Council approved. Everyone watched TV or stared at their devices, all the time, it seemed. Recreation time still appeared, superficially, much the same, with people in her area of the country spending their time rock climbing, camping, hiking, and riding bikes and horses, as did her family. There were still phones and computers. Natural parks and cities. Farms and malls.

People were not really free, though, no matter that Council's official message stated otherwise. The controls on daily life were strict. The controls on a person's life choices even stricter.

CHAPTER 1

Rebecca knew something was wrong when Jonathan was not at breakfast that morning. She clicked on the monitoring screen in the kitchen, which was rarely used, to find that the display indicated that her brother was still in his bedroom. The home's energy output screen showed that his lights were off. Highly unusual. Jonathan was always the first up in the mornings.

Their parents marveled at his energy. Most teenagers wanted to sleep all day. And stay up all night. With Jonathan, it didn't seem to matter what time he went to bed, he was always up in the morning by 6:00 a.m. ready to greet the day.

In other words, the opposite of Rebecca. Mornings were not for her. She could easily stay up all night—reading, watching videos, doing her homework, messaging friends—but getting up in the mornings was a painful process. Every Monday morning, she longed for the weekend, when she would not have to wake up to her alarm to get ready for school.

Half the time, Jonathan would have to come up and rouse her out of bed because she'd hit her watch's snooze button too many times and was still sound asleep. He usually woke her in the most obnoxious ways. Running into her room and pouncing on her bed, bouncing up and down until she had no choice but to get up, for instance. Or tiptoeing in and taking something soft and brushing it lightly under her nose to tickle her relentlessly, until she gradually went from a dozed and dazed instinctual swatting away at the intrusive object and scratching her nose to a wakened and very alert batting away of Jonathan's hand and grumpily admonishing him to get out of her room NOW. He wouldn't comply, of course, until he saw that she was physically out of bed.

This morning, however, she'd roused herself out of bed. She couldn't believe Jonathan hadn't waken her as late as it was and that he wasn't down for breakfast yet either. She opened the fridge and pulled out a container of leftovers, not caring much what it was, and warmed it up. While she waited, she propped herself against the counter, needing its support to stay upright, opened her mouth in a loud, groaning yawn, and stared out the window above the kitchen sink. It looked like a perfect fall day. The skies were blue, the birds were doing their dance around the trees and ground in their own hunt for breakfast. They were lively. Awake. And Rebecca just longed to crawl back into her cozy, warm bed.

The timer dinged, startling her back to the task at hand. Rebecca retrieved her meal and a fork and headed to the table to eat her unconventional breakfast. She didn't really care about breakfast, and on weekends, when she could sleep in, she wouldn't even bother eating until lunch. This morning, she ate her food quickly without tasting it, downed a glass of tomato juice, and wondered again why Jonathan wasn't down yet. It was starting to worry her.

There was still no Jonathan after she'd finished her morning chores and was heading up to get dressed for the day. But first, she knew she had to check on her brother. Climbing the stairs, her stomach was already fluttering with the beginning twinges of anxiety. It was not at all like Jonathan to sleep in. Not like him to get sick at all. She couldn't even remember the last time he was sick enough to miss school. He hated missing school. There would be no reason for him to not already be standing by the door waiting for her to finish getting ready, so they could ride the transit to school together.

In normal times, she would be a little bit worried about him if he wasn't up before her, but these were not normal times, and her worry was understandably intensified. As she reached the top of the stairs and put her hand on the door sitting slightly ajar, she knew that what she would see was not going to be good news. She knew before she pushed the door the rest of the way open what she would find, even though she hoped against hope that she was wrong, that Jonathan was too strong to catch this virus in the first place.

Her inclination, under normal circumstances, if she were ever given the chance to turn the tables, would be to do just that, and rouse Jonathan from sleep in the most obnoxious of ways. Not that she would ever be given that chance. This morning, however, she opened the door into Jonathan's darkened room as quietly and slowly as she could. Not wanting to disturb him if he were sleeping, and not quite wanting to come face-to-face with the virus in her home, taking up residence in her brother.

Jonathan was not asleep. But it was obvious he was not well. He was sitting on the edge of his bed, feet planted on the floor, his shaggy, dark brown hair dangling over the tops of his hands, cradling his head, elbows braced against his knees. He did not lift his head when she first came in, though she knew he knew she was there.

"Jonathan," she whispered in a barely audible and shaky voice, "are you okay?"

He responded after a brief pause, also in a barely audible voice, "I'm fine, Becs. I just need a minute to wake up."

"I don't believe you. Please look at me, Jonathan. Let me see your face."

He surprisingly complied, raising his head and looking her in the eyes. She could see it, then, for certain. The thing that she feared most was written in the pain etched around his eyes and furrowed in the lines on his forehead. It showed in the set of his jaw and the look he gave her. The look he could not shield from his gaze. The look that said he knew it, too.

"It's just a headache, Becs. I'll take something for it and then I'll be good to go."

"You and I both know it isn't just a headache. You don't get just headaches. Ever. And we both know that this is how it always starts."

A drawn-out silence filled the room. The silence had a physical presence. A weight that settled heavily and refused to budge. The heaviness made it suddenly hard for Rebecca to breathe. She had to concentrate on the intake of each breath, focus on the feeling of it entering her nose, making its way to her lungs, and, with great effort, filling up each of the tiny little sacs made for the exchange of air. In. And out. In. And out. If she focused on her breathing, she wouldn't be thinking about the fact that her brother was going to die. In. And out. In. And out.

Jonathan was the one to break the silence. "I'll fight this, Becs. Don't tell Mom and Dad. Not yet. I don't want them to worry…Not yet. I'm *going* to fight this. It'll be okay."

Wanting to believe him, Rebecca responded, "I'll help you, Jonathan. Just tell me what you need, and I'll do everything I can. I *won't* tell Mom and Dad just yet. I'll wait to see if we can fight this, but if we need their help, I'll have to say something. And if…"

Her voice trailed off. She was unable to form those final words, but that silence that had filled the room and weighed down the air a few moments before finished her sentence for her.

****

Their plan to not tell their parents lasted exactly 12 hours. Rebecca had had no choice but to go to school. The trackers were always on and she could not feign illness with Jonathan staying home. In his final year of high school, Jonathan had more leeway. His entrance exams were coming up. It was understood that seniors who were slated to go on to university would take days off to prepare for exams. He could take up to three days without raising any eyebrows. He took one of those days on this day, so that neither his parents or the school would know he was sick. It was Friday. That would give him the weekend to recover. And, besides, he'd told Rebecca, he really *could* use that time to study. After he slept for a while and after the medicine kicked in to dull the headache.

Phones were not, of course, allowed to be used at school. You could not send messages without being discovered, so Rebecca spent the day with her mind on her brother and not on her teachers or her school work. Her friends commented on how quiet she was and asked if everything was okay. At lunch, she read a book, claiming she had to finish it for homework, and did her best to drown out the daily chatter that these days always, *always* circled around to the virus and rundowns of who in their school or who of their schoolmates' families had gotten hit with it and who had been lost and who might be next. Rebecca kept her nose in her book, but she could feel her best friend Cassidi's steely blue eyes on her, with that intense look she would get whenever she was trying to figure something, or someone, out. Rebecca did not dare look at Cassidi, because Cassidi would know, without a word from Rebecca, that something was wrong.

Rebecca and Cassidi had known each other for as long as they could remember. Their dads worked together in the Citizen's Advisory Division. But they had not become friends, really, until 4th grade when they were partnered for a school project. Through that project, they started getting together outside of school to work and found that they ended up hanging out long after they had finished. After that, they quickly became inseparable. Now Cassidi knew nearly everything about Rebecca and could read her like a book. And vice versa. They had few secrets, and Rebecca knew she would have to tell her best friend sooner than later, but she opted for as much later as possible. After all, maybe there would be nothing much to tell. Maybe her brother would be fine.

Rebecca raced home after school, avoiding the usual gathering of her friends on the front steps by leaving through a different door. Her phone, now in the back pocket of her school uniform, buzzed with the unique pattern identifying the messenger as Cassidi. Rebecca did not stop to look. She would get to that later. She had to get back to Jonathan first.

She opened the front door to a perfectly still house. Nothing stirring except for curtains that gently billowed in front of the window cracked open to welcome the late fall breeze. Rebecca noticed with her now too keen senses—heightened by the adrenaline coursing through her veins in anticipation of walking up the stairs in front of her—the flutter of the curtains and the long shadows cast across the living room from the deep orange glow of the low sun. She noticed the specs of dust dancing through that light. She noticed the sound of her footsteps on the hardwood floors as she crept stealthily up the stairs, and the creak in the fourth step from the top that sounded louder to her ears than usual. But she noticed no sounds coming from Jonathan's room at the top of the stairs.

Her heart thudded to the floor of her stomach when she opened the door to find her brother curled up in a ball on top of his covers. Even with the blinds drawn to darken the room she could see his hair matted against his face, framing the strong jawline and clinging to the stubble there. Jonathan was strong. He had a strong personality, he showed a strength of character in the toughest of situations, and he had strong physical features and an athletic build from years of climbing and sports. He looked anything but strong now, with the pain contorting his face even in sleep.

Clearly, the fever had begun. Clearly, she would not be able to keep this from her parents. And, clearly, she was going to lose her brother. Her friend. Her role-model. Her sometimes unwelcome protector. She was not prepared for this. Never did she think this virus would hit her family, and never in a million years would she have thought it would strike Jonathan first.

CHAPTER 2

Jonathan's memorial and visitation had taken place three days ago. Family and friends gathered in the assigned room at the Quadrant 1 Civilian Center to pay their last respects before representatives of the Health and Medicines Division arrived to take Jonathan away. No longer did citizens decide what would become of family members upon death. Council had changed that after The Reckoning. Now this was in Council's control. Rebecca and her parents could only watch as Jonathan was wheeled out, never to be seen again.

Rebecca sat cross-legged on the floor, leaning up against Jonathan's now empty bed, alone, still wearing the t-shirt and shorts she'd slept in. Which was the same t-shirt and shorts she'd worn each day and night since her brother's funeral. She hadn't showered and had to brush her unruly hair repeatedly from her eyes. Her brown curls, nearly the same color as her brother's but much curlier, were tangled and standing out at all angles from her head. Hard to control on the best of days, now it was just a bird's nest, impossible to tame. But whatever. She had no control over anything these days, it seemed. She couldn't help her brother, couldn't stop the virus or control the pain, couldn't control her tears, couldn't make her heart stop lurching at the memories of that last week with her brother. What did it matter what her hair did?

Her parents were back at work. The Citizen's Advisory Division, of which her dad was a part, had established Emergency Rules for Bereavement. The Division was instructed to create a set of rules for the city shortening the period of bereavement from 7 days for immediate family members to 3. If you were not an immediate family member, your period of bereavement was zero. It had to be done, they said, because so many people were falling to the virus. Many others were affected by the fallen because they were family members. The city would cease to function, they said, with so many workers not working, either because they were grieving, or dead. School-aged children old enough to stay home alone were exempt from the Emergency Rules for Bereavement.

Rebecca still had her 7 days. So, on day 4, she sat alone in her room, while her parents had to return to work.

She had retrieved the secret box Jonathan had hidden with his notes for what he'd seen, suspected, and uncovered so far. When she had gone into his tidy, organized closet, she had wondered, just a little, if there would be anything to find, or if Jonathan had been speaking from his fevered brain. But he had been clear-eyed in the moments he spoke to her urgently and, necessarily, briefly about his discoveries and suspicions, a focused intensity and level-headedness that recalled the healthy Jonathan. Rebecca's head fell back against Jonathan's mattress as she remembered their first conversation.

****

"Where is your phone?" he'd asked.

"It's still in my room." She had responded, a bit confused as to why he would ask, but assuming, at first, the question had no bearing in reality, that it had to do with whatever his fevered brain was telling him. That assumption was dispelled immediately when he had taken his own phone, handed it to her, and motioned towards the door. She knew he wanted his phone out of the room, along with hers. It's what you did when you did not want private conversations to be monitored. It was at that moment she noticed that his eyes did not have the fever-induced glaze. It was one of his touches with reality, when he came back to them over the week before he died.

The Council monitored its citizens in two ways. Their phones and the implants submerged just under the skin in every individual's bicep when they were born. Every citizen received a Council-issued phone at the age of 10. Every child could not wait to receive that phone. To a child, it signaled a new freedom: they could message friends, make phone calls, play games, listen to the music they wanted to hear, and watch their favorite shows. But what it really meant was that Council could start monitoring their messages, phone calls, recreational habits, and conversations…because the phones were always listening, always watching.

The implants were placed at birth in order to be able to keep citizens safe, or so said the official word from Council. Originally, they were placed in adults as a way to keep track of work time. A new way to punch the clock with no risk of defrauding the government, since Council was now in charge of the entire work force. In short order, however, Council began placing them in children and newborns as well. They were sold as a way parents could ensure children would be found if they were in danger. That rebellious teenagers could be monitored and reined in. That college students would be prevented from getting out of control. In this way, Council could monitor the movements of all of its citizens. Every move was recorded and monitored using AI, named SMALS (Safety Monitoring and Location System...Council loved acronyms), which could spot irregularities faster than any human.

Citizens were free to move about their assigned quadrants within their city units. They could engage in recreational activities as long as they were accessible using transit. In Quadrant 1, climbing, hiking, cycling, and camping were all available. If Rebecca wanted to ride Cedar, she was free to ride anywhere within her Quadrant as long as she did not go further than the transit district. She and her friends could meet up to go shopping, for coffee, or to the movies. But your every move was recorded. Your patterns of movement established. And if your patterns varied too far from what was considered "normal" for you, the questions started coming in on your phone. A message from SMALS inquiring about your current activity and the reason for said activity.

A response was required. If SMALS was satisfied, you could go about your business, for the time being. If "she" was not satisfied with your response, your presence was requested, or actually demanded in the all too motherly vernacular of the AI system, in front of the Disciplinary Action Division for further review. SMALS had a "female" voice, making it seem more nurturing and caring than a system designed to control the population could be. An alert was simultaneously sent to the Disciplinary Action Division, or DAD, and Council. If you did not show up within an allotted time, determined based on your current whereabouts, SMALS automatically sent out guards to cart you off to one of the detention centers.

When Rebecca came back in the room after depositing Jonathan's phone with hers, he spoke to her softly, still in great pain, but present, "We need to talk. I have to tell you some things I've found out about…this…this so-called *virus* that is killing so many of us."

"They don't know what this virus is. Though it doesn't seem to me they are looking too hard for answers. They haven't told us anything else, anything more, since this all started. We still don't know *anything*!" Rebecca hurled that last word at Jonathan almost like it was his fault, but, of course, it wasn't. She was just angry that she was going to lose her brother and that Council had provided them no answers. No hope. No more understanding of what was happening than they had when it all began last summer.

"Becs, I don't think this is a virus at all. I think it's a toxin. Or something. Not a virus, and not naturally occurring. That's why we don't know anything more. Council doesn't want us to."

"But why wouldn't they want us to? Wouldn't they want to get to the bottom of this? Even if it is a toxin, or whatever, and not a virus?"

"Maybe. Unless they are protecting someone because it serves them to protect them. Or unless they want this to happen."

****

Rebecca shook off the memory as she lifted her head off the mattress and opened the lid to the box she had taken from its hiding spot behind the vent. Jonathan had placed in the box a couple of notebooks and loose pieces of paper where he'd obviously jotted down his thoughts on anything he could find.

Rebecca braced herself to read what Jonathan had written. Up until now, she had pushed their conversations to the back of her mind. Dealing with his death had been almost more than she could handle. But she knew she couldn't put this off any longer. His last wishes were for her to pick up where he left off. It was time now. Time to begin. Time to find out what it was Jonathan knew and to see if she could do what he had been unable to complete.

CHAPTER 3

The night before she had determined she would need to climb the face of the mountain to see what was happening on the other side, she had seen the light her brother had been talking about. Her bedroom was on the opposite side of the house, so she'd never noticed when the light started glowing faintly behind the mountain in the distance, even though she certainly stayed up late enough on a regular basis to do so. She had set her alarm for 2:00 a.m., just to be sure she was awake at that time.

Jonathan had written in his earlier notes that he spotted the light just by coincidence one night when he was up late, unable to sleep. He had sat up in bed, intending to grab his device to read, looking out of his window before doing so. It was something he had done countless times before, on other sleepless nights, but this time, he noticed the sky looked different. He noticed the faintest of bluish-purple light glowing from behind the mountain. It made the outline of the mountain just a little more distinct than it would have been in clear skies with a moon shining above. The color of the light made it almost hard to discern. It was light, for sure, but faded quickly into the blue-black sky. Barely visible. Hardly noticeable.

Rebecca did not need her alarm. She hadn't fallen asleep, too curious to see if she would see what Jonathan saw. She had waited until 2:00 a.m. because, according to Jonathan's notes, that is when the lights always came on. Never before. Never later. Always, right at 2:00. At a few minutes before the hour, Rebecca crept across the hall to Jonathan' room, not wanting to wake her parents. She raised a blind and looked across the dark expanse to the mountain in the distance. There was little evidence of human intrusion between her house and the mountain.

The land was primarily ranchland and Quadrant 1 Recreation Land, with few residential areas. The center of city, and consequently where all shopping needs could be met, was five more miles in the other direction. The Avairs lived in a

Limited Residential District in Quadrant 1, outside of the main occupied area of the Montrose city unit. This residential district was reserved for people who worked in government or who had enough pull with Council to occupy—because the land belonged to the government, no one could actually own land anymore—a plot of land this far out of the city center. Out here, houses were spread further apart. There was land, space, between homes. Unlike the city's nucleus. The closer into the city's central districts you were, the closer the neighbors. What you were assigned to do for your work assignment determined where you lived. The only ones who lived further out than the Limited Residential District were the ranchers and farmers, who obviously needed the larger plots to raise food for the masses and meat for those in the upper Tiers. Out here, there weren't many who would see the light behind the mountain because there just weren't many people living in these parts.

Rebecca stared hard into the darkness, barely able to make out the outline of the mountain from the light of the moon. She thought about what was behind that mountain. She knew who lived out that way. That was ranchland, worked by the parents of a boy she went to school with. He was a year older than her. Daniel Morgan. She didn't know him other than to recognize him in passing in the halls. He was one to notice. Jet black hair. Green eyes. Gentle smile. Tall and lean and just so perfectly muscular from helping on the ranch. But. He was off-limits. He was of a different social Tier, and those lines could not be crossed. Council was quite clear on this. They allocated people and societal groups to provide, in the words of the Vision, "optimum societal conditions in order to provide for the happiness and needs of our country and its citizens." Much as she would love to strike up a conversation with Daniel, get to know him, it could never be. "So why waste time in thinking about him?" she murmured to herself while staring into the darkness.

Rebecca glanced at her watch. It felt like she'd been waiting for much more than the three minutes that had passed since she first came to the window. 1:59 a.m. Her eyes shifted back to the darkness and the ghost of a mountain in the distance, just as a change started to occur. Jonathan was right. It was oh so subtle. She didn't think she would have noticed it without Jonathan's guidance. The lines of the ridge became a bit more distinct, and the hue above that ridge changed from a faint cast of moonlight white overlaying the blue-black sky to a more purple than black tinge to the sky above, fading into the blackness and star speckled night beyond the reach of the light. She casually wondered if it would look brighter on cloudy nights and made a note to check it out one night, more from curiosity than any sort of additional information it would provide.

Rebecca realized she was taking a mental detour from the task at hand. Probably because she did not really want to face the possible implications or what was next for her. Jonathan was right about the lights. It was strange, for sure. But did it have anything to do with the death of her brother and the now seemingly countless other citizens? She could not imagine how the lights had anything to do with ranching, but she also could not imagine how they had anything to do with the illness either. When did the light start appearing? Had it been there always, and Jonathan just happened to notice it one evening? Or did it really only start appearing recently? She had a hard time believing that Jonathan would not have noticed it earlier if the light had been there for any substantial length of time.

This brought her back around to the question of why the light was there. And brought her further back to the realization that she had to find out. That Jonathan was right: it was now up to her. She did not relish that thought. She had no idea how she could do this on her own or figure out where to start.

No, I know exactly where to start. I have to see what the source of the light might be. I have to find out what is on the other side of the mountain.

****

"Becs, I know I'm right about this. I'm on to something. And I think Council was on to me. I felt like I was being monitored more closely than usual."

"What makes you say that?" Rebecca was growing more anxious by the moment. If her brother was being monitored more closely, was it because he really had made some discovery about the whole virus situation? Or just because his patterns were changing, and SMALS took note of this change?

Reading her mind, Jonathan said, "I don't have time to go into all the details, but I have been very careful not to change my patterns, and I was still getting messages asking me about my current actions and demanding explanations for what I was doing throughout the day. I hadn't been brought in for questioning, but I can't believe it was SMALS detecting changes in my patterns. I think I was too careful for that. And the messages seemed...I don't know...less...automated. Less programmed and more specific to me. It's hard to explain, exactly, but it all comes down to the fact that I think somehow Council caught wind of what I was learning."

Jonathan was so calm as he spoke these words. So unafraid. How could he not be terrified? While there wasn't much that she had found to be afraid of other than heights in her 14, almost 15, years of life, the words Jonathan was speaking now *did* terrify her. Rebecca felt the room expanding, Jonathan becoming more distant from her as she spoke. His voice hollow, less real. She could hear her blood start to course through her veins, a whooshing sound in her ears, as the fear for her brother rose. Not just her brother, she realized, but now for her and her whole family. For their entire city. If Jonathan had discovered something he wasn't supposed to know, and Council found out or at least suspected? And now he was suddenly dying from the very illness he was suspicious about? What did all this mean for her and her family if she started poking around in the same places Jonathan did?

"Listen, Becs. Listen closely. I know this is scary to hear, but you have to hear it. Council is up to something. They know what is going on and they are choosing not to do anything about it. This isn't a normal virus we are dealing with. It is an attack on our city. I don't know why we are being targeted, but Council is behind it. Or at least they are allowing it to happen for some reason. They aren't trying to stop it. That is why we don't have any answers yet. I've been able to find out a little about the organization operating on the other side of the mountain, but not much. What I've found is in my notes."

"In your notes?" Jonathan had notes. Of course, he did. The ends of Rebecca's mouth turned up in a hint of a smile. She should have expected no less from her brother.

"Yes. They're in a box in my closet. The only place I could think of to hide them in case something happened to me or in case someone came here snooping around. You'll have to dig behind my gear to the vent and remove the cover to get to the box. It isn't much, I'm afraid, but it's something for you to go on."

"Something for me to go on." It was a statement, and not a question. Rebecca was letting those words sink in. Something for her to go on. Jonathan was expecting her to pick up the trail where he, unwillingly, left it. He was expecting her to accomplish what he could not. And he was far more capable than she. He was 17 and she 14 after all! He was expecting a miracle.

"You can do this, Becs. You are smart enough to figure this out. You're much smarter than I was at your age. You've got a mind for solving problems. You can solve this one." He had yet again read her mind. And probably the look on her face, as well. She was always so transparent. "I don't really have to tell you this, but I'm going to anyway. Be even more careful than I was. You can't get caught. They can't do this to you, too. You will have to find a way to get past the tracker, and be careful with your phone, too."

This was too much. She did not know how to take it all in. How did her life get here? Her brother was dying, possibly because he knew something he shouldn't, and now not only was she going to have to deal with a life without him, but she was also supposed to somehow stop this madness in her city. Stop whomever was behind it, and that meant going up against Council because they were either directing what was happening, or they were allowing it. Either way, she was supposed to do the impossible.

****

Pulling herself out of her memories and peeling her eyes from the mountain and the strange glow, Rebecca made her way quietly back to her room, crawled into bed, and stared at the ceiling, looking for guidance in the darkness. Looking for a way out, though she knew there was none. She had to climb a mountain.

CHAPTER 4

She didn't dare look down. Or up. The only way she could keep going was to look just far enough for something to grab onto to pull herself up a little closer to a point along the ridge where she could see over to the other side. That meant getting to the crest, at least. She knew her tracker would be sending signals to SMALS. She was waiting for a message, but so far, nothing. Which made her even more nervous, though she had no idea of what her response to SMALS would be when it came. Climbing a mountain was definitely not within her normal pattern, as far as she knew. Unless SMALS equated hiking with climbing, lumping them in the same category of behavior.

Still, she was climbing *this* mountain. It really wasn't considered ranch land, the Morgan's ranch, until on the other side of the mountain, but there were no official trails here. Not up this high. She had never been one to test the trackers. They weren't officially told to stay on trails out in the areas designated as Recreation Land. People did go mountain climbing around here, and she rode Cedar across the wide-open parklands and that was never an issue. Perhaps this wasn't either. *Except that Jonathan had believed he was being watched. Would they start watching me too? I am his sister, after all. Have they been watching me already?*

Feeling a little nauseous at this line of thinking, she forced her mind back to just getting up this wall. It was daylight, midday on the 5th day of her mourning period. She had determined last night, in bed, that the sooner she got this over with, the better. After reading through Jonathan's notes, she decided to just tackle it. If she didn't, she would probably be able to talk herself out of it. So, she got dressed, put on her boots, and headed for the trail that would lead her to the base of the granite wall, and then to her current position somewhere up that face.

It wasn't that the climbing itself was difficult. Really, this wall would not have been hard at all, except for the whole fear of heights thing. It was steep, but there was a lot she could hold onto, and solid footing, as well. At least so far. She didn't think she could have too much further to go. She'd been making her way up for a while. She didn't dare so much as glance upwards, however. She did what she had to and kept making her careful way up.

Twenty minutes later, Rebecca crested the ridge. It leveled out for a bit, with some sparse growth and larger boulders littered about. Once on the top, she felt safe again. That is, until she realized that she would have to peer down the other side in order to see what lie below. She made her way to a spot where there were large boulders near the edge and pulled her binoculars from the inside pocket of her jacket. Taking a deep breath, she wedged herself between two closely placed boulders, thinking they would offer support and make her feel safer as she inched closer to the drop-off. She peered over the edge and immediately felt the sensation of falling. Quickly, she jerked her head up and affixed her eyes on her hands on the boulder in front of her. She took a few more deep breaths, letting her equilibrium, and stomach, settle. She tried a different approach. Rebecca lifted the binoculars to her eyes before looking over the edge. She then shifted her gaze to the valley. The scene below was a blur, so she slowly adjusted the focus until found herself peering at what lay below.

Trees. This was all she saw. A forest stretched out below, reaching to the place where the land rose up again to meet the sky across the valley from her. At first, this was all she saw as she scanned the area. How could that be? There was definitely a change in the light last night, so shouldn't she see *something* up here that might give her a clue as to what was causing the light?

Sighing, she pulled back and leaned against one of the boulders, dropping the binoculars from her eyes. She took a moment to let it sink in that she had looked down from this height to the depths below without getting too dizzy or nauseous. Even as she scanned the area. Amazed, she tried again, lifting the binoculars to her eyes as she leaned forward one more time, this time with a little more confidence and certainty than the first time. *Huh. I'm doing okay!* She smiled. The first in more than a week. *Do you see this, Jonathan? I'm okay!* She continued in a deliberate and slow scan below. She started on the far side of the valley, moving from left to right, and back again, before shifting just a bit closer.

Her eyes reached a clump of trees near the edge of the valley, against another rise to the north, and she started to scan back to the left, when she quickly—that made her a little dizzy—retraced her visual path back to the clump of trees. What was it that struck her as odd just then, without her even realizing she'd noticed anything?

"Rebecca, right?" Came a voice from behind her.

Nearly pitching herself over the side in a startled effort to move in the opposite direction from the voice, she dropped her binoculars and gave a yelp. A hand shot out to catch her before she went too far, pulling her safely back from the edge. Well, safe was a relative term here. She wasn't exactly sure which was the safer route: being here with someone who just came upon her while she was spying on who knows what or falling from her perch to the trees jutting out from a ledge below.

"You're Rebecca, aren't you?" Green eyes and a not unkind face stared down at her. Daniel.

"Yes," she replied in a barely audible voice that came out shakier than she'd intended. She was nervous for more reasons than being discovered where she didn't belong.

"Daniel. We go to school together. I'm sorry to hear about your brother." He sounded like he meant it. He didn't seem to care that he had happened upon her spying on the land his family worked.

Rebecca tried to get her nerves under control. Tried to get ahead of what could turn out to be a very bad situation, if she said or did the wrong thing. "Thank you," she said, in a stronger voice than the one that previously escaped her lips, and then added, "Speaking of school, how are you here and not there?"

Daniel gave a little laugh at that before responding, "Us farm and ranch kids are required to spend a portion of our 'education' time learning the ropes from our parents so that we can slip right into our roles when we graduate. Don't you have to do the same?"

"Really? I had no idea. And, no. We don't get to do the same. We are expected to go to school and then go to university after that, so that we are 'properly prepared with the worldly and historical knowledge and wisdom to fulfill our place in government upon maturation'." Did that really come out sounding as bitter as she thought it did? Daniel just smiled in response, appearing not to notice her tone.

"I guess that makes perfect sense for what your parents do, and what you are going to be expected to do after your training." Rebecca nodded. She did not like the idea that she would be forced to work either in the CAD, like her father, or the Citizen's Assignment and Training Division, like her mother. It wasn't that she thought either of their work assignments unpleasant—well, actually, maybe her father's assignment would not be much fun—it was more just the idea that she couldn't *decide*. If it were up to her, she would do something a little more exciting. Something that involved travel. And the outdoors. She had no idea what kind of assignment that would be, but it would be an ideal assignment for her. If they had a choice. Instead, she, like everyone else, was required to play the game. Don't push the boundaries and you don't get disappeared. At least she could spend her free time outside still. Travel was a lot trickier…

Rebecca and Daniel stood for a moment in an awkward silence as Rebecca shifted her pack on her back and Daniel watched her intently, as if assessing her. For what, she did not know, but she was uncomfortable under his confident demeanor and intense gaze. She was certain her nervousness, and even the guilt she felt over being discovered on his turf, with binoculars observing the grounds below, was clearly evident on her face.

"I was sent to find out who was climbing our mountain and lurking on the ridge, "Daniel said with a grin and a lightness of tone that belied the serious implications of the statement. "Dad and I saw you on the camera when we were running a perimeter check," he added.

Rebecca held his gaze for a split second before she had to look away, afraid he'd be able to read the guilt and fear in her eyes.

"Just me," she smiled, trying, almost successfully, to match his lightness. He had a presence and a way of speaking that could put you at ease. Or make you very nervous, Rebecca reminded herself, recalling the intensity with which he had looked at her just moments before.

"Wait. *Your* mountain?" she tried a smile. "I thought the ranch property was on this other side. Down there."

"It is," he returned the smile. "The ridge here is the perimeter."

"I had to get out of the house for a bit. I went for a hike, and ended up here, somehow. I climbed without thinking, and now I'm not sure how to get back down, so I was looking for a different, easier, way, than the way I came up. I'm a little afraid of heights," She knew she was saying too much, explaining too much, but the words all tumbled out of her mouth in a rapid-fire attempt to make her presence seem an accident.

This time, he thoroughly surprised her by laughing out loud, tipping his head back a bit, sending the deep resonance of his voice into the air around them. Rebecca did not find her very real predicament funny at all. Even though she covered up the intent of her presence on his turf, she really *was* at a loss for how she would get back down. Making it safely to the top was not even close to a guarantee that she would have the same luck going down. Going down was much harder than going up. Even she, as inexperienced as she was, knew that.

"You're lucky I came around, then, aren't you?" Daniel said, with the laughter still in his voice. "There is a much easier way down than the route you chose to get up here. Follow me, and I'll show you."

Daniel led Rebecca across the top of the ridge to where a path descended down the back side. She followed him, staring at the back of his head as he made idle, comfortable conversation. Strangely, she did feel at ease with him. Now. It made no sense to her. She also knew it didn't mean anything. It couldn't. When she returned to school, everything would be as it always was. It could never be otherwise, no matter where her foolish thoughts carried her as she followed his footsteps down the mountain.

CHAPTER 5

"Give it to me straight, Becs. How are you holding up?" Cassidi sat across from Rebecca on her bed. She had come over after school, on day 6, her next to the last day of mourning before she would be required to go back. Required to face the looks and the whispers from strangers and acquaintances, and, worse, the words of condolence tinged with fear because now this hit too close to home for her friends. Worse still, she would be heading to school without Jonathan. She would not see him in the hallway during passing, or from across the lunchroom where she'd be sitting with her friends and he with his. And she would come home from school to a house that still felt empty, the life drained from it when it left Jonathan. Her parents were doing the best they could to return to normal, but it was of course almost too much for them to bear, even though they had to.

"I still can't believe he's gone. How is it him and not me? I just don't get it. He was so much stronger than me. I mean, he never got sick!" The tears rolled down Rebecca's face. She realized she hadn't cried since her parents went back to work. She had been so focused on what Jonathan had asked of her, she hadn't had time to cry. Now, though, sitting with Cassidi, the feelings of emptiness and loss returned.

"None of this makes sense, Becs. And definitely not Jonathan." Tears trickled down Cassidi's face as well, which was an odd thing for Rebecca to see, as her friend always seemed so together and strong. But she also knew this had to be hard on Cassidi, too. Though she'd never admitted it, Rebecca could see that Cassidi was more than a little drawn to her brother. Like every other girl she knew. Unlike every other girl she knew, however, Cassidi wasn't one to display these emotions. Not even to Rebecca. She would never want to be seen as vulnerable, or as just another love-struck freshman crushing on an older guy.

"I've been thinking a lot about all of this since it started," Cassidi continued, "and I can't see a pattern in who gets the virus and who doesn't. It seems so random."

"That's exactly what Jonathan said," Rebecca noted, immediately hoping she hadn't given too much away about Jonathan's suspicions.

"It isn't like it takes the weakest among us. If so, you're right, it would *never* have been Jonathan. It can strike anyone, girls and boys, men and women. It gets people from every social Tier, even if the people from these groups don't have much to do with each other. It doesn't seem to spread like a virus. Otherwise, you'd be out with it now, too. So would your parents. But here you are, sitting in front of me, looking perfectly healthy. You *are*, aren't you?" Cassidi said, looking her over closely.

"Yes, I *am* perfectly healthy. Absolutely nothing going on with me physically. Not even the slightest of headaches. Nothing. And I've been thinking about the same things as you and Jonathan, about how strange this virus is." Rebecca hesitated. She wanted so much to bring Cassidi in on her secret. It sure would be nice to have someone to help, especially someone with a mind like Cassidi's.

"What's going on in that mind of yours. I can see your wheels turning. You're thinking something, so out with it," said Cassidi, as if to prove Rebecca's point about her keen mind. And about the transparency of Rebecca's expressions.

****

"One more thing, Becs," said Jonathan, "be very careful who you trust. It would be best if you did this on your own, but I know how hard that is. I just don't know enough about what is happening to know how deep this goes and who is involved. Dad works in government. Mom works in government. All of our friends' parents work in government. That means that the people you know best, the ones you'd be most likely to want to trust, are also the very ones whose families are potentially involved."

****

Remembering Jonathan's warning, Rebecca felt trapped. Unsure what to do. Her friend was so incredibly perceptive, she would know right away if Rebecca was holding something back, and Rebecca desperately wanted her friend's help. She would feel so much better if she had another person to talk to about all this, to help her find out what was killing everyone in the city and why. But, should she trust her? Could she? Cassidi already seemed to be suspicious of the virus. Rebecca decided she had to trust her.

She picked up her phone, tipping it towards Cassidi, raising her eyebrows, and then gesturing towards Cassidi's bag, where she assumed her phone would be stashed. As she did so, she said, "I need something to eat. Haven't had much today. Want to come downstairs while I fix something?" Cassidi, of course, knew exactly where she was going with that comment and jumped right up, grabbing her bag as she did so, and headed for the door.

The girls took their phones downstairs and into the kitchen. Rebecca made a show of fixing something to eat, though she had no intention of actually eating the food she made. Cassidi probably would eat it for her. The girl could always eat. When she was done preparing the food, they walked out of the kitchen, leaving Rebecca's phone and Cassidi's bag containing her phone on the kitchen counter.

Back in her bedroom, Rebecca plunged ahead before she could think too much more about it, and hoped she was making the right decision. Cassidi listened intently, not interrupting. Rebecca couldn't read what she was thinking. Of course not. When she got to the part about Daniel, she almost skipped over it, not wanting to give away what felt like a secret between the two of them. It was silly. She knew that. Daniel had been sent up to see who the intruder was on the ranch and why this person was there. And that was it. He was just nice enough to help her get down when he learned of her predicament. Though he admittedly did not have to lead her down all the way. He could have pointed her in the right direction and left her to it. The path wound its way back to the side of the mountain that faced her home.

He had also known who she was. He had to have known even when he saw her in the camera. Rebecca wondered if Daniel's dad was aware that he knew who Rebecca was. Something felt odd about that situation, but she couldn't put a finger on it. Not wanting to leave out anything that could be important later, she decided to go ahead and fill Cassidi in on that as well, ignoring the smirk on Cassidi's face as she obviously keyed in on Rebecca's feelings about the whole Daniel episode. Cassidi kindly refrained from saying anything about it, thankfully.

Instead, when Rebecca finished, Cassidi asked her what it was she thought she saw just before Daniel came upon her. Good place to start.

"I have no idea what I saw. It didn't register that I'd seen anything until I'd moved away from that spot, so I was moving my aim back that way when Daniel interrupted me."

"Something has to stick out in your mind about it. Anything at all we can go on?"

"Not really. I've been thinking about it a lot, trying to place what it was I saw, but I can't, specifically. I have one more day before I have to go back to school, so I thought I'd go back tomorrow to check out that spot in particular. I've been going over Jonathan's notes again today to see if anything he said in them would help me recall what it was that seemed out of place or different with that clump of trees, but nothing did. I just got the feeling that what I was looking at wasn't exactly what it appeared to be."

"You mean they weren't really trees, even though they looked like trees?"

"Yeah. I guess that's what I mean. I don't know. That's why I'm going back. I don't know what I saw exactly."

"Becs, do you think that's a good idea? I mean, you know Daniel and his dad spotted you before. Who's to say they won't see you again? I don't think the same excuse would work twice."

"Daniel told me that they do the perimeter check three times a day: sunrise, noon, and just after dinner. I can get up there and back after the noon check and before Daniel gets home from school. I'll take the trail, now that I know about it. It'll be quicker that way, and I think I'll be more hidden in the trees. Until I get to the top."

"I'm coming with you."

"There's no way, Cass! You'll be at school. I wish you could, but you can't get in trouble just to help me now. I might need it more later." Those words were a little difficult for Rebecca to spit out. She wanted nothing more than Cassidi's company and help when she went back up the next day, but she meant it when she said she might need her more later. She couldn't possibly ask her to risk getting caught skipping school just for this. What help would she be then?

"Right. I guess you're right, Becs. But I don't like this. What time are you going?" Cassidi gave in, the logic hard to deny.

"I'll leave the house at noon. I'll take Cedar. It'll look like I'm just going for a ride. She could use the exercise anyway. I should be at the trail by the time Daniel's dad finishes his checks. Daniel will be in school. He is only on the ranch twice a week. Tomorrow is Wednesday, so it isn't one of those days."

"Okay. I'm coming over here tomorrow, straight from school. Make sure you're back by then, or I'm coming to find you. And Becs, please be extra careful. Don't get caught, or I'll kill you."

With that, Cassidi got up to go, leaving Rebecca to contemplate the wisdom of telling Cassidi so soon, and to worry over what she had to do, again, tomorrow. At least she would be on a trail this time.

****

Rebecca spent the next morning reading through Jonathan's notes again. He had found out that the company, that had set up camp on the land Daniel's family worked, BRO (Bovine Research Operations), was apparently a research firm for cattle. That seemed logical. Cattle was the Morgan's line of work. They were ranchers—maybe even a research designated ranch—responsible for growing high-quality, safe meat for the upper three Tiers. Which would be Rebecca's family, now that she thought of it. Usually, Rebecca did not consider the social organization of citizens. That structure had been dictated by Council since before she was born. There was little to no way to escape the Tier to which you were born, so it did little good to give that structure much consideration. Even less so for Rebecca where the consumption of meat was concerned.

Rebecca's family did not eat meat, though they could. It had something to do with how her parents lived before, when there was still some choice in what you did and how you lived. Anyone who wanted to could eat meat. Her parents didn't. Rebecca, therefore, did not grow up thinking about the fact that there were those whose choice to eat meat or not was dictated by the social structure Council had arranged 20 years prior. That was strange to think about, too. Just over five years before she was born, and three years before Jonathan, the country had functioned differently.

Her parents knew a different world than the one they currently lived in. And it had all happened so fast, the unraveling of society that lead to The Reckoning. Adults didn't talk much about the time before. It was a painful time to think about. Life before The Reckoning seemed a distant memory, a dream, and one better left alone. For those who survived, that period of history had nearly broken them. Many wondered if they actually *were* the lucky ones. But then they adjusted to this new way of life, the new structure and controls, and left their memories of real choices and a freer life tucked away and out of sight.

Rebecca returned her attention again to Jonathan's notes. It seemed that this company was responsible for research on the optimization of nutritional intake, the quantity and quality of the meat produced by cows, and the food and land needed to reach this optimal level. To Rebecca, BRO's presence on the Morgan ranch made complete sense. What didn't make sense was why they would operate at 2 a.m., under the cloak of darkness, and, apparently, in secret quarters. BRO had come onto the Morgan ranch two years ago. She vaguely recalled that. It was mentioned on Council News as an exciting new opportunity for Montrose's ranchers and citizens to be the first to benefit from BRO's research. She only remembered it because it was about Daniel's family. Nothing else about the arrival of BRO would have been notable to Rebecca.

In Rebecca's few moments on top of the ridge, all that was visible was a valley with trees. There weren't any cattle in that location, and there weren't any obvious structures that one would expect a research firm would need to conduct the kind of work this company was supposed to be engaged in. Yes, these could be located elsewhere. The ranch was huge. But why, then, was the mountain glowing at 2:00 in the morning every morning just above a valley that did not appear to be used for ranching purposes? That made no sense at all. And yet, the mountain was glowing, so something was happening there. She could see why Jonathan was suspicious of what BRO's real purpose was for setting up camp on the Morgan ranch.

Jonathan's notes about BRO provided no other clues. The information he'd discovered about the research firm was the most recent in his notes. He'd learned this information just before getting sick. She was not sure where he had found the information. It didn't seem to contain anything that would not have been mentioned on the Council News at the time BRO moved in. If he had been looking through the news archives for information on BRO, that might have tipped someone off that he was investigating the virus. But only *if* BRO had something to do with the virus.

Frustrated, she stashed those notes away, wishing, as she did so, that she'd had more time to talk to her brother after reading his notes. She wished that he had had more time to tell her more, to find out more himself, to help her solve this mystery so people would stop dying. More than anything, she just wished Jonathan had more time. Period. Tears fell onto the lid as she pressed it into place, sealing the contents within the protection of the box.

I hope I can do this. I don't know what I am doing here, and I'm in way over my head. The tears that fell from her cheeks sat in droplets on the surface for a brief moment before being drawn into the fabric of the box lid, becoming only a wet imprint of her sorrow. Rebecca carried the box back to its hiding place, stowing it securely and placing Jonathan's gear gently back in place. Closing her eyes, she ran her hands over his climbing helmet and ropes, calling his presence back to this world she still inhabited.

Opening her eyes again, Rebecca stood up, shut the closet door, and looked at her watch. Already 11:03 a.m. With no appetite for food, she skipped eating altogether. The knots in her stomach would not have allowed any food to enter anyway. Instead, she got dressed and headed out to the pasture to round up Cedar. Her beloved mare came to her when she called. She must have missed her, or at least missed going out into the fields and forests, because Cedar usually took her time to mosey over to the barn when Rebecca called.

Cedar nuzzled Rebecca in greeting and retrieved a handful of oats gently from Rebecca's hand. She took a few moments to look her horse over, checking her shoes and making sure Cedar looked to be her normal healthy self. She murmured endearments and told Cedar about Jonathan, apologizing for not taking her out for a while. She then grabbed a simple bridle to loop over Cedar's muzzle. She would not have even bothered with that if she didn't have a need to tie Cedar out when she got to the trail. Rebecca preferred to ride Cedar bareback. She got a much better feel for Cedar's movements without the saddle between her and the horse. When she rode bareback, she and Cedar felt like one creature, moving in response to and in rhythm with one another.

    It felt great to be riding Cedar again. She and Cedar took it slow at first. They had some time. Rebecca had taken off a little sooner than planned, but she had been itching to go and didn't want to kill any more time. She'd rather feel like she was on her way, even if moving slowly. When she and Cedar reached the trail, Rebecca hopped off and walked Cedar a bit further off the trail and into the woods, where she would be less likely to be seen in the off chance someone happened this way. Or at least she hoped it was an off chance. She really had no way of knowing what kind of system was in place for monitoring the ranch or this trail. Technically, the trail was not on the ranch land until it wrapped around the front of the mountain and headed up to the ridge. The ridgeline itself marked the outer boundary of the ranch. She wouldn't be trespassing until the end of the trail, but that didn't mean there wouldn't be monitoring devices all along the trail.

It made her nervous to leave Cedar, but she knew she had no other choice. She would be far easier to detect on the trail riding Cedar than on her own. She could step off the trail and hide, if need be. She also would be able to duck into the trees and walk parallel to the trail in the places where the trail was not directly under the canopy of the trees. She reluctantly tied Cedar to a sturdy branch of a large tree. As she turned to go, her horse dipped her head down and began contentedly munching away on the grasses at the base of the tree. She would be fine, Rebecca reassured herself.

CHAPTER 6

Rebecca's trip up the ridge went off without incident. Admittedly, she was half hoping to see Daniel again, even though it definitely would not have been a good thing. But of course, she didn't. Having returned Cedar to pasture, she herself was not quite ready to go in the house, and she had some time before Cassidi would be here. The day was warm for fall. The sun was out, and the air was still. She wanted to feel the sun on her face and the ground beneath her.

She left the barn and walked towards her favorite tree. A giant spruce with its soft, graceful blue-green needles and a trunk much larger than the width of her arm span. In the summer, it provided wonderful shade. Today, she wasn't looking for shade, but rather for the feelings of protection such an old and sturdy form provided. The low autumn light meant that the shade fell mostly on one side of the tree. She sat at the base of the tree on the sunny side, leaning back against the trunk, pulling her knees in close, closing her eyes, and raising her face to the warmth of the sun.

Now that she was back, safe, she let her mind wander back to the ridge. She again was curious as to why she hadn't received any of the automated messages about breaking the patterns of her usual behavior. *Maybe, this time really wasn't breaking any patterns. I was on a trail, hiking. Normal. Except the part about riding Cedar out to the trail. Not normal.*

The fact that she wasn't contacted for the second time should have given her comfort, but, instead, it made her just as anxious and suspicious as the first time. Either SMALS was not as sensitive to changes in patterns as you would think, or even as citizens were led to believe from the warnings given and examples shown in Council News broadcasts. Or, her pattern changes had been detected, and she was allowed to proceed anyway. The first possibility had all kinds of positive implications. The second, on the other hand, was more likely than not to mean trouble for Rebecca. Unfortunately, she had no way of knowing which possibility was the actuality. And that made her anxious. And nervous.

Once she reached the ridge, Rebecca made her way to the same set of boulders she had propped herself up against previously. It took her a few minutes to locate the trees she had seen the last time, but she did find them again. The first thing she noticed is that they were growing closer together than the other trees surrounding them. But more than that, something else seemed…odd. While staring through her binoculars, she caught the hint of movement from within the trees. She trained her eyes on the area where she caught a glimpse of motion and zoomed in closer. There! What *is* that, she'd wondered. It was the same color as the rock, but too symmetrical.

Just then, the object moved again, opening to the inside of the mountain, and two men came to stand outside. They held coffee cups in their hands, but talked with heads bent close, as if trying to ensure they were not overheard. Who would possibly overhear them here? They were in a valley and just emerged, apparently, from inside a mountain. They definitely seemed to be being secretive, though. One of the men looked like an older version of Daniel, but not old enough to be his father. Did Daniel have an older brother? He easily could have one who had graduated from his schooling already, and she could easily never have known he existed.

"Hey. There you are. I was just getting ready to come look for you because you obviously didn't answer the door when I rang. And you didn't answer my message, either." Cassidi loomed above her, blocking out the sun's rays.

"What time is it? Sorry. I've just been sitting here thinking. I guess I lost track of the time," Rebecca responded distractedly.

"You really had me worried. Now, I'm just kind of annoyed. Anyway, I'm glad you're okay. I did nothing but watch the clock this afternoon. Mr. Bussman called on me twice before I even heard him. But I digress. What did you find out? I assume you didn't run into any trouble since you're sitting in front of me in one piece."

"Yeah, I had no trouble at all. And that kind of worries me. It just seems like this was too easy. Unless there *is* nothing to discover there and Jonathan was wrong about all this."

"You don't honestly believe that, do you?"

"No. I don't. Especially not after what I saw today."

"Okay. Fill me in," Cassidi said, unnecessarily, as she dropped her heavy pack, and then herself, on the ground in front of Rebecca.

"Just checking…do you have your phone on you?" Rebecca asked, hoping not, because too much was already said if she had forgotten to stash her phone before coming back here.

"What do you take me for? Of course, I don't have it on me…do *you?*"

"Of course not," Rebecca smiled, relieved to know for certain they weren't being overheard.

"Now, get on with it! I'm on the edge of my seat here." And indeed, she looked to be, sitting back on her heels, hands on her thighs holding her up as she leaned in towards Rebecca in anticipation of whatever it was Rebecca had to tell.

Rebecca filled her in, leaving out nothing, including her concerns over not being contacted by SMALS on either occasion about her actions, which was even more worrying since she also did not have any trouble from the Morgans going up there again today. She also reminded Cassidi about what was in Jonathan's notes about this company, BRO.

"What do you think, Cass? Do you think Jonathan was on to something and BRO is at the root of this illness? Why would a company who researches cow production be involved in killing off people with an illness? So far, though, it's the only thing I can see that is suspicious. I mean, if someone found out Jonathan was looking into BRO, and they are behind it, then I'm sure he would be tracked, but isn't it jumping to conclusions to think that it has to be BRO and that's why Jonathan got caught? If he did get caught." Rebecca finally stopped to breathe.

"Whoa. Slow down with the questions, Becs! I'm losing track. First, I think what you saw today is suspicious, but I don't know exactly why, other than the fact that there doesn't seem to be any reason for the sort of company BRO claims to be to be operating in secret *inside* of a mountain. And, second, there is no logical reason for said company to have any reason to kill people with a virus-mimicking-whatever-it-is. Third, it might be jumping to conclusions, but I happen to agree with you. If BRO is behind it, then that would explain why he was being monitored more closely. *If* he was being monitored more closely."

"The dots don't connect at all. Jonathan's notes list everyone who has gotten the illness, their ages, social Tier, symptoms, and how long it took from beginning to end. I have no idea where he got this information. Though maybe this is actually the thing that got him into trouble in his snooping, and not BRO. Or maybe it was both. He said he was careful to keep up his same patterns, but I'm not sure how he got all of this information while maintaining his normal patterns.

"He also mapped the general location of each person based on social Tier, so you can see how many people from each sector within all four Quadrants of the city have gotten sick and died. And then there's the little bit of information about BRO and Jonathan's suspicions that they are involved, but we don't know why he thinks…or thought…so, other than the fact that they seem to be involved in something they don't want others to know about because of the whole lighting up the mountain at 2:00 a.m. thing."

"And now the whole working on the inside of a mountain thing, too," Cassidi added.

"Yeah, that whole thing, too."

"I think we need to investigate more closely. And, yes, I'm coming with you, so don't bother arguing with me." One look at Cassidi's face and Rebecca knew her friend was digging in her heels and would not be budged from this decision. It would be futile to even try, as she'd only succeed in making Cassidi mad. Rebecca sighed. She hated that she was putting someone else, her best friend, in danger. Though she had to admit, she was also glad of the help.

"I have to go back to school tomorrow," Rebecca said quietly.

"I know. Are you going to be okay? Bendi, Selby, and Troy have all been asking about you. They didn't want to contact you after the services because they thought you would need your space. But they have been asking how you're doing. Others, too, of course, but I think some of those are as curious as they are concerned. Sorry. But you know how it is."

"Yeah. I do. I would expect that. I know how we all talked about this when it was happening to everyone else. I don't hold it against them. I just don't know if I'm ready to face it. Even with the rest of the gang. But…I have no choice, right?"

"Unfortunately, no." Cassidi stood up and held out her hand to help Rebecca up. "Let's go inside. It's getting chilly out here. And we still have to plan our next step."

The two made their way back to Rebecca's house, Cassidi retrieving her phone from the rock where she laid it, and entered the kitchen from the always unlocked back door. Rebecca realized she hadn't eaten all day, so she grabbed some snacks and drinks for the two of them and headed upstairs, in case either of Rebecca's parents came home while they were discussing their plans.

"We obviously can't go until this weekend. Do you have anything planned that we have to work around?" Rebecca asked.

"Nothing that can't be rearranged. This is priority. I say we go Saturday, first thing. We have to get down into that valley and have a closer look."

"How are we going to do that without getting caught?" Rebecca knew they had to do this, but the idea of getting caught was not one she cared to follow to its likely end.

"We'll stick to the trees. You know approximately where we are going, right? So, we'll make our way over the ridge, staying in the trees as much as possible, and climb down the other side. Is that possible? I mean, is there a route we can take that keeps us under cover after we cross over the ridge?

"Maybe. I think we might be able to continue on from the path Daniel showed me. It seemed to go down the other side. We can't take the trail, not on the weekend when we might be more likely to run into Daniel or someone else from the ranch, but we can head down a route parallel to it. It should be forested the whole way. It had better be, for more reasons than one."

"Right," said Cassidi, "your fear of heights. But you managed up on the ridge. Not once, but twice! How did that happen? You can't even look up from the bottom of a mountain without wanting to hurl."

"I think it was the binoculars. They made the ground seem like it was right there. I couldn't do it without them. I tried. Not sure how I made it up the first time, and I'm glad Daniel came along to show me the trail. Otherwise, I might still be up there." Just thinking about her climb up and what it would have been like to get down started the butterflies fluttering in her stomach. Or maybe it was the thoughts of Daniel that did that.

"I'm sure you are glad Daniel came along to save you," Cassidi replied with a glint of amusement in her eyes. Turning serious, she added, "But you know he's off limits, so don't get too wrapped up. Besides, we have more important things to think about."

"I know, I know. Cass…how are we going to get around the trackers? Going up the ridge is one thing, though I still don't understand how I got away with it. Going over the ridge and off-trail is another. No way we will get away with that."

"Leave that to me. I have an idea."

"Great," Rebecca said in a tone that implied she wasn't sure how great it really was. "What is this brilliant idea of yours?"

"You won't like it, so I'm not going to tell you. Yet. But you have to trust me. It's our best chance."

Rebecca sighed, not caring at all for that response, but knowing, still, that her friend was probably right. She had no choice. Cassidi was also smart not to tell her. She knew her too well. If Rebecca did not like what Cassidi had planned, she would likely stubbornly refuse to go along with it, leaving them both vulnerable to discovery if they went ahead with the rest of the plans, or leaving only herself vulnerable, with no help, if she decided to go it alone.

"Okay, Becs. I'm headed home. I have some things to do before my folks get home. Try to take it easy. We can't do anything else tonight, and you have to prepare yourself for tomorrow."

"Ugh. Tomorrow. Thanks for the reminder."

"Sorry. I'll see you tomorrow, Becs. I can swing by here to get you if you want some company? We can transit in together from here."

"Yes, please. That might help. You can beat away the onlookers with your dagger looks."

Cassidi laughed, "Careful, or I might change my mind, and leave you on your own."

"You wouldn't."

"No, you're right. I wouldn't," Cassidi got up and gave Rebecca a hug before heading down the stairs to collect her bag and phone and making her way home to begin putting her plan in action for dealing with the trackers.

CHAPTER 7

The start of the next day at school proved to be as terrible as Rebecca expected. She was never one to like being the center of attention, but that is exactly what she was. Not just with her friends, but with everyone else in the school too. Because now she was just the latest victim in this nightmare gripping their city. On top of that, Jonathan had always attracted people like a magnet. He didn't mind being the center of attention, and actually seemed to enjoy it. It sometimes made him a bit too self-assured. Cocky, actually. She wished he were there now, to direct the attention away from her. She'd even deal with his cockiness. Of, course, she said to herself, if he *were* here now, she wouldn't have to worry about being the center of attention. The only good thing about how the day began is that Mr. Grossby didn't call on her once during History class that morning.

History class. A bore. Somehow, no matter what lessons were being taught that day, it always ended up sounding like Council propaganda. The lessons were meant to make Manglebee look like the savior, like the days before The Reckoning were nothing but war and starvation and a free for all violent wreckage. Today's lesson was yet another on The Reckoning. She didn't blame Mr. Grossby. Council's Education Division supplied the lessons teachers were supposed to teach.

There was very little flexibility in content, though some of the teachers got creative in delivery. Mr. Grossby was not one of them. He seemed as bored with the topic as his students were, but, as with everyone else, he was trapped in his allotment in life, unable to do anything different from his assignment to teach high school students about the Council-approved history of this country. He was old enough to have been assigned based on his occupation before The Reckoning, and not because it was what his parents did. He had been a teacher before, and he remained a teacher after. There had been some shifting around of workers and jobs, to reduce numbers in areas that were deemed saturated or unimportant and to fill in in those areas that did not have enough workers.

If you were good at what you did, and Mr. Grossby apparently had been, then you were most likely assigned to do the same job after The Reckoning, even if the parameters of the job changed a bit.

"I don't have to remind you of what life was like for the ten years prior to The Reckoning. This country, formerly called the United States of America, was not united as we are today. This was a greatly divided country. There was no balance in our system, as we see today," droned Mr. Grossby, as he occasionally glanced down at his script to be sure he got the phrasing right. "Head Councilor Mangabee's Vision provides stability, balance, and security for all citizens."

Mr. Grossby went on to lecture about the 10 years leading up to The Reckoning. The country had been growing unstable for several years. Probably actually decades, but these types of things have a way of sneaking up on people. Conditions grow a little more uncomfortable over time, rather than major changes, and you don't notice until the accumulation of changes amounts to conditions that are entirely unpleasant. There was a growing population and decreasing energy and food supplies. The economy was also taking a hit, with too many people and not enough jobs. Most of our work was conducted overseas, and AI was taking over the workforce for jobs that did remain here, rendering people unnecessary. This all meant that more people were hungry, fewer people could afford to heat or cool their homes or drive to work, which meant even more hungry people and fewer jobs as businesses closed or AI took over.

"Excuse me, Mr. Grossby, but doesn't AI still do most of the work?" That was Sam, at the front of the class. Always one to challenge the information being taught, but somehow evidently not pushing it far enough to get into too much trouble since she was still here.

"Yes, Sam, you are right. Though not most of the work. AI does a lot of the work, in oversight, quality control, and sensitive jobs such as surgery, where there is too much room for human error. We still need doctors, of course, but AI performs the surgeries. With AI, we see far fewer mistakes leading to patient death, in this example with using AI in the medical field. We also see a much more efficient system altogether. There is another difference now, however. We have fewer people because so much of the population was, sadly, lost during The Reckoning." In this, Mr. Grossby still remained dispassionate. These were still explanations he was obviously directed to give, and Sam was certainly not the first student to pose this sort of question.

"AI is used to make our system function in an effective and efficient manner. Workers are still used in some places where AI *could* be used because it makes sense to do so. It helps maintain the balance in our system because people need something to do. And since we no longer trade with other countries like we did before The Reckoning, we can make everything here. Anecor is completely self-sufficient now. Council's rules about jobs and family size, subsistence credits and living quarters all work together to create a balanced, healthy, and happy society." Mr. Grossby finished his canned response to Sam's question. Rebecca could see that Sam didn't buy it, but she wisely kept silent.

Mr. Grossby picked up where he'd left off before Sam's question. The food supply was already diminishing, but then the country also saw continued crop failures, more people getting sick from airborne illnesses and viruses..." Mr. Grossby paused at this last word, letting it fall away from his lips, trailing off into a silence. He stared off into the distance for a moment, lost in his own thoughts. Rebecca knew he must be thinking about his wife, who had died from this current illness. Glancing around the room, she could see students looking away or shifting around in their seats. Everyone understood.

Rebecca felt his pain acutely. Tears welled up in her eyes before she could force them back. She blinked a few times, trying to stop the flow. Lowering her head to hide her eyes, she felt the gaze of several students shift to her, wondering if Mr. Grossby's words were affecting her, too. She wouldn't look up. She couldn't. Fortunately, Mr. Grossby directed the attention back towards him, readying himself to continue on with class with a slight shake of his head and a deep breath in an effort to regain his composure.

Her teacher moved on. The government was not functioning. There was fighting and discontent within the government. People engaging in violent protests. Crime at all-time highs. Nothing was working anymore. A complete collapse of our system and society. When Head Councilor Manglebee was elected to office, he knew he had to do something drastic to ensure this country did not completely fall apart. With the help of people who he brought into his fold because they had the same vision for this country— they did not want the country to continue down the same road—he made the hard decisions and he and his team did what had to be done.

This small group of men took over the country and dismantled the dysfunctional government. They broke the system in order to heal it, and then completely reorganized this country into the great place we live in today. Head Councilor Manglebee crafted the Vision. This masterpiece was the culmination of all of the hard work these men did to fix the social, economic, and environmental issues killing this country. It provides the structure for our healthy society.

Rebecca heard a few giggles escaping from somewhere in the room, and then quickly stifled before the guilty parties were found out and sent down to the Principal's Office to be dealt with. The Reckoning was no laughing matter. Not here, in school where your teacher could see. While this current generation was the first to grow up completely within the new government and structure, they also knew enough from the little things they picked up from parents, instigators, and others along the way to know that Council's words, Manglebee's Vision, were not as wonderful as the history lessons and Council News and bulletins would have them believe. If everything was as peaceful and balanced as Council would have them believe, there would be no need for the disappearances.

Rebecca watched the clock. Waiting for the tone that would indicate the end of class, and the break for lunch. Five minutes left. She let her mind drift. There was nothing new in these lessons anyways. They had heard the same story since entering school at age 5, with just a bit more elaboration, or embellishment, of the details each year to match the age of the audience.

The tone sounded. Rebecca gathered her books and put them in her bag. She took her time. She was not looking forward to lunch. The class schedule did not leave a lot of time for questions from her friends or anyone else, so she had been largely left alone. She and Cassidi timed their arrival to have just enough time to get into the building and to their first classes. It didn't stop the stares, or the murmurings of condolences on the way into the building or between classes. It didn't stop the looks of pity on her teachers' faces, or the looks of renewed pain from those, like Mr. Grossby, whose own losses were recalled and made fresh by seeing Rebecca.

Dragging her feet to the cafeteria, Rebecca prepared herself to face her friends. They were all already there, including Cassidi, as she knew they would be. As anxious as she was, she wasn't really hungry but got in line to get her food anyway because it was a good way to stall just a little bit longer. As she made her way to the table, Cassidi caught her eye and gave her a reassuring look. She took her place at the table next to Cassidi.

"Heya Becs," Troy said, making every effort to sound as if nothing was different.

"Yo, Becs. Good to see you," Selby, acting as if Rebecca had just been away on vacation.

Bendi was the last to greet her. Gentle and kind, sensitive, Bendi. She had an even harder time trying to act like nothing was different, but she managed a, "Welcome back. We missed you."

Obviously, Cassidi had gotten to them ahead of time to warn them not to draw attention to Jonathan's death. She appreciated her friend's thoughtfulness but wasn't entirely sure if it made it any easier.

The rest of the lunch passed with Rebecca picking at her food and moving it around on the tray. Her friends made idle chatter, talking about everything *except* the virus and Jonathan's death. The boys tried to engage her, to make her smile in their tales of school happenings in her absence, mostly at the expense of other students. While Bendi was even quieter than usual, looking on the verge of tears and not eating much of her own lunch. Cassidi stayed on top of the conversations, keeping the ball rolling when the silences settled in on the group.

At last lunch was over. The group of five got up to make their way out of the cafeteria, with Bendi pausing to give Rebecca a hug. "I know we aren't supposed to talk about it, but…" she swallowed hard, "I'm so, so sorry, Becs." And with tears now falling down her cheeks, she hurried out of the lunchroom.

"Sorry," said Cassidi, "you know how Bendi is. She's taking this really hard because she cares about you. Sometimes she just hurts too much for others."

"It's okay, Cass. Thanks for doing so much to help today. Bendi is thoughtful. I didn't mind."

The boys were walking ahead of Rebecca and Cassidi as they made their way out into the hallway, where Rebecca and Troy would split off from the other two to head to their

Robotics and Technology class, and Cassidi and Selby would be heading to Calculus.

"Meet at your house after school?" Cassidi asked.

"Definitely," Rebecca responded, as Cassidi gave her hand a quick squeeze, imparting her own strength into Rebecca to get her through the rest of the day, and turned to join Selby. Rebecca and Troy walked together to class. He filled her in on what she'd missed in RT class while she was out, telling her he would be happy to help her catch up when she was ready.

Rebecca gladly took him up on that offer. Troy had a knack for any techy, geeky subject. He was miles ahead of everyone else in the class, often even correcting the teacher if they made an error. Which, come to think of it, actually meant the Education Division and Council had made an error since they were the ones who dictated the lessons. But no one dared bring that up in class. Troy apparently came by his gift naturally, as both of his parents were genius in the same area. Their talents were put to use in the Security Division of government. It was entirely clear that their son would be able to slide right into the same department after university, if not sooner. He was that smart.

They entered class and took their seats. Rebecca did not have time much to wander off in her own thoughts during this class. Or for the remainder of the afternoon, for that matter. After lunch, her classes were comprised of her most difficult subjects: RT, Trig, and Advanced Chemistry. They required more of her attention than History, Speech Comm, and Advanced English. Rebecca was glad for the distraction.

When the final tone sounded, Rebecca, as she had done the day she raced home to Jonathan, avoided her gathering of friends by leaving through the school's west door. This time, however, all of them would understand, and Cassidi would soon be meeting her at her house. Hopefully to let her in on the plans to get around the trackers.

CHAPTER 8

Rebecca was waiting for Cassidi downstairs, looking at her phone to distract her while she did so. She needed to not think about much for a little bit. She had to let down from the day. Let herself just *be*, if only for a few minutes.

It turned out to be a longer few minutes than she had anticipated. Just as she was growing concerned about what was taking Cassidi so long, the doorbell rang. When she opened it, Cassidi stood there looking pale and a little ill.

"Cass! What's wrong? You're not getting it now, too, are you?"

No response, though Cassidi looked like she was trying to find the words for whatever she wanted to say.

"Please don't tell me I'm going to lose you now, too," Rebecca's face started to crack. That thought was more than she could possibly bear.

The words seem to bring Cassidi around. She shook her head no, and came into the house, dropping her bag, with her phone in it, and nodding her head in the direction of the stairs. Rebecca left her phone on table. The two girls made their way up the stairs and into the safety of Rebecca's room, where they could talk without their phones listening, before either of them spoke again.

"Cass, you're scaring me. You are white as a ghost and I've never seen you look spooked before."

"I'm not sick, Becs, but you might wish I was when I tell you."

"Don't even joke about that, Cass!"

"I wish I was. You might want to sit down for this. Preferably across the room from me."

She complied, feeling more anxious by the moment. Cassidi was always so calm, no matter the crisis. She could be counted on to keep everyone else together. She and Selby both had that ability. So, there was no way Rebecca could imagine anything other than her or Cassidi getting this illness that would cause her to act as she was now.

"Okay. I'm sitting, so you need to start talking, fast, because my mind is racing ahead, and I can't imagine for the life of me what is making you act this way."

But Cassidi didn't start talking immediately. She took a moment to sit in the desk chair across from where Rebecca sat in her usual spot on her bed, knees tucked up, with her arms wrapped around them, chin set between her knees, and terror on her face. Cassidi sat straight back, feet planted on the ground. She rubbed her hands firmly across her thighs, rocking slightly back and forth as she did so, before coming to a stop, with her hands still resting on her legs. She was pointedly avoiding Rebecca's gaze. Cassidi closed her eyes, and then blurted out the words,

"I told Troy."

"You WHAT??"

"Listen, Becs, I had to!" Cassidi opened her eyes now and looked at Rebecca imploring her understanding. "It was the only thing I could think of to get past the trackers. Who else do we know that could help us? How else could we possibly get down into the valley if we didn't get help?"

"So, where is he? I take it your conversation with him didn't go well," Rebecca said.

"I don't know where he is!"

Rebecca suddenly hopped off the bed and started pacing the room. Cassidi pulled her knees up, much as Rebecca had just been doing, feet propped on the edge of the chair, and buried her face in her knees in a very un-Cassidi-like posture. Rebecca saw her friend and took pity on her. She knew Cassidi had to be feeling awful. She was right though; how else could they get past the tracking system? Ultimately, it was her own fault for bringing Cassidi into it in the first place.

Rebecca sighed and forced herself to stop pacing, taking a seat again on her bed, before saying, "I know you were trying to help. It was a good idea, even if it didn't work. Just tell me what happened."

"I caught Troy after school, just as we were all breaking apart to go our separate ways. I let Troy head off towards his transit stop but caught up with him after I was sure none of the others would see me. He was walking through the park when I got to him. Since I didn't want to talk with our phones by us, I indicated that we should put them inside our bags on the picnic table, and then we walked a safe distance away. I filled him in quickly on what we know so far and what you saw the other day. I asked him if he would help us to get past the tracking system on Saturday."

"What did he do? What did he say?"

"He got mad! He said that we were insane, that there was no way the government would be involved in any of this, or his parents would know about it. He said we were even crazier if we continued to snoop around in other people's business, trespassing on their property and spying on them. And then, he stormed off, grabbing his bag and heading away from the transit station, so I guess he wasn't going home, which is why I don't know where he is."

"Oh, Cass, what if he tells someone? We could be carted off to a detention center. Or worse."

"I don't think he'd do that, Becs. Troy isn't like that. He might not believe us, or maybe he is scared of the idea that we could be right about this, but I don't believe he would turn us in."

"I hope you're…"

Rebecca was interrupted by the doorbell. The girls looked at each other, both thinking the same thing: who else could it be? Rebecca ran down the stairs, with Cassidi right on her heels. As the doorbell was ringing a second time, she opened the door to find Troy standing outside, impatience and anger both moving across his face. Rebecca gestured him inside, a little reluctantly, given the obvious state of his emotions at the moment, but there was nothing else she could do. Cassidi stepped aside, pinning herself against the wall, as Troy charged through the entry and into the living room.

He was getting wound up to speak, when Cassidi gave the "cut it" sign, slicing her hand across her neck, and then pointing to the phones on the table and then jabbing her finger in the air towards the stairway to indicate everyone should head up there before speaking. Fortunately, not only did he get the hint, but he followed Cassidi's directive.

Before either Cassidi or Rebecca could say a word, and when the door had barely clicked closed, Troy laid into them: "Seriously, what are you two *thinking*? Don't you understand the trouble you could get in? Do you not get that there doesn't have to even *be* anything to find out? All you have to *do* is act suspicious, which you most certainly *are*, and off you go. Trust me. I know this. I hear it from my parents all the time. Start poking your nose in other people's business, or, worse yet, acting on suspicions of government activity is a fine way to end up put away for life or disappeared. I can't *believe* the two of you! And now dragging *me* into it? Especially with what my parents do, and with what *I'm* expected to do for my assignment?"

Troy didn't even stop to breathe during this tirade. His pale face was red by the time he was finished. His glasses repeatedly having slipped down his nose while he was flailing about in his rush to get the words out, he had finally given up and held them in a fist that threatened to crush them. He'd raked his hands through his thick sandy blond hair enough that it now looked as if he'd just crawled out of bed. When he stopped speaking, finally, to draw in a breath, he also had to wipe the back of his hand across his mouth to remove the spittle that had escaped with his rush of words.

"I know you don't believe us, Troy. But I never would have brought you into this if we didn't desperately need your help. We aren't asking you to go with us. Just tell us how to get around the trackers. If we got caught, neither of us would ever spill. We would never tell them you were involved on any level. And I'm sorry. I'm sorry I had to come to you. But we are going to do this, with or without your help," Cassidi rushed through her own words, trying to get them out before Troy had a chance to start in again.

Cassidi continued, "Something is going on here. Jonathan was figuring it out, and then he got sick before he could solve this. We owe it to him, and to everyone in Montrose, to find out what is really the cause of this illness. Answer this: does this virus behave like any other virus you've ever seen or heard about or read about?"

"No." Cassidi smiled at this, feeling a small victory in getting him to agree to something she said.

That smile faded almost before it was fully formed, when Troy responded, "But viruses evolve all the time. Quickly. Who's to say that this is not just some newly evolved strain that spreads in a way the scientists have yet to detect?"

"So, how do you explain the lights behind the mountain and the people coming *out* of the mountain that Becs saw?" challenged Cassidi. She was not one to give in easily.

"I can't, but it doesn't mean that there isn't an explanation. Just that I don't know what it is."

"Please, Troy. I know Jonathan was right. It isn't what it seems. I have no idea exactly what it is, or even if the government is in any way involved. Maybe they really have no idea about what's happening and are as perplexed as the rest of us. Or maybe it's something that is happening outside of your parents' division. Whatever it is. I need to do what I can to find out. And if I'm wrong? Well, then I'll deal with that, too." Rebecca pleaded with Troy, in the hopes that she could break through with a gentler approach than Cassidi's.

And maybe she knew that Troy was more likely to cave into her than he was to Cassidi because he'd had a crush on her for years now. He'd confessed as much in 6th grade. They were at a school dance. He was teasing Rebecca about another boy who kept asking her to dance. She had responded that no one else was asking, so she just kept dancing with him, but it didn't mean she liked him. So, Troy had asked her to dance. Once out on the floor, a minute into the song, he had apparently gotten up the courage to admit he had liked her for a long time and asked if she felt the same. Rebecca recalled how awful that was. She'd had to tell them that she liked him. A lot. As a friend. A close friend, but still a friend. He had turned red, swallowed hard, and looked off into the distance for the remainder of the song. They parted ways after that and it took Troy weeks before he could look her in the eyes again, and the summer break before he was able to talk to her like old times.

Rebecca wasn't sure if it was her softer approach or the still harbored feelings he had, but she could see the rigidity leave him. His frame deflating as he exhaled in an exaggerated sigh. He was coming around.

"Tell me again what you know and what you plan to do," he finally said.

Cassidi opened her mouth to speak but was stopped in her tracks.

"Becs, I want to hear it from you."

Cassidi shot Troy one of her sharp-edged looks that could slice through any armor. Luckily, Troy was looking at Rebecca and missed the look. Rebecca did not and issued her own warning glance to Cassidi. Troy hadn't actually agreed yet, though it seemed he was on the verge of doing so. Unless Cassidi pushed his buttons again. She wisely refrained, and sat down in the desk chair again, one leg crossed over the other, swinging back and forth in her obvious frustration at being shoved aside.

Rebecca recounted everything to Troy. Including the meeting with Daniel. She didn't think it would be fair to hide anything from him if they were expecting his help. He apparently did not pick up on how she felt about Daniel, as

Cassidi did, but, well, he was a guy, so what else could you expect? She was happy for that, at any rate. It made her feel better that Troy seemed not to read her too-readable face.

Another deep sigh from Troy when she was finished. "You sure don't give a guy much of a choice, do you?"

"Sorry, Troy. I wish there was another way," Rebecca said.

Troy sat in silence for what seemed an eternity. It sounded like he had agreed to help them, but the situation still felt too fragile and Rebecca was afraid to break the silence for fear of scaring him off. Cassidi's look said she felt the same.

"Okay. When are you guys planning this insanity again?"

"Saturday morning."

"As in *this* Saturday morning? As in, the day after *tomorrow*?" Troy looked aghast at this revelation.

"You sure don't give a guy much time, do you?"

Rebecca chanced a hesitant, "Does this mean you'll help us?"

Yet another sigh. With an edge of exasperation. "I don't think you've left me much choice, if I don't want to see two of my best friends locked away for life, since you've already told me you're going through with this madness with or without my help. I guess it has to be with, then, because I honestly don't want the guilt for the rest of my life if you guys get caught by the trackers."

Rebecca leapt off of her bed and threw her arms around Troy in a rib-crushing hug, thanking him profusely.

"Don't thank me yet. I still have to figure out how to help you. In a day. With school and homework. I can't make any promises. But I won't be able to do any of it if you continue to crush my ribs and squeeze the life out of me," Troy squeaked out with the little air left in his lungs. Rebecca abruptly let go, at which time, a tiny look of disappointment passed Troy's face. He might have not been able to breathe, but he apparently wasn't really ready for Rebecca's hug to end, either.

At this time, Cassidi stood up from the desk chair and crossed the room to Troy, extending her hand, rather than giving him the exuberant hug Rebecca had given. Back to her controlled demeanor, but still with appreciation written across her face.

"Thank you, Troy. We owe you one."

"Yes, you do. Big time."

Cassidi did her best to keep the irritation from showing, and Rebecca thought she did a fine job of it. Troy seemed not to notice it. He headed for the door.

"Well, I'll leave you girls to it. Whatever it is you're doing. It seems I've got a long night ahead of me, so I best be making my way home. Meet me at the west side entrance before school tomorrow and I'll let you know where things stand. I don't expect to figure it all out tonight, but I hope to at least have an idea if what you're asking is possible. And if I don't show…well…I guess you'll know I was only successful in getting found out."

"You're too smart for that," Rebecca said.

"Yeah, you're right. I am."

This time, Cassidi could not refrain from a groan and a roll of her eyes. Troy just laughed. He seemed back to normal, in spite of what they'd just asked him to do. This relieved Rebecca, and she felt her shoulders drop, a little of the tension she didn't know she was holding, leaving her. She closed the door, and leaned back against it, looking to see a similar reaction from her friend.

"Okay, so I get why you did this, and right now I appreciate that you did. But this doesn't mean you're totally off the hook, you know. That could have gone very badly."

"I know, Becs. Believe me. I know. But it didn't, and now I feel much better about what we are doing on Saturday."

"Yeah, so do I."

CHAPTER 9

Cassidi and Rebecca entered the school together on the following morning. They had the same first period: second floor, west wing. After depositing their bags in the room, they retraced their steps to the first floor, and then down the west wing and out the side door. Troy was already there waiting. He looked terrible. Like he hadn't slept at all the previous night.

"What took you two so long?" Troy said with an attempt at humor, glazed with a bit of testiness.

"How long have you been waiting?" Rebecca asked.

"Five minutes," Troy smiled, seeming more himself.

"You look awful," Cassidi chimed in, offering her usual blunt two cents.

"Why thanks, Cass, you're looking mighty fine yourself," Troy retorted, but with a smile. Everyone was used to Cassidi's no-nonsense-call-it-as-she-sees-it commentary. It was true, as well, that Cassidi was looking a little rough. They all were.

"I'm sorry, again, Troy, for Cass dragging you into this." Cassidi gave Rebecca an elbow jab at this. "I'm glad she did, because I don't know what we'd do without you. Your help at least makes me feel just a little less nervous about tomorrow. A little. That is, if you are able to figure out what to do. Did you? Figure anything out?"

They all glanced around instinctively to make sure no one else was around. Troy chose the west door because it was rarely used. Usually, everyone entered through the front or back doors. Occasionally, students would leave through the west door, as Rebecca had, but that was only if they had someplace to go in a hurry. Typically, the time just before and after school was when everyone caught up with friends, clustering in groups in the main hallway, before dashing off to their classes to beat the sounding of the first tone or wandering away to make for the transit stations. This morning, the group of three was unsurprisingly alone outside the west door.

"Maybe. I have an idea, at least, but I won't know if it will work until tonight. Or, to be more precise, I won't know if *I* can make it work. Theoretically, my idea is possible. I won't know if I can do it until I work on it tonight."

"Okay, Troy, you're getting a little ahead of us. Do *what* exactly?" Cassidi asked.

"Oh, yeah. Sorry about that. I haven't really slept. I was thinking last night about these trackers that are in our arms. That's what we really have to worry about. We can leave our phones at home."

"Wait. *We?* No. Just Becs and I. I might have dragged you into this by asking you to do this for us, but I won't have it on my head if we get caught and you're with us when we do. It's too dangerous." Rebecca gave a start at Cassidi's comment. She had been so caught up in what Troy was trying to say that she didn't even pick up on the "we" comment Troy made.

"Cass is right, Troy. It's too dangerous. We are already asking too much of you."

"I'm not giving you a choice. If you want me to do this, I am coming with you. Listen. I'm still not sure if I believe you guys. In fact, I don't think I do. But the only way for me to know for sure is to come with you to see what you two are making such a big fuss about. I need to see for myself. So, if you want me to help you, I am coming with. I'm already in deep, putting my neck on the line by helping you at all. I might as well go all the way."

Cassidi and Rebecca looked at one another, reading each other's thoughts on what Troy just said. Cassidi gave a shrug, as if to say it was Rebecca's call, she didn't care if Troy wanted to put himself in more danger than he was already. Rebecca gave a slight nod of acknowledgement, then turned to give Troy a long, uncertain look.

Making up her mind, she said, "Okay, yeah. I guess now it's me who really doesn't have a choice, isn't it?"

"Not if you want my help," responded Troy.

"Okay, you can come with us, but I don't like it. This is my burden, a risk I have to take, and it makes me highly uncomfortable to be dragging others into it."

"Becs," said Troy, "you aren't forcing us into this. Neither one of us. *We* are making the decision to help you and I am sure both of us are well aware of what the potential risks are."

"Yes. Exactly. Troy is right, Becs."

"I still don't like it. But I'll accept it. Go ahead with what you were saying, Troy. We are running out of time before first period starts, and I don't think I want to wait until lunch to hear this."

"Right. So, the thing about these trackers is that they are essentially mini computers in our arms. More accurately, they are GPS devices, but they communicate position data points to SMALS, which we all know is a computer. The way that our trackers know our positions is because of the satellites we have. Basically, our trackers pick up on signals from these satellites that then tell our trackers where we are, based on our distance from the satellites. Our trackers then send this information back to SMALS, where the data points are compiled to detect our standard patterns of movement on the surface. You with me so far?"

Both girls gave impatient nods, just wanting Troy to get to the point, but knowing better than to say so when his argument would likely take longer than letting him talk.

"Okay. Good. Since our trackers have an element about them that acts like a computer, I think it is possible to trick our trackers into sending the same data points repeatedly to SMALS. To do this, I will have to break into the system through my dad's computer. Maybe not actually break in. This is something he already works with. I just have to gain access past his sign-in screen. Anyways. Once I do that, I can open each of our trackers in the system and shut off the GPS element. What I believe this will do is to then hold the pattern at the last data point."

"But won't SMALS detect that the GPS was turned off?" asked Cassidi.

"I don't think so. I think if I disable it within the system itself, it'll be fine. There are occasions, I know, when this happens. I've heard my parents talk about it, but never in enough detail to know why, exactly, which is something I've wondered about for a while now. But that's another story. What is important here is that I will have to access the system to turn off our GPS within our trackers."

"Do you think you can do it?" asked Rebecca.

"I sure hope so. I think I can. I'll test out my theory tonight, after my parents are in bed."

Rebecca glanced nervously at her watch and saw they had less than 5 minutes before they had to be in class.

"We gotta run, or we're going to be late," she said to the others.

"Right. We have to work out a system for how to communicate whether I am successful or not. Becs, can we meet again briefly at your place after school today? I don't think we can all three just disappear without talking to the other two after school. They'll get suspicious."

"Sure. No problem."

The three dispersed, with Troy rushing down to the east wing for his first class and Rebecca and Cassidi making their way quickly through jostling students all trying to make it to class before the tone would sound at any moment.

****

The day passed in a blur, especially for Troy, as he had not slept for more than two hours the previous night trying to figure out what he could do. Rebecca and Cassidi weren't much better off. Both had lain awake a good portion of the night worried about what they were going to be doing and all that could go wrong. And hoping Troy would be successful in his attempt to get around the trackers. They did their best to cover up how tired they were from the other two, not wanting the questions and not wanting to risk getting yet two more people involved. Troy was the least successful as he tried to stifle multiple yawns at the lunch table. Selby and Bendi seemed to accept his explanation that he was up late working on a project for RT class.

The gang met briefly to catch up at the end of the day, but as soon as Troy made his excuses to go because of how tired he was, everyone else quickly dispersed as well. Cassidi and Troy headed off towards the transit stops for their respective homes, but then made the detour once out of sight to head back to the transit line that would take them to Rebecca's house. Once there, before heading upstairs, the three dumped their bags in the living room, as was now protocol when the three of them met up. Ditch the bags with the phones in them before making more than idle small talk.

"What's our plan going to be for tomorrow? Anyone come up with any ideas for how we communicate?" asked Cassidi.

"We have to be able to somehow send a message saying that I was or was not successful, without actually saying it," said Troy.

"I was thinking that later today, we could message each other about getting together for coffee tomorrow morning, so we establish a meeting. That will be the basis of what we communicate tomorrow. Our code. If you are successful, Troy, you will message the excuse that you can't meet up because you are still trying to get a class project done and you've got too much left to do on it. That'll be your cue, Cass, to also decline our coffee date, saying something maybe about your Mom roping you into helping around the house. Something like that anyway. Whatever it is, it has to be an excuse that keeps all of us in our homes, so that it makes sense that that is the position being sent from the GPS in our trackers," Rebecca said.

Troy's eyes widened in a look of surprise, followed by what could only be described as pride, as if he had something to do with Rebecca coming up with this idea in the first place.

"Well done, Becs! I'm impressed. Not only did you obviously follow my explanations yesterday, but your little plan nicely covers our tracks perfectly."

"Uh. Thanks, Troy. Not a big deal," said Rebecca.

"Nice, Becs. Now that we have that part easily sorted, what exactly *is* our plan for tomorrow. And what will we do if Troy doesn't succeed tonight?" Cassidi said, steering the conversation back on track.

"First, let's make sure we've got this straight. If I succeed, we cancel our coffee plans. If I don't succeed, we confirm our plans. Does that sum it up?"

"Yeah, that sums it up," replied Rebecca.

"That covers it. Let's start with what time we should plan on meeting, tomorrow," Cassidi said, adding, "I think we should plan on as early as possible, but we want to make sure we give Troy enough time."

"I think early is good. That way, if I get the trackers disabled, it won't be too long afterwards that we can get going, reducing the time that we look like we are in one place. I think the later it gets, the more suspicious SMALS will get. It isn't often we all would stay put in the same place, the same position, even within our homes."

"Excellent point, Troy. Becs, are you okay with an early start?"

"The earlier the better. How does 7:00 sound to you guys? Maybe by going early we'll have less of a chance of running into anyone else on a Saturday."

"I probably won't be sleeping much again, so 7:00 is good for me. Then maybe after we find out that this is nothing and you girls are as insane as I originally thought, I can get home and catch up on some zees."

"Sure, Troy. Whatever," said Cassidi with a roll of her eyes, "So we'll meet here at 7:00?"

"Better not actually meet here. I wouldn't want my parents to be suspicious since we'll just be turning around and leaving again right away. I also don't want to be delayed because you know they'll want to catch up with you guys."

"Good point, Becs," said Cassidi, "but your place is still closest to the direction we need to head. Do you think it's safe to meet out behind your stables? We can probably cut through the fields without being seen that early in the morning on a Saturday. When we reach the stream, we can follow it under the trees until we get to the base of the mountain."

"That should work," replied Rebecca, "We can then cut back to where the trail leads up. Or maybe we can just head straight up through the forest from there. It's close enough to the trail that I think it should still take us to the right place. We already said we don't think it's safe to be right on the trail."

"No, any trail is not a good idea, even that early on a Saturday morning," agreed Troy.

"Can I ask an obvious question?" said Troy.

"Shoot," replied Cassidi.

"What is it we plan to do exactly if we succeed in making it to this supposed door in the mountain without getting caught?"

"I guess we hadn't thought past just getting there," said Rebecca, "but I don't think we should do much more tomorrow than just check things out. See if there is anything once we are down there that will tell us more about what is going on."

"I think Becs is right. Our first goal is just to see if this can be done. If we can get any more information about BRO than we have already, which is almost none."

"I'm all for not putting ourselves at any greater risk than we have to but consider that I'm not so sure how often we would get away with disabling our trackers before SMALS gets suspicious or catches on," Troy said.

"Another good point, Troy," Cassidi said, "Right now, we have no idea what we will be greeted with when we get down there. I say we still go check it out, first, then plan our next step when we see what there is to see. Keeping in mind that we might only get a couple of chances at this."

"Okay, I think we have our plan then. 7:00 a.m. tomorrow. I'll message you by 6:15 so that we have time to get here by 7:00. If my message says I wasn't successful, what do we do? We can't meet here, for obvious reasons," said Troy as he was making his way to the door, obviously barely able to stand from sheer exhaustion.

"Let's hope that doesn't happen. I'm afraid if it does, I have to go it alone," Rebecca responded with a quavering voice.

"Becs, you can't!" Cassidi and Troy said at the same time.

"I'll have to. I have no other choice. Let's just hope your genius brain figures this out tonight, Troy. I'll feel a whole lot better if I have some company. Much as I hate to admit it, since I don't really like the fact that I'm bringing you guys into this. Troy, you better get home and take a nap, first. You look dead on your feet."

"I am. Maybe I'll sleep a little. There really isn't anything I can do until my parents go to bed anyway. If I leave now, I can take a nap for an hour or so before they get home," Troy said as he looked at his watch.

"Then get going!" replied Rebecca.

"I'm going to go, too. I think we could all use some extra rest this evening. If at all possible."

Cassidi and Troy showed themselves out, as Rebecca flopped across her bed and fixed her eyes on a tiny bug of some sort crawling across her ceiling. Watching the little bug move this way and that, with an aimless determination, was somehow hypnotic to Rebecca. Her mind cleared. She was focused only on the movements of the bug, and before she knew it, she was sound asleep.

CHAPTER 10

It was morning already. Rebecca awoke as if in a fog, moving through her morning routine in a daze. She couldn't believe she slept through the night, and that her parents didn't wake her when she didn't come down for dinner.

"Hey, Becs. We're on for our morning coffee meeting. Finished that class project," came the message from Troy. Rebecca's stomach sank to her feet. She waited for a message from Cassidi, but none came. It didn't matter, she was doing this alone.

She knew she had to move quickly, leaving before 7:00, just in case Cassidi got the bright idea to turn up anyway. That would be just like her. But her legs felt like lead. She found it difficult to move at more than what felt like a snail's pace. And her head was *so* foggy, like she had been drugged. She hadn't realized just how she tired she was.

Somehow, she made it to the stream and then to the base of the mountain and found herself looking up at a tangle of trees and brush. Her progress felt so slow. Each movement she made was an effort, and she kept getting caught in the underbrush it seemed at every step, causing her to trip and stumble. She must sound like a herd of elephants moving through these trees.

Surely, she must be getting to the top. It felt like she'd been climbing up through the trees for hours. She was just so tired. She eyed a particularly large tree that looked to her tired mind like a good place to lean back against and shut her eyes. Just for a few minutes. It couldn't hurt, could it?

"Becs, get a hold of yourself," she said out loud, as she kept fighting her way through the forest. She looked up ahead and it seemed to her the trees started to level out a short distance up. "Finally," she thought, "This is taking forever." Putting her head down, she willed her leaden legs to move a little bit faster.

"Just…a…few…more…"

"Fancy meeting you here, Rebecca Avair," said a familiar voice as a hand reached out and grabbed her much more harshly than the first time, causing her to jump, and cry out in pain…

****

Rebecca awoke to the sound of her own voice crying out. She instinctively reached for the arm Daniel had grabbed in her dream. It took a moment for her to calm her breathing. Just a dream, she said to herself. *Just a dream. Just a dream.*

It was still light outside. She couldn't have been asleep for long. Still laying down, she lifted her phone from her nightstand and checked the time: 5:21 p.m. She had been asleep for almost an hour. She felt more tired than she had before falling asleep. Her parents would be home shortly. Dropping her phone by her side, she looked at the ceiling for the bug she had been watching when she fell asleep. It had apparently found a better place to be.

Lifting her phone again, she sent the message to Troy and Cassidi: "Coffee date tomorrow, guys? Has to be early for me. 7:00 sound okay?" She set the phone down, yawning so big her eyes watered. She heard first Troy's sound pattern and then Cassidi's, one immediately after the other. She knew they'd both just respond something in the affirmative, since they had pre-arranged to have this exchange of messages to put in place tomorrow's communication strategy, but she checked her phone anyway.

"It's a bit early, don't you think, Becs? But I'll do my best to be there bright and shiny," came Cassidi's typically sarcastic reply.

"I'm game. Up early anyway," was Troy's response.

With that done, Rebecca sat up, stretched, and got out of bed, not wanting to fall asleep again. She also did not really want to think too much about tomorrow. Instead, she decided to head downstairs and busy herself making dinner for her and her parents. *Won't they be surprised*, she thought rhetorically.

CHAPTER 11

It was 12:30 a.m. by the time Troy switched on his dad's computer. Their Friday movie night had lasted longer than normal. He was glad he at least got some sleep before they got home. He had a really hard time staying awake through most of the movie. What did he expect? Not only was he exhausted, but he'd also let them pick the movie, ensuring that it would be something that he found exceedingly boring. He didn't manage to stay awake for the whole thing, which meant he got a few more minutes of sleep while the movie was playing. This he accomplished without raising the suspicion of his parents, who simply assumed he did not like their movie choice. True enough.

His parents were in bed by 11:30 p.m., but Troy had waited the extra hour to be sure that they had had time to fall asleep and neither was making any last-minute trips to the restroom (his mom) or kitchen (his dad). He was a little nervous about getting the correct password for his dad's computer. It would not be good to get locked out. Not for the task at hand and not for what would follow when his dad found out his computer was locked. Hoping his dad was as transparent with his computer password as he was with the other password enabled devices around the house, Troy held his breath while he typed in his first guess and pressed enter…

Success! His cheeks puffed out with an audible release of air. He was in. He pushed his glasses back up on his nose, hovered his hands over the keyboard, taking in the fact that what he was doing could ruin him if he were found out. Finding out something had happened to Becs because he did not even try? Well, that would ruin him more. He laid his fingers on the keys and began to type in the search box. He searched for the tracker database, and then found all three trackers by each person's date of birth. Now for the truly hard part.

****

Cassidi lay awake, across her bed, fully dressed. She had been for an hour. It was only 5:00 a.m., but she hadn't been able to sleep much, and when she did, it was fitful. She would personally kill Troy if he got this wrong. Too much was riding on this. She knew she would never let Becs go it alone, even if Troy failed in his attempt to disarm the GPS on the trackers. Certainly, he could do this. He was a genius at the computer. She glanced at her watch again. 5:02 a.m. This was going to be a long hour's wait.

Pacing her room, Cassidi looked for something to take her mind off of the time but couldn't find anything that wouldn't just agitate her more. She was anxious. She stopped in front of her mirror, staring herself down. Cassidi had become an expert at building up the walls that would keep anyone from knowing what she was thinking or how she was feeling. Not even Rebecca knew everything she was thinking and feeling, unless she told her. Rebecca was transparent. Cassidi opaque. If she hadn't drawn this shield of safety around her emotions and thoughts, she wouldn't have survived her own family. She raked her fingers through her straight, closely-cropped auburn hair, and looked into her own light blue, almost cat-like eyes. For a moment, the walls came down, and a life of pain and sadness fleeted across her features, before she caught herself, and resurrected her hard look. Turning away from the mirror, she returned to pacing her room like a tiger trapped in a cage.

****

Her stomach was in knots. For the thousandth time, she wished her brother were here. She was sure getting herself into some risky business for a girl who tended to play it safe. Rebecca was thinking about how sheltered her life had been. Up until now, nothing had challenged her belief in her abilities to do whatever was asked or required of her. Nothing had challenged her idea of how strong she was, except for her fear of heights. She might not have needed or liked being the center of attention, but she never felt insecure about who she was. Now, she was confronting a task that challenged these perceptions she held of herself. At every turn, she was doubting her decisions and doubting her ability to do what had to be done.

"I'm sorry, Jonathan," she said to her empty, dark room. She didn't really know what she was apologizing for. She kicked off her covers and climbed out of bed. She moved quietly around her room, beginning to get herself ready for the message that would soon arrive to her phone. Rebecca was going to assume Troy would succeed. It was the only thing she could let herself think at the moment. Regardless, she would be going, one way or the other. She would have to get dressed anyway.

****

Her phone buzzed. It was Troy.

CHAPTER 12

Head Councilor Manglebee had been making a statement when he placed the Capital Complex at the geographic center of Anecor. Moving the location of the capital from its previous location served a purpose. It marked a separation of the old from the new. It signified a new beginning. Manglebee reasoned that this physical separation would create a mental separation in the minds of the citizens between what had been the United States of America and what was now Anecor. Privately, he also wanted the citizens of this new country to recognize that he was at the center of it all. He was the figure of utmost importance, the one who made it all happen, and the one who would now control the government and the country. This was not a truth he relayed to even his closest advisors.

Head Councilor Manglebee sat now with these 12 advisors in a large, sparsely furnished meeting room. It was the room used for strategic planning and consultations. When the 13 men were in this room, imprisonment was the punishment for staff interruptions of any sort. There was a special facility on Complex grounds specifically constructed for this purpose. It had only been used once. That was all that was needed. From that point onwards, no one dared to defy this one rule. Those who came aboard Council staff in the years after the poor soul who had thought his message important enough to break the rule had been imprisoned were immediately brought up to speed on why it was important to take that rule seriously.

A map of the 7 regions of Anecor was displayed on the screen at the front of the room. A few lighted red blocks simply labeled with a number and letter were dispersed in the unoccupied areas, known as the Borderlands, that separated each region. Each occupied city unit was lighted yellow, and several of these were flashing. One of Manglebee's advisors, Gaff, was standing next to the screen, prepared to brief his boss as soon as he was given the go ahead.

The other 11 men were getting situated, pulling out their devices prepared to provide information if called upon and take notes. Manglebee waited, sitting back with his forefingers steepled and resting under his chin, watching the men, looking like he had all the time in the world, until one noticed the look in his eyes. When at last all the fidgeting stopped and all eyes were focused on him, Manglebee shifted his gaze to Gaff.

"It seems we are ready now. Proceed with your update."

Gaff zoomed into the first blinking yellow light. "We continue to have an increase in incidents across the country. You can see here in Barstow that the numbers from last week have gone up from 6 to 9, with occurrences happening most often in the more densely populated areas. All instigators have been dealt with, as you've directed. But it doesn't seem to be slowing the numbers down. The same is happening everywhere."

Gaff zoomed in on each of the blinking city units to reveal how many incidents were occurring and the location of each within the city unit's boundaries. "Have you been able to make any connections between the instigators? Do we know yet if they are working together in a coordinated effort?" Manglebee's voice barely hinted at an underlying tension, though all men in the room had worked alongside him for long enough to sense its presence.

Spencer spoke from his place at the table. "No. If it is coordinated, we haven't been able to see how. We are still working on this. It seems there is a connection between *some* of the individuals in each city unit, but not all of them. Sir, we believe these are mostly individual or small group actions."

"If, as you say, these instigators are not working in a coordinated manner, it means that citizens are getting more out of control."

"Yes, sir. It does appear that way. It doesn't seem to matter that they see that we deal with whomever engages in civil disobedience. They keep at it." Gaff said, still at his place next to the map.

Manglebee turned his attention to the man sitting directly on his right, "Cord, what kind of progress are we making on MBD?"

Cord looked uncomfortable. He knew Manglebee was not going to like his response. "We are coming along, but our numbers just aren't where we would like them to be yet. We seem to be running into some snags with some of the programming."

"We need this operational now. Not next year, not in six months, but now. You are to eat, sleep, and breathe MBD until you get it where we need it to be. Am I clear?"

"Yes, sir." Cord responded. Several other men looked down, presumably at their devices. Each relieved that they were not the focus of Manglebee's attention at that moment, but each recognizing that they could be, at any time.

"Good. By next week's meeting, I expect to hear a more promising report from you." Cord's eyes displayed the fear he felt. To be able to give Manglebee what he asked for was a monumental feat. His people were already putting in long days and often nights to accomplish the tasks required of them. He knew they were doing everything they could to be successful. Next week's results were bound to be a disappointment. What that would mean for Cord was something he preferred not to imagine.

"Unless we have any other pressing issues, I think we are finished here," Manglebee said. No one moved to speak.

"Okay, then. Spencer, I want you to increase the number of people you have investigating the instigators. The rest of you are to continue with your current assignments." A general round of consensus around the table.

"That is all." With that, Manglebee gathered his belongings and left the room. As usual, the 12 advisors waited until he was gone before they, too, gathered their things and left, without speaking a word.

CHAPTER 13

This was really happening. Now. Rebecca crept quietly from her house, slipping out the back door into the dawn light. Daylight was just breaking, but the sun was not yet above the mountains. Her parents' bedroom overlooked the back of the house, but when she looked up, the blinds were drawn, as expected. The entire family tended to be slow to get moving on Saturdays. Her parents stayed in their small suite of rooms reading the Council News and drinking their coffee. Her dad would venture down at some point to round up some breakfast for them, and then putter back upstairs. Rebecca always slept in, except when there was a reason not to. Like today. Jonathan would often be up and out of the house early. It was not unusual for any in the family not to see one another until sometime in the afternoon. Her parents would never know she wasn't in her room when they ventured out, even if she weren't back by then. She hoped she was.

She moved quickly, just in case her parents were already awake and decided to open the blinds to the early morning sun. She rounded the corner of the barn and moved along, out of sight of the house now, until she reached the back side. She leaned back against the structure, listening to the soft noises of the horses inside.

"Mornin' sunshine," Cassidi said in almost a whisper, though there was no one else around to hear. Rebecca jumped at the sound of her voice.

"Hey. You made it." Rebecca noticed how calm Cassidi looked, and immediately felt just a little bit better at the sight of her.

"Of course. Was that ever a doubt? So, Troy isn't here yet?"

"I'm here," Troy said as he came into view.

"Are you sure you're up for this, Troy?" Rebecca asked. "You can't have gotten much sleep at all, and you don't have to put yourself at any more risk than you already have."

"I'm good. There's no way I'd be sleeping now anyway."

"Awww. Worried about us, are you? How sweet," Cassidi said with a smirk.

"Dream on, Cass. Curiosity has the best of me. I want to see what it is Becs thought she saw. And I'm too wired on all the caffeine I had so that I could work on getting the GPS disabled. My parents didn't go to bed until 11:30 last night. I didn't get started until 12:30. For a while there, I wasn't sure I was going to be able to figure out how to get it done. It wasn't simply pressing an off button, you know."

"I know. I'm relieved you got it done. One less thing to worry about," Cassidi said. "Are you guys ready? The sooner we get moving, the sooner we get this done."

"Just waiting on you two," quipped Troy.

"I guess I'm as ready as I can be," said Rebecca.

"Lead the way, Becs," Cassidi said, gesturing towards the field in the direction of the stream.

None of them said anything as they crossed the field. They were more exposed here than they would be once they reached the stream, lined as it was with a narrow buffer of trees. Once they reached the stream, they did not talk much, each lost in their own thoughts about what they were doing. A half hour later, they were at the base of the mountain. It was time to make a decision about the route over the ridge.

"The trail is a little ways that way," Rebecca pointed back along the base of the mountain. "Should we go up and over here, instead?"

They all looked up, trying to discern a path over. It was impossible to tell how the going would be from where they were. It was all trees. Rebecca knew from studying the ridgeline from Jonathan's room that they would not have to go as high up if they went this way, and she knew it was entirely covered in trees, but she could not tell anything more about how hard it would be.

"What do *you* think, Becs?" asked Cassidi.

"Yeah, I'm game for whatever you think is best, Becs, as I know less than either of you about what to expect."

"I could not tell from my house what the terrain will be like here. We could easily follow the trail from in the trees, and, at least on this side, it would not be too dense. But it would be longer. If we cross here, we won't have as far to go, but it could be harder climbing. If we can get straight over, we are also closer to where the door into the mountain is. We won't land on top of it, or anything, but it'll be closer. I think. I guess I don't actually know where the trail leads once it goes beyond where I entered and left it at the top."

"Sounds like a very round-about way of saying we should head up here," said Troy, trying for lightness, but failing since his voice came out in something of a croak.

"I think so. It seems like the shortest route, at least by distance," Rebecca replied.

"I say we do it, then," said Cass.

The three headed up, taking turns taking the lead as one noticed a path that looked easier to follow. It was slow going. The slope was steep, the understory often dense. They didn't quite have to bushwhack their way through, though Cassidi's knife came in handy more than once to cut away a tangle of vines that had wrapped around someone's legs. They had to pick their way among roots and rocks, slick slopes with little to grab onto in the loose dirt, and fallen trees. Moving up, always up. Except for the occasions when they had to backtrack to look for an easier path.

Eventually they crested the top of the slope, still covered in trees, much to the relief of all of them. Cassidi collapsed on the ground, lying back in needles and dirt. Not that it mattered. All of them were covered in a layer of dirt already. Sweat drenching their shirts despite the cool air. Troy paced, working to catch his breath, his face redder than Rebecca had ever seen. He didn't look good. Rebecca took off her pack and tossed it on the ground, and then dropped to the ground herself, sitting among the roots of a large tree.

"Well," said Cassidi once her breathing had slowed enough to talk, "that was fun. Let's do it again."

"You go ahead. I'll wait for you here," Troy gasped out between breaths. He was a sit in front of a computer all day type, not a hike in the woods all day type. This was more physical exercise than he'd done in an entire year put together. "It's 9:00. Do we have a few minutes to catch our breath?"

"I think we need to," said Rebecca. "We don't know what's ahead of us yet. But not long. Because we don't know what's ahead of us yet."

Cassidi sat up, opened her pack, and ruffled around inside until she found what she was looking for. "Snack anyone?"

Rebecca shook her head. *How could Cass eat?* Cassidi could always eat. It seemed she was a bottomless pit. She was tall and lean, a runner and a biker, so she could pack it away.

"Not unless you guys want to be treated to a second viewing after it comes back up," Troy said.

"Thanks for the visual," said Cassidi.

"Any time."

Troy finally sat down, putting his head between his knees. Cassidi ate her nuts, followed by an apple, happy no one else wanted any, as she finished it all. Rebecca closed her eyes, calling up a visualization of where they had to go based on where she thought they were now. It would be helpful if there were a way to see down the mountain. She opened her eyes and looked around, and then got up and started wandering in the area to see if she could see an opening in the trees.

A few minutes later, she came back to where Troy and Cassidi sat.

"I found where we are going from here," she told them. "There's an opening in the trees where it overhangs the valley. I could see it through my binoculars again."

"Was anything happening?" asked Troy.

"No. I didn't see anyone at all."

"How does it look for getting down there?" asked Cassidi.

"Not as bad as our way up. It isn't so steep. I think it'll be best if we cut a diagonal going down. It'll get us closer than going straight down. Troy, are you okay to move again now?"

"Yep. I'll make it. Might not move tomorrow, but I can now."

"Becs, neither one of us has seen this door we are heading to…how about we go to the overlook before we head down so Troy and I can see where we are headed."

Rebecca led them over to the spot she had found a few minutes before and handed her binoculars to Cassidi.

"Okay, flying blind here, Becs. Point me the right direction and tell me exactly what I'm looking for," said Cassidi.

"Look down and to your right, follow the base of the mountain until you get to a clump of trees that are closer together than all the others. I think you'll know what I mean when you see it. It doesn't look natural."

Rebecca and Troy watched as Cassidi scanned, moving her binoculars right slowly, then left a little, then quickly right.

"Got it! You're right. The trees stand out if you know what you're looking for," Cassidi said and then pulled the focus in closer. "I see the door, too. Geez, that door would be noticeable to anyone if it wasn't hidden by the trees."

"Let me have a look," Troy said, holding out his hand to Cassidi, impatient for a chance to see what there was to see.

"Just a sec! A little patience, would you?" Cassidi had an edge in her voice but handed the binoculars over after another quick look.

"Thanks, Cass," Troy said as he aimed the binoculars in the general direction he'd seen Cassidi looking. He found the trees quickly and had to acknowledge that what he saw was…weird. It didn't mean that what they were looking at was at all what Rebecca and Cassidi suspected it was. Not that they knew exactly what they suspected, only that they thought it was some nefarious dealings having to do with this illness. No way to tell that from their current vantage point.

"I see it, too," Troy said, "and I think you're right about cutting a diagonal as we go down. It does seem like the quickest way, and if we get closer, but stay above it, we should be able to get a better idea of what it is."

"Right, or at least see if it's safe to get any closer to check it out," Cassidi added as they began making their way in the general direction of their target.

****

The way down was much easier. The trees were still abundant, but the understory was thinner, and it was definitely not as steep. They made quick work of it, now that their destination seemed attainable. However, the view from where they stood just above and at an angle to the trees and door did not provide them with any more information than what they'd seen through the binoculars. It was harder to see much of anything, really, since they were now much more level with the surrounding trees, making it difficult to see through them. This left them with only one option. Move closer.

So, they did. Slowly. Anxiously. Cautiously.

It was quiet, with only the sounds of their footsteps breaking sticks and crunching pine cones. Until Rebecca's foot caught on something in the ground causing her to yelp as she stumbled and lost her balance, landing with a crash on the ground and sliding down the slope a few feet before coming to a stop. She lay there staring up through the tree branches, and then Troy's face as he moved in to look down at her anxiously.

"Becs! Are you okay? Don't move too quickly. You could have really hurt yourself."

Rebecca didn't respond right away. Instead, she took a mental assessment of what hurt and slowly moved body parts, starting with fingers and toes. Everything seemed in working order, so she carefully sat up, with Troy's assistance.

"No, I think I'm alright. Thanks, Troy," Rebecca said as she further inspected arms and hands. "I'm just a little scratched up. Maybe bruised."

"You've got a scratch across your cheek. Does it hurt?"

"I hadn't noticed," Rebecca said as she drew her hand up to the cheek Troy had pointed to, and then she winced. "Yeah, it stings a little. I'll survive," she said with a small smile.

"Um, guys? You might want to come have a look at this," Cassidi called from the spot where Rebecca had tripped. "Are you okay to walk, Becs?"

"Yeah, I'm good. Have a look at what?"

"This thing you tripped over."

"You mean it wasn't a root or rock?" Rebecca said as Troy helped her the rest of the way up to a standing position.

"No. Definitely not a root or a rock. Come look." Cassidi was crouched on the ground inspecting whatever she was looking at.

Troy and Rebecca climbed back up the slope, with Troy following behind Rebecca, hands out, watching her nervously to make sure she was truly as okay as she said she was and not about to take another spill. Rebecca *was* favoring her left ankle a little, though she managed the short climb back up to where Cassidi waited without too much trouble.

"That's a pretty mean scratch you have on your face," said Cassidi, as she looked up at Rebecca and Troy approaching. "You sure you're okay? You're limping."

"Yeah, I'm fine. Just twisted my ankle a little. It doesn't feel too bad."

"Good," Cassidi said, already distracted again. "Look at this…" She pointed to an object protruding from the ground. It was easy to see how Rebecca didn't notice it. It was only an inch above the ground and black. It blended in well with the soil.

All three peered as closely as they could, with three heads bent over the top of a cylindrical metal piece several inches in diameter. Troy moved closer to it, lying down on the ground and examining the tops and sides.

"It looks like it telescopes. See these ridges on the top here? They aren't attached to one another. It isn't one solid piece."

"Well, we'd see it much better without your head in the way," said Cassidi.

"Oh. Yes. Sorry." Troy moved aside and Rebecca and Cassidi kneeled down to get a better look.

Cassidi opened her mouth to say something, but before any words came out, there was a scraping noise from below. All three instinctively flattened to their stomachs, looking at each other with wide eyes. Cassidi, quite unnecessarily, put a warning finger to her lips. The sound came a second time. Then voices. The voices belonged to a man and a woman, and it did not sound like the conversation was a pleasant one. The words spoken were inaudible, though the tones were harsh and tense.

"Wait here. I'm moving closer," whispered Cassidi as she got up into a crouched position and moved behind a nearby tree. Staying low and moving swiftly, but quietly, Cassidi moved down the slope, making her way from tree to tree. Rebecca watched for a moment, shot Troy a look and a shrug, and then moved to follow. Troy looked on in disbelief and uncertainty. He was not as stealth in the woods as the two more outdoor experienced girls, but he was not so sure he liked the idea of being left behind either. Both choices, to stay put or to follow, were equally bad choices, but at least if he followed, he would have company if something happened to them. Out here, he was on his own. Frustrated, he made his decision.

He found Rebecca and Cassidi behind a tree, looking from above the opening in the mountain at the scene below them. There was no more room for Troy behind that tree if he wanted to see anything, so he made his way to one adjacent and slightly behind theirs. From their vantage point, they could see that the two people arguing below were a middle-aged man with a full head of greying hair and broad shoulders and a woman who looked to be in her mid-30s with glasses and sandy blond hair pulled back in a loose pony tail that did not quite capture all of her hair.

"This is going too far, Karl. *You* are going too far."

"I have my orders, Bryn. And so do you. Including the order to follow my directives, along with everyone else in this Division. You do not have to like it, but you do have to do what we have been sent here to do. This is for the greater…"

"Oh, Karl, stop. Now. I don't need to hear any more of your 'greater good' lines. I might have been ordered to do what you say, but, no, I do not have to like it, and I do not have to buy it. And I don't buy it. I don't buy that you actually believe this is for any *greater good*."

"Bryn, you are getting close to crossing a line here. Just because I have shown you lenience in the past because I knew your father does not mean that I will or can continue to do so. Watch yourself."

And with that, Karl turned and went back inside, not looking to see if Bryn would follow. She did not. She paced in front of the door, still agitated. Pulling a phone out of her pocket, she punched in something, waited a moment, and then put the phone back in her pocket before going inside.

Once the door closed behind her, Troy crept over to where Rebecca and Cassidi stood. "Did you see her phone? It wasn't a Council issue phone. At least not like any I've ever seen."

"I did notice," said Rebecca.

"I wonder what she was doing on it right before she went inside. We're too far away. I couldn't see anything that would give a clue about whether she was sending someone a message or doing something else," Cassidi said.

"I should have pulled out my binoculars," Rebecca realized too late.

"It happened too fast for that," said Troy.

"I wish we had gotten down here sooner. Maybe we would have gotten more information about exactly *what* they were arguing about. Obviously, Bryn doesn't like what's going on here, but it doesn't tell us *what* is going on here," Rebecca said.

"Did you guys notice anything else?" asked Cassidi.

"Anything you're asking about in particular, Cass?" said Troy.

"Okay, so did you guys notice that when they walked out, the door closed behind them, and they did not use a key or anything that I could see to get back in."

"Door's unlocked," said Rebecca.

"Yes, so what?" said Troy.

"It's *unlocked*," said Cassidi.

"Oh no. No way," said Troy, catching on. "There is no way you can be thinking about walking in there, Cass. Not even you are that crazy."

"We don't have to go *in*," replied Cassidi. "We could just crack the door and peek in, see if we can see anything inside.

"What if they are right inside the door? Or if someone comes outside?" Rebecca asked, joining Troy in his dissent.

"You two can stay here if you want. I'm going to go look. Standing here isn't going to give us any more answers. I'll listen closely before I open the door, and I'll only open it just enough to have a quick look."

Just as she was taking her first step from behind the tree, the door scraped open again, and Bryn came back outside, followed by the same man Rebecca had seen before. The man who looked like Daniel. The two spoke briefly and quietly. The man did most of the talking, with Bryn nodding her head, a worried look on her face, and only interjecting twice. They both then headed back inside. Cassidi let out a breath and fell back against the tree.

"I think it's safe to assume that going down there right now is out of the question," Troy said.

"He's right, Cass. We can't go down there now. We have to figure out what is next for us. It's getting late. We will need to make our way back or I know my parents will become concerned about why they haven't seen me yet."

"Mine too," Troy agreed.

"Mine won't notice," said Cassidi, "but you guys are right. We need to regroup and figure out our next step. Obviously, there's *something* going on here. And it seems like it's not good, which makes me think Jonathan was looking in the right place."

"There does seem to be something here, but we can't know what it is yet. I know you both want Jonathan to be right about this, if only because you think you might be able to do something about it, but those two people weren't saying anything that would tell us for sure it has to do with the virus." Troy was still holding onto his doubts. It was to be expected. He analyzed everything and was reluctant to come to any conclusion until he thought he'd been thorough in his analysis. It was no wonder completing his independent projects always took so much time. Sometimes his genius was more of a hindrance than a benefit.

"Always the optimist, Troy," Cassidi replied. "Let's head back over so you two don't get in trouble. We can talk about our next move when we get down on the other side."

"Wait a second. What is Daniel doing down there?" Rebecca had caught another movement out of the corner of her eye as she was giving the area below one more scan to see if she saw anything new. Daniel was below, near the entrance into the mountains, but he looked as if he was also hiding.

Cassidi noticed the same thing. "He looks like he doesn't want to be seen. I wonder how long he's been down there."

"I hope he didn't see us. That's the last thing we need. Well, almost the last thing, but it wouldn't be good, I'm sure," said Troy, speaking barely above a whisper. "I think we need to get out of here as fast and as quietly as possible."

"I agree," said Rebecca, as she glanced one more time down to Daniel. He did not seem to have any idea they were there. She moved quietly up to another tree, with the other two closely behind. With an unspoken agreement, they made their way first to the object Rebecca had tripped over for one last look.

"I wonder if there are more of these, or if this is the only one," whispered Rebecca.

"And what *is* it? What does it *do*?" added Cassidi.

"It seems likely connected to something underground, and we have to still be above whatever that door leads into, unless the underground structure is really small, which seems highly unlikely," said Troy.

"Whatever it is, it isn't operating now. Now, it's just a black tube that is sitting there waiting for someone to trip over it," Cassidi said. "Let's keep moving, since this is another mystery we aren't going to solve right now."

"Keep your eyes peeled for more as we go, just in case," said Troy.

"Good plan. They're hard to see this way, but if we are looking for them, we might be better able to see them," added Rebecca.

CHAPTER 14

Even with the black metal object being so difficult to see, they found three more on their way back up the slope. They were all relatively close together and seemed to disappear before they got too far up the slope. Rather than looking for more, they had decided to continue on their direct path up the slope and discuss the object further when making their plans.

After having made their slow way down, the three sat under the trees by the stream to catch their breath and plan. After Cassidi voiced the thought that maybe the metal tubes had something to do with the lights, they decided that they should do an overnight visit. This had the added benefit of not raising any alerts for their tracking devices reading an output from their homes for several hours. As long as no one noticed that they were actually shut off. If Troy timed it right, it seemed the chances of that happening would be minimal.

Knowing they all needed some sleep, they decided that they would meet up on Sunday night. This would give them a chance to have a full night of sleep and give Troy an opportunity to see if he could gather any more information from the files on his parents' computer. They did also decide to meet up for coffee Sunday afternoon so that they could discuss anything Troy had discovered before finalizing arrangements for that night.

They made their way back towards where the stream met the field behind Rebecca's house. The sun was as high in the sky as it would get for a fall day. It was after noon, Cassidi was hungry again, and they were all beat. The walk along the stream was quiet. The stream itself hypnotic, with the gentle bubbling of water and the occasional leaf flowing downstream in the same direction they were walking. The trees provided shade as well as cover from anyone who happened down the nearby road or passed by on the transit line. All three were lost in their own reveries.

Rebecca and Cassidi were thinking about whether the black tubes had anything to do with the light Rebecca and Jonathan saw at night, and they were both trying to connect the dots between what BRO could possibly be doing in the mountain that was causing these illnesses. Rebecca was also wondering why Daniel was hiding in the trees, and if he had noticed them there, but just wasn't saying anything because he didn't want to be caught either. And Troy? His mind was busy thinking about where to look for more information, how he could dig for it without getting caught, and what, if anything, his parents knew about BRO and the virus. They reached the field and decided it would be best to part ways there.

"Same plan as before? Becs, you message us to reschedule our coffee date. It just seems we ought to do that in order to keep consistent for SMALS monitoring," Cassidi suggested.

"Yeah, I'll message you guys. Oh! Troy, are you going to be able to get in to turn our GPS back on? We didn't even think of that," Rebecca exclaimed, the thought having just occurred to her.

"I thought of it, of course," said Troy with a grin. "Your GPS will automatically turn back on in…oh…" he looked at his watch, "about 45 minutes. Lucky for us, they had parameters that could be set for start and stop times for turning off the GPS on the trackers." Troy puffed up a bit, looking quite proud of his accomplishment.

"Thanks for telling us we were on a deadline ahead of time," said Cassidi. "Though, come to think of it, maybe it was better not knowing," she added, trailing off, almost as if talking more to herself than Troy and Rebecca.

"You both would have been stressing the entire time about our deadline, so, yeah, I decided not to tell you unless you brought it up or unless it became necessary. For your own good." Troy was looking at Rebecca in particular. Truth be told, it was she he was most concerned about. She worried enough as it was, so if he could lighten her load a bit, he would.

"Okay, so we have 45 minutes to get home. We should go, then, so you guys can make it back in plenty of time," Rebecca said, starting to look a little anxious.

"Uh, Becs?" Cassidi said staring at her.

"Yeah?"

"What about your face? That scratch looks pretty bad. Not something your parents aren't going to notice."

The worry lines deepened on Rebecca's forehead, and she furrowed her eyebrows, thinking for a moment before responding. "Maybe I can tell them I was just out with Cedar and I didn't duck in time to miss a branch hanging from a tree."

"Do you think you can get away with that since your parents will probably think you have been in your room this whole time?" Troy was looking concerned now as well.

"I think so. I don't think they will think much about it. They are more…distracted…these days."

"Even more importantly," said Cassidi, "do you think *you* can pull it off? You know everyone can read you like a book. Can you make them believe you?"

"Well, I thought I could until you just mentioned it!"

"Sorry, but I had to state the obvious, Becs. You aren't a good liar."

"No, I know. But, again. They're very distracted these days, so I think that will help. I hope."

"Good luck with that," Cassidi said with a flat look that indicated she wasn't actually joking. She turned and started heading in the direction of home.

"Yes, good luck, Becs. You'll be fine, I'm sure." Troy wasn't joking, either. He gave her a last look before turning towards the nearest transit stop heading for home himself. "Don't forget to message us!" He called over his shoulder as he was walking away.

"I won't. Thanks for all your help!" Rebecca called back. Troy gave a quick wave of his hand in return, without looking back again.

Rebecca watched him walk away, without really seeing him. Her mind was drifting back to Daniel's presence and the conversation the three of them had overheard, wondering what the connection was between all that they had seen and heard and the death occurring in ever larger numbers all around her. Could it be that Daniel was suspicious too? There was no way she could approach him, of course. But she did wonder. What did he know? What about his brother—for now she was certain that that had to be his older brother she had seen on both discovery missions—how was he involved in all this?

Too many unanswered questions. She realized that they had now gone far beyond the point where Jonathan's investigations had ended. His information on BRO did not provide anything useful. She had confirmed the lights, found a possible source for them (but not why they were there), and discovered some obvious conflict among the people working inside the mountain. None of this provided any more answers as to why so many people were getting sick and dying, but with no connections between the people who were getting sick. It all still just seemed so random.

Rebecca was staring into the water now. She noticed for the first time the scratch on her cheek. She cupped her hand and scooped up some water, doing her best to clean off the wound and render it less noticeable. She peered a bit closer at her reflection. Ouch. She looked rough. Rebecca splashed more cold water on her face and raked her fingers through her hair. She stood up and brushed as much dirt and tree debris from her clothes and shoes as possible. And hoped her parents would be too preoccupied to notice. Better yet, she hoped they weren't in the living room so she could at least go up to her room and change clothes. Maybe practice the delivery of her story for getting the scratch before facing her parents' possible questions.

She need not have worried. When she got home, her parents weren't even there. They had left a note on the kitchen table telling her they were going to be gone for the afternoon and possibly into the early evening, leaving her to fend for herself for dinner. No indication of where they were going. Rebecca hoped they were doing something to help take their minds off of their grief. She was worried for them, but they all kind of tip-toed around one another now, encased in their own thoughts and feelings.

Rebecca had noticed that her parents seemed withdrawn from each other, too. It wasn't that there was any tension. They were never ones to openly argue or fight. Not like Cassidi's parents did, even in front of Rebecca the few times she had gone over to her friend's house. That was one area where Cassidi did not reveal too much. Rebecca had asked, more than once, after witnessing some of Cassidi's parents' arguments, about whether her parents were alright and whether Cassidi was alright. She always brushed Rebecca off, making light of the situation, though Rebecca could see there was more to it. She knew better than to push, though.

Rebecca's own parents were quieter. If they had their disagreements, and surely they did, they handled them quietly.

The tension never got to be too high nor last too long. Since Jonathan's death, though, her parents' usual quiet way of living seemed to become now lonely as well. They did not act angry with one another. It was more like they just didn't really see one another now. Or her. They went through the motions of the day. They would ask Rebecca how she was doing. Check on her. Tell her they were there for her if she wanted to talk. They would worry, she knew, if Rebecca disappeared for a whole day, if they didn't see her at all. Or, at least she thought they would. She suddenly realized that she didn't actually know for sure.

For now, Rebecca was glad that they were not there at the moment. It saved her from worrying about explanations. It left her with her own time, with no need to tiptoe around them or try to make any sort of light conversation, which was not easy for any of them. She hated feeling so relieved that they were not home, but somehow the house felt less empty, less silent, with her parents not in it. Tears rolled down her face. She felt a heavy sadness for what the loss of Jonathan had done to her family. Rebecca wondered if their family would ever recover, if her life would ever approach the calm ease of earlier days. She doubted it. Little did she know, however, how much her life would change in the coming months. Little did she know how much she would actually long for just the mere presence of her parents, even in their sadness and grief and only half there-ness.

CHAPTER 15

"What've you got for us, Troy," Cassidi asked, before Troy even got seated, across from her, with his coffee and a cinnamon roll.

"Well, hello to you, too Cass. I'm doing great, thanks for asking," Troy quipped in reply. He did not respond to Cassidi right away. He took off his jacket and hung it over the back of his chair, where it promptly slid off and to the floor without his notice. He took a somewhat noisy sip of his hot coffee, made a face at how hot it was, and then picked up his cinnamon roll and took a big bite. Cassidi sighed and drummed her fingers, while Rebecca sipped her own coffee while waiting for Troy to decide he was ready.

Troy certainly seemed to enjoy his power in this situation. He liked being the one with the knowledge. He always did. And he definitely enjoyed making Cassidi wait. Though friends, those two knew how to push one another's buttons. They were continually in these types of personality struggles, each one subtly, or not so subtly, trying to get just a little bit of a rise from the other, without pushing it too far. It got tiresome to watch, sometimes, thought Rebecca, looking from one to the other. Drawing attention to it only made it worse, so Rebecca sipped her much needed coffee…and waited.

"Not much, I'm afraid," Troy finally spoke. "I searched some of the files on my dad's computer, but I didn't have a lot of time. I did find out that the company BRO has been appointed by Council to do research. None of that is a surprise. It just confirms some of what Jonathan already found, right?" Rebecca nodded in response.

Troy continued, "The one odd thing that I did find is that they have High Security Clearance. That's why my dad has something about them in his files, I guess. But there was nothing in the clearance file to indicate why they have or need such a high clearance. I found this information on a spreadsheet of companies and individuals with High Security Clearance. Your dad is on it, Becs. Maybe that makes sense with his role as head of the CAD."

"Probably," agreed Rebecca. "Any other names on that list? Are any of the Morgans on that list?"

"You would think Mr. Morgan would be on it, wouldn't you? Since BRO is operating on his ranch. But he isn't. I looked him up and he has no security clearances at all. It seems BRO is just set up on his land, or in his mountain, but he is not directly involved in what they are doing. But his son is."

"Daniel?" Rebecca asked, a little too quickly, a little too anxiously. Troy actually noticed and shot her an odd, inquisitive look. "I'm just trying to figure out why he was snooping around yesterday, and hoping he wasn't there to spy on us." Rebecca added, attempting to cover up her real concerns about Daniel.

"No. Not Daniel." Troy's tone implied that he was not completely buying her explanation. "Remy. His older brother, apparently. Which would have been the logical guess since that is who we saw talking with the woman Bryn outside the door just before Cass was about to go and get herself into really big trouble with her brilliant plan."

"Oh, yeah, right." Rebecca responded, growing red in the face with embarrassment, while Cassidi simply rolled her eyes at the both of them.

"Anyways. I didn't find anything else last night. I can dig a little deeper before we meet up tonight. Maybe. I'll try to.

Now that I know that BRO and Remy both have High Security Clearance, I might have something more to go on when I search the files."

"Both of your parents work for Security, right Troy? You just looked at your dad's computer. What about your mom's?" Cassidi asked.

"They both work for Security. I was hoping to find what I need on Dad's computer, since he works off of his desktop at home. Mom works on her laptop, mostly. She keeps it in her briefcase in their room. Accessing that would be nearly impossible. So that's off limits. I won't risk trying to get my hands on my mom's computer. Not unless it becomes some sort of absolute imperative."

"No, you're right, Troy. You shouldn't even consider that," Rebecca said.

The coffee shop was beginning to fill up. Students were filing in for afternoon meet ups with friends or to get away from the house to work on assignments for school. There were also a few families coming in after spending a day outside enjoying the fall weather. Rebecca, Cassidi, and Troy all noticed the crowds as they looked up from their table when a family of three walked by, the father accidentally bumping Cassidi's chair as he tried to wrangle his young, rambunctious, son to a nearby table.

"I think we need to finish up here," Troy said in a stage whisper.

"Yes, let's wrap this up fast. We are meeting behind Bec's barn tonight at 1:00, right?" Cassidi spoke in a loud whisper as well, leaning in over the table so that she was not overheard by anyone who happened to be close by. High school kids talking about meeting up at 1:00 in the morning would certainly rouse suspicions. They didn't need that. You never knew who would report you if they overheard something they thought might score them some points with Council.

Troy nodded an affirmation and Rebecca spoke a quiet, "Yes." At this point, there wasn't much else to say. No one tried to shift the conversation to small talk. It just wasn't in any of them to do so. They were too wrapped up in their mission to be able to think of much else. Too tired as well. The late nights and worries were beginning to catch up with all of them. Tomorrow, they would be back at school. None of them liked the idea of pulling an all-nighter on a school night, but they didn't have a choice. There was no way they would wait until next weekend, so it had to be tonight, and tomorrow they would have to face another day of school and trying to act normal around Selby and Bendi. But, first, they had to get through tonight.

****

It was 1:00 a.m. and Cassidi and Rebecca were standing behind the barn waiting for Troy. When he hadn't arrived by 1:10 a.m., the two girls started getting worried. Troy wasn't always the first to arrive, but he was not one to be late either. They could wait no more than 5 more minutes before they would have to take off without him.

"Do you think he fell asleep?" Rebecca mused aloud.

"Could be. I almost did," Cassidi responded.

"He has been spending a lot of overnight hours on this. None of us has been getting much sleep, but I bet he's gotten less than both of us," said Rebecca.

Looking at her watch again, Cassidi said, "We really can't wait much longer. I know you said the lights go on at two and stay on, but I really want to be there when they come on, and we are already pushing it, even though we know the route now."

"I know. Let's get going. I hate to leave without him, but he can catch up with us if he gets here after we leave," said Rebecca.

They had been on the river trail for less than 5 minutes when they heard the sound of footsteps crashing through the trees. Both girls started and then froze in their tracks looking behind them in the direction of the noise. Troy came into view from behind the trees. His face was red, and he was out of breath, surely from the speed he had to keep up in order to catch them, as the girls were moving quickly themselves since they'd already lost 15 minutes waiting for Troy.

As Troy got closer, it became apparent that it was not only exertion that was getting the better of Troy. He looked…well…he looked spooked. Like he'd just seen a ghost. Rebecca and Cassidi waited for him to catch his breath, though both girls were getting impatient. The clock wasn't standing still while they waited and they were losing the time they'd made up in traveling fast, which they'd be much less able to do with Troy along since he was not as athletic as they were. At the same time, his appearance was disconcerting and worrying.

"Is something wrong, Troy? Sorry we had to leave without you, but we waited until 1:15. We had no choice but to get going," Rebecca said.

Troy was bent over, hands on his knees, using his arms to prop himself up. His breath was ragged, with a hint of a wheeze. At Rebecca's question, he raised an arm into the air, giving a signal to give him a moment before he responded. Rebecca and Cassidi looked at one another with both concern and an underlying impatience. Cassidi looked at her watch. Three times.

Troy finally answered but did not move from his hunched over position. His voice came out pinched and higher than usual, "I almost didn't make it. Almost got caught. Dad got up as I was getting ready to leave. Must…*gasp*…have…*gasp*…heard me."

"Did he *see* you?" Cassidi asked, with a stricken look on her face. Troy's dad catching him would be bad. Very, very bad.

"No…close call," Troy finally stood up, though he did not look or sound much better. "I was just about to open the door when I heard their bedroom door push open. Barely made it into the living room before I heard Dad coming down the stairs. I had to crouch on the other side of the couch. He looked into the living room briefly, but then I heard his footsteps head into the kitchen. I had to wait while he wandered around each of the downstairs rooms before heading back upstairs. Then I waited some more to make sure he was really in bed."

Cassidi was staring hard at Troy. It looked like there was something he wasn't saying. It occurred to her that maybe he had found something in the files on his dad's computer. "Did you find anything else out about BRO?"

"Sorry. I didn't. I didn't even get a chance to look tonight. Dad was on his computer until late. There wasn't enough time after he went to bed for me to really go digging," Troy responded, but Cassidi could have sworn he wasn't telling the whole truth. There was something in the look that flashed in his eyes that indicated fear. Or guilt. She wasn't sure which.

She glanced at Rebecca to see her reaction to this. Rebecca's knitted her brow and narrowed her eyes just slightly. It seemed she had caught it, too. She gave a sidelong glance towards Cassidi, who returned the look, and then gave a slight shrug of her shoulders. There was nothing they could do now. They didn't have time to press him. They needed to get over the ridge, and fast.

Getting up the mountain in darkness was a trick. They had headlamps, but they still had a difficult time seeing too well since there was no path. They had discussed the option of going up the trail, but they had no idea if their presence there would be detected. Rebecca led the way, doing her best to pick their way through the path they had gone on Saturday. In many places, it was easy to see where they'd trampled down the brush, but in others, their path was less obvious. Still better to try to stick to the path they had already made because in the difficult places they had already done the work.

Two o'clock came as they crested the hill. They did not make it down to the lights in time to see how they operated. That wasn't necessarily a big deal. All of them had just been very curious to see how they worked; how they came up out of the ground. They would still get to see them in action once they reached them, if indeed the metal fixtures they had seen were actually the sources for the lights. From where they stood at the top of the hill, that seemed to be a distinct possibility.

"At least with the lights on, it will be easier to track our way down to where they are," Rebecca commented as the three of them began to make their way down through the trees.

"This light gives me the creeps," said Cassidi after a few minutes of silence. "I'm not sure it actually *is* any easier to see. Everything has an eerie, purple glow."

"Do you guys notice that it is also starting to disappear as we get lower?" Troy said, and then he looked up. "Check this out. You can still see it above us, but it isn't at ground level. Must mean those devices raise up pretty high above the ground."

"If they are the source of the light. We don't actually know that yet," Cassidi chimed in.

"True enough," responded Troy.

Rebecca, still leading the way, suddenly stopped. She halted Cassidi and Troy with her hand. Her head was cocked to the side. "Do you hear that?"

"Hear what?" asked Cassidi.

"That low hum. Shh. Listen. It isn't very loud," Rebecca said.

"I hear it. More like a buzzing sound. Like a quiet swarm of bees," said Cassidi.

"Yeah, that's it," agreed Rebecca. "Do you hear it, Troy?"

"Not with the two of you yammering away," he responded. "Hang on."

They all stopped talking again and listened. Troy nodded his head. "Yes, a quiet swarm of bees. That's a good description, Cass. Very quiet."

"I wonder what it is. We didn't notice it the other day, so maybe it has something to do with the light," Rebecca said.

"Hopefully, these questions will all be answered when we get down there," Cassidi commented.

As they continued further down the slope, the sound got a little louder, but was still just barely audible. When they approached the spot where the metal fixtures were, it became obvious that they were indeed the source of the light. From the ground, black poles rose up into the air above the height of the surrounding trees. The purple glow emanated from the tops of the poles. The top was a short, but wide, cylinder with openings in the sides from where the light shown.

The light had an odd quality about it. As it left the cylinder, it came out in waves that almost looked like liquid smoke. It dispersed as it traveled further away from the source, looking more like the dull, barely discernable light Rebecca, and Jonathan before her, had seen from Jonathan's window. Except one thing. The light flowed only in the direction over the mountain, towards city, in spite of the fact that there didn't seem to be anything sending it in that particular direction.

"That's strange," Rebecca said. "It isn't acting like a regular light at all. I've never seen anything like it."

"No. Me neither. You ever seen anything like it, Troy?" asked Cassidi.

"Not at all. It is behaving very strangely for sure. And do you guys see…there are tiny points of white light that flash occasionally?"

"Yeah, I see it," said Rebecca.

"So do I. More questions. More mystery. Still no answers. None of this makes sense," Cassidi said, frustration evident in the tone of her voice.

"I know," said Rebecca. "I feel like we are getting nowhere."

"Let's move down closer to the entrance to see if there is anything to see down there," Cassidi suggested. This time, neither Rebecca nor Troy disagreed with the suggestion. Not only did they think it less likely they would be discovered in the dark in the middle of the night, but they felt like their options were rather limited at this point. If they had any chance of learning more, they were going to have to get a closer look. The idea thrilled none of them, except perhaps Cassidi, just a little. She was a risk taker, so, though she was frightened, she was also just a little bit excited.

CHAPTER 16

The entry was dark, and all was quiet, except for the buzzing from overhead. Looking around the grounds outside of the door, they noticed, for the first time, a gravel and dirt track that led to what looked like a garage. It was so well camouflaged and hidden by trees that none of them had noticed it from above. Like the door, the garage was built into the side of the mountain. The top of the structure was covered in a layer of earth, with trees sprouting from the top and vines hanging over the sides, providing more cover for the entry.

"This explains the unnatural clump of trees we saw from above. It's bigger than just what is hiding the door. This must be how they get inside with their vehicles," Rebecca said to the others as they all continued their inspections.

"Hey guys, check this out," Cassidi called out as she was touching the bark of a tree. "These aren't all real. This is a really impressive fake. Wouldn't have noticed it at all if I hadn't touched the bark."

"Whoa," said Troy with wonder in his voice. "You really can't tell until you touch them. This is amazing!"

"What is *really* amazing is that none of us even thought about a road. It only makes sense. This is in the middle of a valley with nothing else around. Hiking in here every time seems obviously unreasonable," said Rebecca.

"It's a dirt road. Well, not even a road. Just two sets of tracks. But the garage door is large enough to fit something pretty big through it. Or at least tall," Troy said, shining his head lamp down the road first and then turning to point it towards the garage door.

"Should we fol—" Cassidi began before she was cut off.

"I hear something! Headlamps off. Now!" Rebecca shouted in a loud whisper.

All three headlamps were off almost instantaneously, and just as a pair of headlights came into view, bouncing around with the rocking of a vehicle over uneven terrain. Reflexively, Rebecca, Troy, and Cassidi hid themselves behind the trees and waited as the lights moved slowly closer. Behind the first set of lights, a second set became visible.

Troy shrank back at the sight of the two sets of lights approaching. He pinned himself against one of the fake trees, hugging himself as if for protection, and squeezed his eyes closed, willing himself back home and safely in his bed. Why did he ever get mixed up in all this? He never should have made his way to Rebecca's house after Cassidi had approached him for help. Never should have agreed, furthermore, to help the girls. Let them put their lives on the line. Not his.

Cassidi and Rebecca watched as a truck with an enclosed container on the back moved slowly into view. As the driver came parallel, they could see a large figure behind the wheel. Bulky, but not at all with the appearance of softness. From the set of his shoulders and the sharp edges of his face, he looked like a figure cut from Greek mythology. He looked like someone you did not want to catch you lurking behind a tree spying on what he was doing. The car followed closely. Even in the slight light cast by the headlights, the girls could tell from the grey of his hair to the outline of his face that it was most likely Karl, the man with whom Bryn argued outside the entry a few nights before. Troy missed it all, as his eyes were still squeezed tight against the reality of what he was doing.

As soon as the car passed far enough along that Karl would not see her, Cassidi moved closer towards the garage door, following the truck and the car. Rebecca tried to get her attention but could not call out to Cassidi for fear of being heard. "Stay here," she whispered to Troy, who had no intention of doing otherwise. Rebecca followed Cassidi's path, scared of and irritated at her friend's impulsiveness. As she moved between trees, she caught the garage doors slowly and quietly edging their way inwards towards a cavernous interior, overhead lights dimly glowing. She could make out nothing else.

Cassidi had already reached a tree abutting the side of the doors and watched as the truck began its passage through the opening. Rebecca eased her way closer, more cautious than Cassidi in her approach. If Cassidi was afraid, her actions and her demeanor did not show it. She wore a look of concentration: eyes narrowed, brows furrowed. She leaned as far forward as she could while still being hidden, mostly, by the tree. Rebecca held her breath as Karl's position in the car moved parallel to Cassidi. His head did not turn, his focus apparently remaining on his own movement forward. Before he was completely inside the structure, the doors began to swing slowly closed.

"No. Oh no," Rebecca muttered, anticipating Cassidi's next move before she made it. Cassidi glanced back towards

Rebecca, briefly, made a barely discernable hand signal indicating that Rebecca should wait there, and disappeared around the closing door. Rebecca froze as the doors quietly clicked closed, her friend gone from sight. With shock and disbelief, she stared at the door for a solid five minutes. It did not open. Cassidi was really and truly inside, and there was no way of knowing what she was doing or if she had been caught. Rebecca tried not to think of Zeus—as she was now mentally naming the hulk of a man driving the truck—discovering Cassidi's intrusion. Somehow, she doubted Karl would go easy on her either.

"Cass did *not* go in there," Troy's constricted voice squeaked from behind, causing Rebecca to jump half out of her skin, emitting a yelp.

"Are you insane, Troy! You could have given me a warning you were coming up on me. And, yes, Cass is inside. Cass is inside there with Zeus and Karl doing who knows what, and if she gets caught…"

"Zeus?" Troy asked.

"Yeah, that huge monster driving the truck. He looked like he could break Cass like a twig using only his thumb and a finger."

Even in the dark, she could see Troy stiffen. He swallowed hard. "I didn't see. I couldn't look," he admitted.

"Yeah, well, there was Zeus driving a truck and that Karl guy, I'm almost positive, following him in a car. And Cass got the bright idea to follow them into the mountain, with nothing to protect her. I couldn't stop her. I was still too far away," Rebecca responded with the hard edge of anger. "Not that that matters, who stops Cass from anything once she's set her mind to something," she mumbled to herself more than to Troy.

"What are we supposed to do now? We don't have much time left before daylight and before our trackers will automatically turn back on. Does she expect us to just wait for her?" Troy's voice rose in pitch and volume as the realization hit him that this could be the end for all of them.

"I *have* to wait for her. But you don't, Troy. You can go back. I wouldn't blame you at all if you did. There's no point in all three of us getting caught for this."

A growl erupted from Troy's throat. Rebecca could feel his frustration and uncertainty more than she could see it. She felt terrible for him being here, but also a bit annoyed. She did not like the position she was in. She blamed herself for bringing Cassidi into this mess and Cassidi for bringing Troy into it. But she couldn't help but be annoyed at Cassidi's rash behavior and Troy's whining. All of it left her in a worse position, she thought, than she would have been had she done this on her own. She took a deep breath and exhaled audibly.

Speaking softly and as gently as she could, she said, "Troy, maybe it's best if you head back. If you get back in time, maybe you could change the time for our trackers to turn back on. It will look like we just overslept. Certainly not unusual for me. That would buy us a little more time."

"And what if it isn't enough?" Troy said.

"Let's just hope that it is." Fear crept into Rebecca's voice with this last response.

"How will I know if you make it back okay? If Cassidi makes it out?" Troy was not going to pretend that he didn't want to leave, and he knew that Rebecca was right. If they were to have a chance at all, he would have to get back home quickly and change the time that their trackers would be turned back on. He would have to be home before his parents got up to get ready for work.

"I'll message you when I get home. If we are both safe, I will say that I need to meet you before school to ask you some questions about RT homework. If I have to leave without Cass, I'll say…huh…not sure what I'll say. Not sure I'll leave without her," Rebecca raised her hand to her forehead, rubbing it with her fingers. When she lowered her hand, she realized it was trembling. Her whole body seemed to be quivering. She made two fists at her side, set her jaw, and willed herself brave.

"If you don't hear anything from me, assume the worst. If I do decide to leave without Cass, I'll message you something. Don't know what yet, but if it isn't about RT homework, you'll know I made it back, but Cass didn't," Rebecca continued with a firm voice.

"You didn't make her go in there, Becs. If you have to, leave without her, and we will figure something out to get her back," Troy urged. "I have to get going now or I won't make it back in time. I'll give you guys until 6:45 before your trackers turn back on. Any more than that and you will have big problems no matter what."

"That works. It gives me another hour to wait before I have to be worried about getting back before the trackers are operating again," Rebecca said after raising her arm to activate her watch and checking the time. "Will you be okay going back by yourself? Do you remember the way?"

"Yes, of course. I might be clumsy and not exactly made for the forest, but I can certainly remember directions." Troy sounded more than a little offended.

"Right. Of course, you can. Sorry, Troy. I didn't mean anything by it. I just want to make sure you're okay since you should never have been brought into this mess," Rebecca reached out and squeezed his shoulder reassuringly.

"Thanks, but it wasn't your fault, and I'm glad I can help. I hope it's enough. Be careful, Becs, *please*. Please don't wait too long. I'll be waiting for your message." With that, Troy gave her one last, pleading look, then turned uphill and began quickly, if a bit awkwardly, making his way back towards the other side of the mountain. Rebecca watched him for a few moments before he disappeared into the darkness, and then she listened to him go for a few minutes more, glad at that particular moment for the closed doors keeping Troy's noisy departure from being heard.

Rebecca stood in the dark, listening to the fading sounds of Troy and becoming acutely aware of her own vulnerable situation. Not as vulnerable as Cassidi, but that was her own choice, Rebecca reminded herself again. "And now, here I am," she continued, muttering aloud to herself, "alone in the dark standing outside a garage door leading into a mountain that just swallowed Zeus, Karl, and my best friend."

Rebecca could hear her own heartbeat in her chest, along with the thrum of the lights still heading over the mountain. Looking up at them, she realized she had actually almost forgotten they were there in the recent commotion. Yet, there they were, the strange waves flowing up and out over the mountain and her city, with the tiny sparks of white firing off randomly, almost too small to be seen. She found herself mesmerized watching them, lured into a calm she hadn't felt all night. Or in the last couple of weeks. She leaned back against the solid tree. This one felt real, she noted, as she sank to the ground and let her mind float into nothingness with the lights above.

CHAPTER 17

Out of breath, Troy reached his front door in record time. At least for him. Pure adrenaline got him over the mountain, but now he felt like his heart was going to pound out of his chest and his legs had somehow gone to rubber. Burning rubber. He grabbed the door handle for support, keeled over with his forehead resting on top of his hands, waiting for his breathing to calm. His parents should still be sleeping. He hoped they would still be sleeping. 4:30. Normally they would not be up for another hour.

As soon as he thought his legs would carry him into the house, he stood up and swiped his key to unlock the door, creeping it open ever so slowly. He had to be sure the house was quiet. Once certain, he slipped through the door and headed straight for the office. He closed the door behind him, then thought better of it. With the door cracked, he could hear his parents better if they started moving around earlier than expected.

Still in the dark, he felt around for the sensor to turn on the computer. He heard the hum of the internal mechanisms warming up. So loud. His right leg bounced, and his fingers lightly drummed the desk in nervous anticipation. At last, the sign-in screen opened. Troy typed in the password and navigated to the tracking program. He changed the time to turn Rebecca and Cassidi's trackers back on, made sure no alerts were activated and that everything seemed in order. It did.

Troy prepared to shut down the computer and head back up to bed, then reconsidered. He still had nearly a full hour before his parents would awaken. He considered what he now knew. Rebecca and Cassidi weren't entirely insane. They had definitely found *something*. But what? If there was a security issue with BRO, that could create a lot of trouble for Council. If his dad wasn't even aware of it yet, maybe Troy could figure out a way to alert him without giving Rebecca and Cassidi away. But what if his dad already had information that might help Rebecca?

It can't hurt to check, he thought. He had already discovered that BRO had High Security Clearance, but what else was in his dad's files? His previous efforts to find more information on BRO hadn't been all that successful. He decided to try to dig a little deeper. Maybe he had missed something the last time. He had been in a hurry last time. Missing something would have been easy to do. Of course, he was in a hurry this time as well, but now that he had already changed the time for Rebecca and Cassidi's trackers, he could focus his search more.

After spending a few minutes opening various files on the drive assigned to SD files, he realized he was getting nowhere. Not exactly nowhere. These files were fascinating. So much information in them. He did discover a file that might be useful for them, though he wasn't really sure how at this point. Troy found a folder labeled "Citizens of Interest." This file appeared to be the names of individuals in Region 3 who were creating trouble in the eyes of Council. The instigators. Troy was a bit surprised that this file contained names from all of Region 3 and not just Montrose. He thought his dad's work was only for the Montrose division of CAD. He knew that there was some sharing of information between the divisions, but he was still surprised to find an entire list of names for Region 3.

****

Each of the 7 regions had several occupied city units within the boundaries of the region. After The Reckoning—once Manglebee and his Council had subdued and defeated citizens—Council began the process of reorganization and restructuring. Manglebee used the military to help him accomplish the monumental task of moving people around and maintaining control. Council determined which cities were to be the new occupied city units based on physical size; availability of surrounding land for ranching, agriculture, industrial plants; and degree of infrastructure destruction. In addition, the new city units could not be too close to one another nor to neighboring regions. This last led to the concept of the Borderlands. A buffer between regions that would provide another level of control on citizen movement. There was also the added benefit of creating an area that Council could use however it wanted, beyond the prying eyes of citizens.

During the transition time, food and water were rationed. Where necessary, people were housed in camps until their new location was identified and housing and work assignments determined. Some citizens were temporarily assigned to work forces responsible for any infrastructure demolition and construction deemed necessary and for the creation of the transit systems that would move people around the occupied city units—thus eliminating the wide-spread need for vehicles—before getting their permanent assignments.

As the food, industrial, economic, and governance systems took shape, Council began to cut a majority of trade ties with other countries. Anecor would be self-reliant and self-sustaining. Globally, a movement away from the co-operative and interdependent system already existed, thus the cutting of trade ties was already beginning prior to Manglebee's Vision. He just finished the job. International relations were now kept to a minimum.

Within five years of The Reckoning, Anecor's structure was largely in place. Weary citizens settled into their newly assigned routines. They learned quickly the new rules and boundaries, grew accustomed to the monitoring systems. They had to. It was survival. But it didn't take long for some to become emboldened again. It didn't take long for the signs of unrest to begin. Council reacted swiftly by carrying off the instigators, either from homes or work sites or from right off the street. At first, this happened in secret, as Manglebee did not want anything to appear to be amiss in Anecor, but as the numbers of instigators grew, he decided to make examples of the troublemakers. Even so, no one knew exactly what became of them. They were rounded up, and then simply just disappeared. This is when citizens started to use the term "disappeared" as the action or state of being taken away by Council's strongmen, never to be seen again.

****

Troy opened the folder for "Citizens of Interest." It was no small list. Pages of names. He had no time to go through them to see if anyone he knew was on the list, but he made a mental note to file this information away, noting the location of the folder on his dad's computer, for potential use in the future. He wouldn't tell Rebecca and Cassidi about this yet. There did not seem to be a need, as it did not appear to have anything to do with BRO. But he would be able to locate the folder again if a need did arise.

Not finding anything directly related to BRO on his dad's work drive, he decided to dig a little deeper. He opened each of the other three drives on the computer. Most of what he found was irrelevant: household operations and supplies, documents about him, Council documents provided to all citizens. But buried within the drive containing the Council documents, Troy found a folder labeled MBD-v04. There was an unusual symbol over the icon. An eye, he thought. Kind of creepy. Intrigued, he clicked on the folder.

"SECURITY ALERT" popped up on the screen, as a voice spoke: "Warning. Retinal scan required." Troy jolted nearly out of the chair. He fumbled quickly for the mouse, looking for how to close the folder before the voice spoke again, potentially waking his parents in the process. He managed to get the folder closed, dismissing the alert at the same time, just as the warning voice began its second alert. Troy felt like he would pass out. He sat frozen at the desk, listening for sounds from upstairs that would indicate his parents had been awakened by the voice.

After he heard nothing for a couple of minutes, he closed out of everything and shut down the computer as fast as possible, then slinked up to his bedroom, crawled under the covers—still fully dressed—and waited for Rebecca's message. He would have to be more careful in the future. If he could even bring himself to go digging again. Right now, he wasn't even sure about manipulating the trackers again.

CHAPTER 18

"You're still here?" came a voice from the darkness, rudely and abruptly yanking Rebecca back to the here and now. She was on her feet and behind the tree before she had time to recognize the voice or comprehend the words that had been formed. Cassidi came closer, chuckling at Rebecca's reaction. Her strained features contradicted the sound of her laugh.

"Cass!" Without thinking, Rebecca was around the front of the tree again, flinging her arms around her friend. It lasted just a moment. The relief of seeing Cassidi again. And then came the flood of anger now that Rebecca knew Cassidi was safe. "How could you *do* that? How could you just leave Troy and I standing out here while you dash inside a closing door *knowing* who was on the other side? You could have been captured, or, who knows, even *killed*! You could have ended this whole thing for all of us, before we had a chance to know anything!" Rebecca was only partially succeeding in keeping her voice down, but once the stream of anger was out, her composure weakened, and once again she found herself trembling.

Looking at Cassidi, she realized she was in worse shape than herself. Her friend had no response to the tirade. She just stood there, facing Rebecca, eyes sparking in the glow of a soft light coming from above the garage, a layer of sweat glistening on her skin. Her breath was shallow, but it did not seem as if she had been running. More like that kind of panting that comes from panic or sheer terror. It was then that Rebecca realized the seriousness of Cassidi's state, and that her initial words had been a weak attempt to appear normal. Normal she was not. It had to be bad if it shook Cassidi as much as it appeared.

Rebecca took Cassidi's hand and pulled her out of the light and back into the relative safety of the trees. Another thought occurred to her just at that moment, as she looked up at the garage door. It was still closed, meaning Cassidi did not come out of it. It dawned on her that she must have come out the door, the one they had seen originally. Meaning that she went *through* at least part of this structure.

"Cass, we have to climb up, fast. Troy went home already so that he could reset our trackers to turn back on at 6:45. We don't have much time, but once we get to the stream, I need you to tell me what you saw. Are you okay to move now?" Cassidi nodded but said nothing. Rebecca scrutinized her for a moment through the darkness. Making the decision that there was nothing else that could be done just now, she made the move to go, turning back to be sure Cassidi was following her.

Without Troy, they were able to climb quickly, even with the state Cassidi was in. Rebecca led the way. Cassidi followed. The girls did not talk on their way up and over. They reached the stream that would lead them back towards Rebecca's house before they stopped. Rebecca stopped purposefully, while Cassidi only came to a halt after running into the back of Rebecca. She had been following Rebecca, but moving automatically, not really paying attention to what she was doing.

Rebecca grabbed Cassidi by the shoulders. "Cass. You're really starting to worry me." Strange to be the one trying to bring Cassidi around. Just last week, the roles were reversed.

Cassidi looked up at Rebecca, the haunted look still in her eyes. She shook her head a little and focused on Rebecca.

"Becs, I don't know what's going on in there, but whatever it is, it's...it's...gruesome."

"What exactly did you see?"

"I hardly know where to start."

"Start from the beginning. From when you got inside the garage door. How did you stay out of sight? What were Zeus and Karl doing? Was there anything in that truck?" Rebecca fired off just a couple of the questions she had been holding until they reached this spot. The questions actually seemed to help Cassidi pull out of her shock.

"I hid behind some containers that were beside the door. I saw them through the crack when I got to the garage door. I figured I'd be able to stay out of sight and watch what they were doing. I wanted to tell you, but you were too far away, and I had to just go for it before I lost the chance.

"I hadn't planned to go any further. I thought I could just stay there and watch, then come back out when they left. But—" Cassidi looked away, eyes glazing over as she recalled those first minutes inside. For a second time, she shook her head to bring herself back to the present. She exhaled a burst of air and met Rebecca's expectant and troubled eyes.

"But what, Cass?"

"But...when I saw what they took out of the truck, I had to follow them."

"What was it?"

"Not what. Who. People, Becs. That is what I saw them take out of the truck."

"*What?!* Who? What did they do with them?"

"Yes. People. I couldn't tell if they were dead or alive and just knocked out. They had them on stretchers, like they use in hospitals. They were lying out on them and strapped down. They took out three people, and there was someone else with them. Someone else hopped out of the back of the truck to help them with the stretchers."

"Who was it? Remy? Or that woman we saw…Bryn, I think her name was?"

"No. No, it wasn't someone we've seen before. It was a man. Older than Remy but younger than Karl. It…well, he looked like Troy, Becs. But it couldn't have been, right? There are lots of light-haired nerdy people around. It couldn't have been Troy's dad, could it?"

Rebecca opened her mouth to respond but found that no words came out. She didn't know what to say. It couldn't have been, could it? Could Troy's dad be involved, and Troy not know it? Rebecca was suddenly very glad Troy had already headed home. A sickening thought hit Rebecca with a punch in her gut. What if it *was* Troy's dad, and what if Troy already knew? She pushed that thought away before it had a chance to really take hold.

"No, I can't believe it would be Troy's dad. I can't believe it. I don't believe it." Rebecca attempted to convince herself as much as Cassidi that the possibility that Troy's dad was involved was not a possibility at all.

"What happened after you saw them take the people out? I know you had to have gone into the building further because you came out the door. Not the garage door." Rebecca steered the conversation along, avoiding further exploration of the Troy's dad speculation.

"They went through a door. I followed them. I couldn't just go out the way I came in anyways, so I followed them. They went down a hallway in a labyrinth of hallways. I'm actually surprised I found my way out. It was all hallways and doors. There was an exit sign over the door, so that helped," Cassidi actually chuckled at this last thought.

"Did you see where they took the people?" Rebecca asked.

"I followed them as closely as I could. It wasn't easy keeping up with them because I couldn't get too close or they'd hear me. Plus, it was lit up inside. Not everything, but as soon as they went into a hallway, it lit up, and the lights stayed on after they moved on."

"But did you *see where they took the people?*" Rebecca persisted. Time was ticking away, and 6:45 was rapidly approaching. They *both* had to get back home in less than an hour. While she could have discussed the finer points of Cassidi's observations about electricity use, now was not the time.

"No." Cassidi sounded defeated. "I lost them. I followed them through a door that they had to unlock. Fortunately, I was able to get through before it clicked all the way closed. There was a sign on the door that said, "Restricted Access, Level Three Clearance Only." They turned down another hallway, but when I entered the same hallway, they weren't there. I heard a door click as I turned the corner, but there were too many doors to choose from. I couldn't have followed them anyway. No telling what I would have walked into.

"As I was backtracking my way out of the restricted area, I tried a few doors. After I listened to make sure no one was on the other side, of course. Most of the doors were locked. The ones that were unlocked seemed like storage areas or meeting rooms. Except for two of them. One looked like some sort of science lab, and the other was freezing cold and full of what looked like large metal refrigerators, but I couldn't get them open. They were sealed tight. On my way from the restricted area to the exit, I randomly tested doors. Locked. I did notice more signs for labs and another sign indicating eye protection must be worn before entering."

"We have to go, Cass. I have more questions, but I guess they have to wait."

"There really isn't much else to tell. But now I have more questions, too. You said Troy went home to change our tracker times, right?"

"Yeah," Rebecca responded. "I'm supposed to message him that I need to meet him before school about some RT homework if you and I got out safe. And then we are meeting before school at the west door again."

"So, how much of this should we tell him?" asked Cassidi.

"Good question. No way we should tell him about the guy who looks like him. But we have to tell him something. He knows you went in there. He knows you would have seen *something*. Can you come get me in an hour and a half? We can talk about it on the way to school. I'm going to need a lot of coffee today."

"Can do."

"Okay. Let's get moving. You have further to go to get home than I do, but I'll meet you at my place at 7:45."

The girls made quick work of the walk back to where they split off to go their separate ways home. Rebecca was glad to see that her friend had recovered from the initial shock. This day was going to be eternal. They wouldn't have much time to talk before meeting up with Troy, and even less time to fill him in before first period. Her brain hurt from lack of sleep. She was overwhelmed with all Cassidi had seen. All she wanted was to crawl into bed, sleep for days, and wake up to a world that was still familiar. A world where there wasn't something making the people of Montrose drop like flies. A world without doors into mountains and strange purple lights bending in unusual ways. A world without people being led from trucks into the belly of the mountain for who knows what reasons. And a world where her brother was still there to wake her up when she slept too late. Yes, that too would be welcome, even as tired as she currently was.

CHAPTER 19

Cassidi appeared at Rebecca's door just before 7:45 eating an apple strudel. Good to know the previous night's activities hadn't ruined her appetite, thought Rebecca, who herself was unable to eat a morsel. She'd brought along an energy bar, just in case she could stomach it at some point before lunch. Both girls had large cups of coffee gripped in hands that would have been shaky from nerves and lack of sleep had they not had something to hold on to.

On the walk to transit, Rebecca, after some hesitation, decided to voice her unwelcome thought that if the man Cassidi had seen was indeed Troy's dad, then maybe Troy knew what was happening and was just playing along. He had been poking around on his dad's computer, after all. And he had been really late in arriving last night and flustered as well. Unsurprisingly, this same thought had crossed Cassidi's mind as well. They had decided, however, that they could not leave out what Cassidi had seen. There was no way to deny that she had seen something, and they decided that it would be too difficult to come up with a believable alternative. Cassidi also thought that if they told him about seeing the people, they would be able to watch his response to see if he gave anything away. But they would not tell him the third guy looked like a dead ringer for an older, and not quite so scrawny, Troy. No, they'd leave that last part out.

When they got to school, they'd stashed their bags, as usual, in their classrooms and met Troy by the side door again. Troy obviously hadn't slept either. He looked genuinely relieved to see Rebecca, and even Cassidi, walking through the doors looking rough, but whole. In fact, he almost looked like he was going to hug them. Maybe he didn't know anything. Or he was a really good actor.

"Thank god you guys are okay. I thought for sure you weren't coming out of there, Cass." Troy swallowed hard, gulping down the thoughts of what could have happened if Cassidi had been caught. "What happened when you went inside? And how did you do it? Not get caught, that is?"

"Not get caught at what?" Bendi stepped around the partially open door as she spoke in her quiet voice. Selby followed closely behind.

"What are you guys up to?" Selby asked. "You've all been walking around looking like death…no offense Becs…and being all secretive with these little meetings before and after school. And none of you seems to ever have the time to get together with me or Bendi anymore. So, what's up? What did you almost get caught at doing, Cass?"

"What are you guys doing here? H-h-how did you two know to come here?" asked Troy.

"I saw you walk into school. Selby and I decided to follow you because you guys have been acting so strange."

"We couldn't figure out why you would be going in without meeting us by the front steps like we always do when we get to school early. And when you came out here, we waited under the stairs to see what you were doing. Then we saw Cass and Becs walk by, so we stood just inside the door until just now. That's what we are doing here. Now. What are *you* doing here?" Selby glared at each of them in turn, obviously not liking the fact that he and Bendi had been left out of whatever this was that the three of them were up to.

"Don't blame them, Selby. This is my doing. I didn't want anyone to be involved, really. But I needed help with something, so I told Cass, hoping she could help me." Rebecca tried to smooth things over, while also feeling more than a little unnerved at this new turn of events. Today of all days. She didn't have the mental fortitude to think through this all right now.

"It isn't all Becs fault," Cassidi interjected. "I brought Troy in. Unfortunately, we couldn't accomplish what we needed on our own, and, also unfortunately, I thought Troy might be the only one who could help."

"Hey, what do you mean unfortunately?" Troy asked, offended.

"Oh, get a grip," Cassidi said. "I only meant that it was bad enough that Becs and I were involved without having to bring you in on it too. The more of us involved, the more dangerous it is for each of us. But we needed you, and you've been a huge help."

"Oh. Okay. Okay, thanks," replied Troy. "You're right. You did need me. Or you wouldn't be standing here right now. So that takes us back to where we were when these two popped out of nowhere."

"Yeeees, it does. I don't feel comfortable with going into all this now. Sorry, Bendi and Selby. I know you feel like we should have told you, but it really wasn't because we didn't want to. But now I don't see how to keep you guys out of it, much as I'd like to. I know you won't give up until you know, Selby, and that could mean trouble for all of us." Rebecca was weighing her options as she spoke. She felt that more of this was getting out of her control, slipping away from her with each new piece of knowledge, with each unhappy surprise. Like this one. The five friends had been close for a few years now. She really didn't know how she could keep them at bay now.

"Becs," Bendi's soft voice interrupted Rebecca's thoughts. "We want to help. Whatever it is. It's obviously important, and we want to help. Does this have to do with Jonathan?" Bendi, ever the observer. That girl had a keen intuition to go along with her powers of observation.

"Yes." Rebecca's reply was barely above the sound of a whisper into a strong wind, which is how she herself felt right now. And the wind threatened to carry her away in whatever direction it turned, with her powerless to do anything more than be carried along.

"Listen," said Cassidi, "it's Becs call as to how much she wants you guys to know. Can you give her some time to think? This isn't what we were expecting today, and we've all had a rough night."

"Of course," said Bendi.

"Yeah. Okay, I guess." Selby was more impatient than Bendi and would not want to wait for long.

"We can't talk about this in the open at school. We can't talk about it where we might be heard." As Rebecca said this, she realized Bendi and Selby had also lost their packs. She breathed a sigh of relief. "Can you guys meet at the park after school? We can talk then."

Selby and Bendi responded in the affirmative.

"No word of this at lunch or in the halls. We have to be careful. Got it?" demanded Cassidi.

"Got it. Just normal conversation at lunch. This is gonna kill me you know," Selby said.

"Yes. Yes, we know," Cassidi responded.

****

Somehow, they all got through the day. Lunch was quieter than normal, with three of the gang not really capable of much cohesive conversation, and the remaining two left to ponder what it was they'd find out at the end of the day. Instead of meeting outside the school after classes finished, they all made their way to the park, where they tossed their packs on a picnic table, wandered a few feet away, and sat in a tight-knit circle, knees touching, or nearly so, leaning in as close as possible, but trying to look casual. All eyes turned to Rebecca.

Rebecca recounted everything up to the point of the previous night's events, which is what she and Cassidi had needed to fill Troy in on. They all sat silent. No one interrupted. Not even Selby. When she finished, Selby and

Bendi still sat without a word. Bendi looked thoughtful, and scared. Selby kept looking with disbelief between the three of them, and then gaped at Cassidi when Rebecca had told of her disappearance into the recesses of the mountain.

"And now is the time when you fill all of us in on what happened when you were inside, Cass." Troy had barely been able to keep still during the retelling of events, and now he was more than a little impatient to hear what he had been waiting to hear since Rebecca's message earlier that morning.

Cassidi took over from there. She filled the group in on the events inside, recounting everything except for the part about the third person looking like he could be Troy's father. It was a lot of information for the newcomers. But Troy looked positively ill by the end. Rebecca bumped Cassidi's knee with her own as she sat watching Troy's response, and Cassidi responded in kind, both girls acknowledging that they were watching Troy's reactions.

"This feels like a scene out of a bad movie. And by bad, I mean one that is truly horrifying. The kind that keeps you up at night," Selby finally said after Cassidi finished speaking.

"I don't understand how this could be happening here," said Bendi. "Do you think those people were dead?"

"I really don't know," replied Cassidi. "I'm not sure which is worse, if they were or if they weren't." Bendi visibly shivered in response to Cassidi's comment.

"I can't even *begin* to imagine what they would be doing with dead bodies. Man, cross that. I can't begin to imagine what they'd be doing with live ones, either," said Selby.

Rebecca caught a movement out of the corner of her eye and looked up to see Daniel crossing the park at a distance too close to be comfortable. She thought she saw his eyes shifting in their direction, but she couldn't be sure. He walked with a coolness that suggested he was entirely unaware, or uncaring, of their presence. Somehow, though, she doubted he was unaware. Uncaring might be a stretch, too, given their previous encounter and what was occurring on his family's property. She wondered for the hundredth time if he knew what BRO was up to. And Remy. But she wasn't exactly sure of what Remy's role was. There was discontent there, for sure, but why? Rebecca didn't dare point out Daniel's presence just then. Nothing like five sets of eyes turning in his direction to make a person suspicious of this little gathering.

"What do we do next, Becs?" asked Bendi.

"I have no idea," responded Rebecca. "I'm open to suggestions. But right now, I can't think straight. I'm guessing Cass and Troy are in the same boat."

"Oh, of course you can't! I'm sorry, Becs. We should let you guys go home and get some sleep," said Bendi.

"Bendi and I are rested. We're fresh brains, so let us give it some thought. We can bounce our ideas off the rest of you tomorrow when you can think better." Selby was already feeling better about things now that he knew the whole story. Now that he was involved. He even understood why they hadn't wanted to tell him and Bendi. But now that they knew, they could take some action and help solve this horror movie mystery.

"I hate to leave you two to sort this out without us, but I know the three of us will be useless, so I'll have to take you up on that offer. Just remember you have to be more careful than you think possible. No phones nearby. I know you guys know how serious this is. I just have to say it," Rebecca said.

"We understand, Becs, and we promise we will be extremely careful" said Bendi. Selby bobbed his head vigorously in agreement.

Troy, unable to stifle one of his cavernous yawns, started to stand, saying, "Sounds good to me. Same time, same place tomorrow?"

"Same time, same place," said Cassidi.

"Works for me," confirmed Rebecca. Bendi nodded.

"Yep. I'm in," said Selby.

With that, the group disbanded, except for Bendi and Selby, who remained where they were to rehash what they'd just learned. They spent the next hour going over the details and trying to make sense of it all, and then another hour after that brainstorming what might be done next. The other three made for their homes. Each gave excuses to their parents to disappear into their bedrooms and all three were asleep before heads hit the pillows, blissfully unable to think one more thought about the previous night or what they would do next.

CHAPTER 20

A much-needed (for some) sleep and a school day later, the five met as planned in the park, huddled again in their circle. And, again, Daniel was nearby, though this time, no one saw him. He stayed behind one of the decorative bushes that lined the playground area. The five friends were quiet as they spoke, but Daniel hoped he could at least snatch a few words out of the air spoken just loud enough to carry to him on the fall breeze. He didn't know what they were up to, but he intended to find out. He hadn't quite believed Rebecca's story when he brought her down the mountain two weeks ago. He wanted to believe it. He liked Rebecca. But something just didn't ring true in her words, though he couldn't place a finger on what it was exactly. Daniel made himself as comfortable as he could sitting huddled on the ground, glad the wind and the chill in the air would likely ensure the playground stayed empty.

"You three are lookin' a little livelier today, I must say," Selby was the first to speak. "Bendi and I were here for a couple of hours yesterday. Almost got busted for missin' dinner last night 'til I told them I got caught up working on a paper in the library. They forgave me after that." He grinned.

"Good to know, Selby," said Troy. "You are a clever one." Selby shot him a look that said he wasn't quite sure how to take that last comment, but then he shrugged and dismissed it.

"Okay," Selby rubbed his hands together in front of his face, "so who's ready to hear our brilliant plan?"

Rebecca smiled. Selby could always be counted on for his enthusiasm. It was contagious. Even now. She had worried all day about bringing Selby and Bendi into the fold. Not that she had a choice. Right now, though, she was glad they knew. It was a relief to know they weren't hiding anything anymore from their other two friends. That little charade had been getting increasingly difficult to continue. It took too much of her meager store of energy. Now, they could all focus on the important stuff.

Cassidi looked at Rebecca, reading her expression, and judging correctly that she was feeling okay about all this,

Cassidi relaxed. For herself, she had been happy of the recent turn of events, especially after the night she had had inside the mountain. She figured the more brains in the mix, the better they would be able to devise a plan for what to do next. She was worried a little about Bendi being involved only because she always seemed so meek. She was definitely sensitive, and Cassidi did not think Bendi would handle it too well if she experienced the kind of night Cassidi had experienced. Bendi was smart, but no one would call her tough. Selby, however, was a good addition to the mix. He had a good head on his shoulders and was not easily shaken in any situation she had seen. Not even during the school exams that caused fear in the hearts of most students, as the culmination of the results of those exams over the last six years of school were the only way students ensured their places after graduation.

While it was generally considered a given that you would do what your parents did, the exams either verified the path for you, or, if you did not perform up to snuff, sent you down the ranks to a more "appropriate" placement of Council's choosing. Very rarely did a student ever climb up during those exams. Climbing up was so much harder than sliding down. Council said it was possible, and maybe it was, but Cassidi knew of no such case herself. She knew Jonathan had been really smart, and he wanted to rise up higher in government than his and Rebecca's parents. He always did exceptionally well on the exams, but even he hadn't been given a higher ranking than his parents' Tier 3 position. None of them had, and no one else whose parents were Tier 3 had. Everyone would have known if they had since results were always posted for all to see. Which meant you also knew who moved down in their level rankings.

Cassidi always feared that would be her. So far, she had held on to her Tier 3 position along with the rest of the gang. Her parents, however, were sure she would let them down, that she would be a disappointment and an embarrassment. They told her so often. Cassidi was very intelligent, but her parents made her feel otherwise.

Selby began to lay out the plan he and Bendi had come up with the day before, Bendi interjecting with some finer points along the way. Now that they had more people involved, their plan could be better coordinated than "let's just go in there and see what we find." No one, not even Cassidi, wanted to go that route again. It was quite clear now that they were digging themselves deep into the quagmire of a swamp that could swallow them all without a trace. Dangerous was hardly the word for it. Dangerous is what most people thought of rock climbing, free style, on a class 5.13 route. This was so far beyond that.

There was no doubt, Selby had said, that they would have to go inside again and try to get more information.

Everyone agreed with this, though none were excited by it. It really was their only option. They were at a standstill until they knew more about what was happening. What they would do with the information once they had it was anybody's guess. They could take it to Council, unless Council was involved. If Council was involved? Well, they'd have to cross that bridge once they got there.

The plan Selby and Bendi laid out involved sending Cassidi inside again, since she knew her way around, with two other people to investigate the lab and to try to find where the three men had taken the three people on stretchers. They were also going to go back into the freezer room to see if there was a way to unlock the doors on the individual freezers. If there was still time, they would see if they could find out more information by snooping through some of the other lab rooms Cassidi had found. If there was time. With any luck, they would find out more about the lights' purpose, which confounded the lot of them. The other two would be posted outside, one down the road from the garage so that any approaching vehicles would be spotted, and the other outside the regular door, just as another precaution.

"I see one problem," said Troy. "Well, more than one, but let's just start with the trackers. I'm not sure I feel good about continuing to get into Dad's computer to manipulate everyone's trackers. I almost got caught the last time, and that was one time too many for me."

"Oh man, you've been doing things the hard way!" said Selby. "I can get a hold of something that will scramble our signals for as long as we want. Undetectable by SMALS, and best thing is SMALS won't even know it isn't detecting our GPS signals. How 'bout that?"

"Are you kidding me?" said Troy, baffled. "*You* have access to a device like that? I mean, I'd thought of building one myself, but there wasn't enough time. I didn't know it was something that already existed. And *you* can get it?"

"Of course it already exists, man. You might be a genius, but I guarantee that if *you're* thinking of it, it already exists out there somewhere. No offense. It's just that there's a lot of technology gadgets people already made that most of us know nothin' about."

"And how do you know about this, Selby? How is it that you can get your hands on one of these?" asked Cassidi.

"Because it's in my house," Selby replied, to the utter astonishment of the other four. "I use it all the time when I want to escape the house for a bit without anyone gettin' in my business."

"That's incredible, Selby," said Rebecca. "Much better than having Troy hack into his Dad's computer." Troy looked crestfallen at this, but Rebecca didn't appear to notice. "But if there's only one, how will that help the rest of us?"

"Lucky for you, one is all we need," said Selby. "I set it to locate a tracker. You just have to be standing within ten feet of the device for it to pick it up. Once it locates one of your trackers, I push a button, it pairs with that tracker, and, bam, you're undetectable until I break the link. It can handle up to ten pairings, so we're good."

Looking around the room at everyone's surprised and relieved expressions, Selby added, "See…you shoulda brought me into this from start. Would've saved yourselves a lot of grief."

"How was *I* supposed to know you had this miracle gadget sitting in your house? You never told any of us anything about this!" Cassidi said, taking Selby's remark as a direct affront to her since it was her decision to ask Troy for his help.

"I'm glad you're here now," said Rebecca, wanting to steer the conversation away from a possible confrontation that couldn't lead anywhere good. "Okay," she exhaled, "we've got that covered. Now, who goes in with Cass and who keeps watch outside?"

"I can go in," said Troy. As soon as the words escaped his lips, he wished he could stuff them right back into his mouth. What possessed him to say such a thing?

Unfortunately, he didn't see a way to back out gracefully once the words were out there.

"Becs, where do you want to be? This is your gig," said Cassidi.

"I should go inside. It should be me. At least those of you outside can run if you need to. Troy, are you sure you want to go inside? You were pretty much dragged into this, and you've already put yourself in a lot of danger."

"I can go. I haven't had a chance to do anything yet," said Selby. "I don't mind a little danger."

"Are you alright with that, Troy?" asked Rebecca.

"Sure. Fine. Whatever you want, Becs," Troy scowled, but breathed a sigh of relief, glad he had sidestepped that one.

"Troy and Bendi, you two will serve as lookouts on the outside. Any ideas how to communicate between us?" Rebecca brought up the point no one else so far mentioned in this brilliant little plan until now.

"Leave that up to me, too. My folks also have these old 2-way radios. They're just for communicating over pretty short distances between only the people who have them turned on and tuned in to the same wavelength," Selby said.

"Anything your parents *don't* have, Selby?" Cassidi asked.

"Probably not. You'd be surprised what my folks have in their storage compartment. They might seem like normal government folks to you, same as your parents, but they're what people used to call *survivalists*. They're prepared for *anything*. Stayed holed up all during The Reckoning. Had their own food, supply channels, secret communications, the works. No one knew about it except those connected in the same system. When it all ended, they crawled out of hiding and joined in the new system. They play the part. Just like everyone else. But, man, they sure kept all their goods. They'd be able to do it all again if it all hits the fan again. And so would I."

For the second time, four pair of eyes stared at him, four mouths agape in awe and disbelief. In the bushes, Daniel noticed that the group got awfully quiet. He hadn't been able to pick up on much. A few words here and there. He could tell they were definitely planning something, and now they all grew silent. He'd heard someone say that this was Rebecca's gig. Heard something else about SMALS, but he couldn't make out exactly what it was. And now there was silence. He shifted from his current position to see if he could manage a peek through the branches. The leaves were too full to get much more than a glimpse of someone's clothes or a hint of skin or hair, but it wasn't enough to really see anything of use. He didn't dare move the branches aside for fear of making a noise. Frustrated, he sat back again to wait and listen.

Selby laughed. "Man, you all look like someone could knock you down with a feather!"

"I've never heard of such a thing," said Bendi, the only one, strangely, capable of finding her voice at the moment. "Aren't your parents afraid of getting discovered? That wouldn't be good for any of you."

"Nah. I kept it all from you guys until now, didn't I? No one knows about this except the other survivalists in the group. It isn't something anyone goes around spoutin' off to whoever they want. I never would have told you guys myself if it didn't seem like something you needed to understand right now. And I expect you all to keep this to yourself. Understood? This could mean bad things for my family if any one of you says something to anyone outside of our group. I'm only trusting you now because we all have to trust each other right now. This thing we're doing is big. We need what my parents have if we have any chance of coming out of this alive. And I'm not kidding."

"Are you holding out on anything else we should know about?" asked Cassidi.

"Like I said. You'd be surprised at what all my folks have. I'll poke around in there to see if I can find anything else useful. Right now, we've got ourselves a scrambler and 2-way radios. I'd say that's a good start."

"It is," said Rebecca. "See if you can find anything that might help us get into locked doors. Something that can work on security doors. We need to go back to the restricted area Cass saw. But we need a way in."

"Can do, can do."

"When are we doing this?" asked Bendi.

"I'm not keen on another night like Sunday night. I vote we wait for the weekend," suggested Cassidi.

"I agree," said Rebecca. "Selby, will that give you enough time to get everything together?"

"Yep. Not a problem. I'll do it on the sly, but if we ever need my folks' help, I know they'd be safe to go to. For now, though, I can acquire the goods without them knowin'. We only do drills every couple of months now that I'm up to speed. We used to practice all the time when I was growing up. My parents wanted to make sure I knew what I was doing. In case something happened to them."

"Seriously, Selby. Who *are* you?" Troy asked, to which Selby responded with a shrug and a grin.

The gang settled on getting together first on Friday after school, out behind Rebecca's barn, where they would not be seen by prying eyes. Selby could show them all the gear and how to use it. They'd finalize their plans, what little there was to finalize, as it was all pretty straight forward. After that, they'd all go home for a few hours before meeting up again to execute the plan that night. They all stood up to leave.

Finally, thought Daniel. He had long grown bored and his rear was sore from sitting on the hard ground. He had very little information to go on. The group was maddeningly quiet when they talked, though he did hear a day. Friday. He didn't know what was happening on that day, but it seemed something was. He'd just have to keep his eyes peeled Friday, watch Rebecca and the others to find out what they were up to. At least now he knew the day.

CHAPTER 21

It was Friday. The group was gathered out behind Rebecca's barn. Selby heaved a pack heavier than usual off his shoulders. It landed with a thud and a jangle of metal and plastic. The anticipation was palpable. The intrigue of the gadgets overriding the fear of their precarious situation. At least for the moment. Just seconds before, everyone had been shifting and moving, rubbing hands together or blowing on them, doing what they could to keep warm in the shadows of a day turned chill and damp, but once Selby began to unzip his pack, all movement came to a halt.

Selby first pulled out a device that resembled their phones, only a little smaller and with buttons sharing the space on the face of the device with the readout screen. This was the scrambler. Troy was a little disappointed in how simplistic it looked. He was hoping for something more futuristic looking and, well, cooler.

"I thought we'd just take care of this business right off the bat," Selby said as he held out the scrambler for everyone to see. "Get it outta the way now and we don't have to worry about it tonight. Sound good?"

"Sure. But is it okay that our signals are scrambled for so long? Will they stay scrambled even when we all go home?" asked Rebecca.

"Good questions, Becs. Yep. I've had my tracker scrambled all day and all night before. No problem. You have to be ten feet or closer for the scrambler to pair with your tracker, but that's just because otherwise it would be pickin' up trackers all over the city. Once you're linked, though, you're all good. Like I said, you'll stay scrambled until I unlink your tracker from the device."

"Why would anyone ever want to unlink? That thing is freedom," said Cassidi.

"True enough, Cass," replied Selby. "But my folks don't want us messin' with our safety supplies too much. We're supposed to be just like everyone else, unless we need it. Not sure what it would take for them to replace this baby, if something happened to it, and I don't wanna find out."

"How does it work?" asked Troy.

"Let me show you. You wanna go first, Troy?" asked Selby.

"Yes."

"Okay, step right up." Selby motioned Troy over so that he could see what Selby was doing. With a couple of presses of a button, and Troy's confirmation of his tracker ID, he was linked.

"Not much to it," Troy commented.

"Nope, that's the beauty of it," Selby responded.

Selby continued with the rest of them, one-by-one. Each was curious to see how the thing worked, so each of them took their places next to Selby as he linked their trackers to the scrambler. They could see their IDs show up on the monitoring screen: a simple display that showed tracker ID connections and green lights indicating a functioning connection. Once they were all connected, Selby pulled out the 2-way radios.

"Whoa, those things are huge!" Cassidi said.

"They're big, but they're handy. They're strong enough to work even when we're inside and Troy and Bendi are outside. We shouldn't have any trouble gettin' in touch when we need to."

"Did you bring enough for everyone?" asked Bendi.

"Sure did. That way, if something happens to any one of us, the others will still be able to communicate. Just seems the smart thing to do, right?" replied Selby.

"Yes. Very smart," agreed Bendi. "Can I see one?"

"Suuuure. Here." Selby handed the one he was holding over to Bendi and then pulled the others out of his bag, giving everyone one. He showed them all how to tune into the same channel and demonstrated how to send an SOS signal without talking. They spent the next half hour trying them out, having a bit of fun with the novelty of them as they all moved to different locations around the barn to test them out. They all practiced sending an SOS signal as well. Several times. If the signal was needed, then the situation would be dire. Selby thought it would be a good idea that they could send the signal without having to think too hard about what it was.

"I've got one more thing for us," Selby told the group once they'd all reconvened. "I was thinking that we needed at least a little something for physical safety. No heavy hitting weapons. None of you could handle that. But I got these."

Selby held up the object for them all to see. It looked a bit like an electric razor. When he turned it on, Bendi, Rebecca, and Cassidi all jumped back in surprise. Troy moved in for a closer inspection. "What does it do?" He asked.

"It temporarily immobilizes a person," replied Selby. "It sends an electric current through their body and makes it so they can't move. It buys you a little time if someone catches you. The downside is, you have to be up close and personal for it to work. But it's better than nothin'."

"Up close and personal? How close is that?" asked Cassidi.

"You actually have to press this against the target, on someplace like the arm or the back. The back is best, but any muscular area will do," Selby replied.

"How much time do we have after we use this on a person?" asked Bendi.

"That really depends on the person and where you hit 'em. If you get 'em in the back, you get more time than in the arms or legs. But, best guess, you get anywhere from 20 seconds to almost a minute."

"In other words, not much time," said Troy.

"Nope. Not much time, but enough time to give you a head start in a foot race," said Selby. "But if you need to use it more than once, you can. It'll recharge repeatedly until the battery dies. I'll make sure they're fully charged before we head out tonight, but these batteries are good ones; they can last up to around 50 jolts. It used to be that these babies would only give enough of a jolt to cause some pain. Some tinkering by one of the crew boosted their output enough to temporarily immobilize a person, but not for long. We'd be needin' the big boys for that, and I don't have time to train you on those. Don't want anybody takin' any one of our own out."

"Selby, did you find anything that might come in handy for opening the freezers and the security doors?" asked Rebecca.

"Yes, indeed, I did," Selby said with another of his grins. "I was gonna surprise you with it once we got inside if you hadn't remembered to ask."

Selby dove into his bag one final time. He pulled out a simple card that looked like any other access card. "That doesn't look like it would do much," Cassidi commented.

"Doesn't look like much, but it'll do the trick, assuming they have nothing fancier than a standard electronic lock on the door," Selby responded.

"They didn't look like anything special," said Cassidi. "At least not from what I could tell. Just looked like a regular, electronic pads that use a card to open."

"How does this work?" asked Bendi.

"It has a special chip in it. It's able to read the program on a lock pad to decipher the necessary code to unlock the door. Then it just supplies that code," Selby explained.

Selby passed the card to Bendi, who looked it over and then passed it on so that the others could also have a look. Absolutely nothing extraordinary about the card. It looked just like the cards they all had for their homes. "Are we splittin' up inside or sticking together?" asked Selby.

"I think we should stick together if we can. Two people can look around and one can keep watch at the door, just in case someone is on the inside that we don't know about," said Rebecca.

"Sounds like a good plan to me," Cassidi responded. "I'd feel much better if we had someone standing watch. We might not get as much done as fast, but I think it's a safer route."

"You want the safer route? *You?*" scoffed Troy.

"Yeah, well, it wasn't you who went in last week. After what I saw, I'm a safety first kinda girl now. At least for this," Cassidi responded, with just enough derision in her tone to let Troy know what she thought of his efforts that last trip over the mountains. Troy glanced away, his cheeks and neck turning slightly pink, and said nothing further.

Selby cleared his throat, "Yeah, well, I think that's it. We've gone over everything I have, now we just have to do this thing."

The shuffling of feet started again, much as it had when they all first arrived. Except this time, it was a nervous energy rather than an attempt to keep warm. It was 5:30. They had about 6 more hours before they would be meeting back up at this same spot to take on something that felt much bigger than any of them other than Selby could possibly handle. But handle it they'd have to.

"Anyone have any questions before we take off? About the plan or about the stuff Selby showed us?" asked Rebecca.

Everyone glanced around at one another, trying to size up where the others stood and what they were feeling. All four shook their heads, though not a one looked entirely confident. At that, the band of five broke apart, to spend the next several hours resting as much as they could and fortifying frayed nerves in preparation for tonight.

CHAPTER 22

10:30. She knew she should be trying to sleep, but instead Rebecca found herself in Jonathan's room, on the floor, propped up against his bed, and looking at a framed photo of him after his first free climb on a challenging route. His look was triumphant and carefree, yet still carried the etchings of focus and control needed when climbing. Rebecca always thought this photo captured the whole of Jonathan, as she thought of him. Strong and confident, driven, but with a sense of humor and lightness to him as well.

"Well, Jonathan, you were right to be suspicious of BRO and the light. Even if this has nothing to do with the virus, whatever it is, isn't good," she spoke the words out loud, but half under her breath. "And I'm scared. *Really* scared."

Rebecca sighed, dropped her head back on the mattress, and closed her eyes. *Breathe in. Breathe out. Breathe in. Breathe out.* She took in deep breaths to calm her elevated heart rate. Behind still-closed eyelids, she played out the gang's plans for the night. She felt responsible for everyone's safety, though she knew each of them made the decision to participate. She knew her friends. They were doing this to help her, yes, but also because they all felt it was important for their city. And because they were a naturally curious bunch. Even Bendi. As timid as she appeared, she had a fierce desire to know things.

This was perhaps the trait that linked them all into such a tight group, in spite of the differences in their personalities, and in spite of the friction that sometimes appeared because of the differences in their personalities. They all understood that need to know things. The need to understand. Up until now, the school curriculum and Council-approved information about the world limited the horizon for what could be known. There was an innocence about the group. A naïveté about what it was they didn't understand.

They might not have liked the Council or anyone in authority for that matter. But never did they imagine it possible that there could be the level of deception and potential harm that they seemed to be witnessing with BRO. How far did this extend? Is it possible that Council was behind it? Could someone *really* be killing so many in their city? These were questions every single one of the friends now needed to answer. The need to find the answers would override their fears. The time of innocence was ending.

Opening her eyes, Rebecca raised her arm up high enough to activate her watch and to look at the time without lifting her head. It was just before 11:00 and time to make her final preparations to meet the others. She lifted her head and looked around a room dimly lit by the light of the nearly full moon.

"What have you gotten me into, bro," she said to the framed photo in her hands.

"You've got this," his smile and eyes told her in response.

Taking her fear in hand and shoving it down deep enough to be hidden from sight, she gathered her courage around her like a protective shell. A look of determination and resolve replaced the sadness and uncertainty. At that moment, she resembled Jonathan far more than she would have ever thought possible. Her eyes reflected back the same focus and control she was seeing in Jonathan's in the photo. Standing, she gave her brother one last look. "Here we go," she told him as she replaced the frame back in its place on the desk in the corner of the room.

Rebecca shouldered her pack, left her brother's room, and walked to the other end of the hall where her parents slept behind a closed door. She listened closely at the door for anything that would indicate her parents were awake. Hearing nothing, she risked opening the door just wide enough to see inside. The room was dark. Less moonlight shone through the window on this side of the house. She could just make out the outlines of their forms buried under the covers. She listened for a moment to the even sounds of their breathing, her dad's deep and resonant, almost a snore, and her mom's lighter, airier breath.

"Love you," she mouthed, lips forming the words without sound. Squeezing eyelids tight to hold back any tears, she closed the door with a soft click, stood up tall, and swiped at her eyes, before turning towards the stairs.

****

Selby and Rebecca rounded the corner to the back side of the barn at the same time. They were the first to arrive. The others still had ten minutes before their designated meeting time. Selby was wearing his headlamp, though with the bright moon, turning it on was unnecessary. He lowered his pack and both of them kneeled beside it while he opened it.

"You have everything?" Rebecca asked.

"Yep, I believe so. But let's check just to make sure," Selby responded, taking the items out and placing them in separate piles. "You?"

"Sure do. Not that I needed to bring much with me. Just my headlamp with extra batteries, water, and my pocket cam in case we find anything we think we should take photos or videos of."

"A camera? Nice. I like the way you think, Becs. Since we can't have our phones, a pocket cam is a great idea," Selby flashed her a smile.

The last item Selby pulled out was something Rebecca hadn't seen before. He hadn't shown it to them earlier that night.

"What is *that*?" Rebecca said.

"Extra protection. It's similar to the immobilizer devices I got for you guys, but harder hitting and further reaching. It takes a lot of practice to aim it with any accuracy, so I'll be the only one usin' it. If we need it, I can hit someone with it from across the room, and it'll immobilize them for up to 15 minutes."

"Whoa! What is that?" asked Troy, rounding the corner just as Selby was holding the immobilizer up for Rebecca.

"It's an immobilizer," Selby responded. "Same as what I am givin' you guys to use, but way more powerful."

"Why aren't we getting one? And why didn't you show us this earlier today?" asked Troy.

"Because," Selby responded, "you don't have the skills to use it, and I knew you'd be tryin' to talk me into bringin' one for you anyways."

"Would have been nice to have one, since it's just me and Bindi outside," said Troy.

"True, but without time to train, we've got to use what we can. Not gonna risk puttin' one of these in anyone's hands who hasn't been trained."

"Okay, I get your point. Still would have felt much safer with one of those," Troy sulked.

Bendi and Cassidi arrived together. Both girls' eyes growing wide at the sight of the immobilizer. Selby once again explained its use and why he was the only one who would be handling it. Bendi nodded, looking a little relieved, and Cassidi scowled. Like Troy, she thought it would have only been fair if they'd all had the chance to operate something that had a greater defense potential than a device that was hardly bigger than a phone and that you could only use if you were close enough to touch the intended target. That little thing didn't make her feel much safer than just running away if they got caught.

Selby handed out the 2-way radios and handheld tasers. He quizzed the group on the functions of each and how to operate them, just to be sure they all remembered. Once satisfied that they did, he gave a nod of approval. He turned on his radio, shouldered his pack, and then slung the immobilizer over his shoulder by its strap.

"In the words of my dad: let's get this show on the road," Selby said. "You ready to go get 'em, Becs?"

"Ready," she nodded. Yes, Selby was a good addition. Prepared. Calm. His demeanor bolstered her own focus and resolve. She realized that she was indeed ready. "How about you guys? Are you ready? It isn't too late to back out."

A flicker crossed Troy's eyes, but passed into his own inner sanctum, to be replaced with a hard look uncharacteristic for him. Cassidi's look was similarly hardened, while Bendi looked unafraid, but at peace with whatever they might face. Rebecca was certain they were all as afraid as she had been, but they were all in this together, and they drew strength from that. No one wanted to let any of the others down. They were a tribe. One for all and all for one, and all that. For the first time in their lives, they knew what that really meant. Each stood a little taller, chin held a little higher, as they moved to follow Rebecca across the field towards the stream and the face of the mountain now illuminated by the full moon.

CHAPTER 23

At the edge of the woods at the base of the mountain, Rebecca stopped and turned towards the others. "This is where we head up, Selby and Bendi. It's steep and there is no trail other than the one we've made trekking up here, which is to say: there isn't much of a trail at all. We can follow the basic path we've made in our past two trips. This will save us from having to cut away the vegetation to make a new path."

"Looks like the moonlight disappears in there. We might want our headlamps," Bendi observed looking into the darkened forest.

"Yeah, the footing is not easy, so headlamps would be a good idea. It's late now, but let's not turn them on until we get under the cover of the trees," said Rebecca.

After pulling headlamps from pockets, packs, or around their necks, they put them in place on their heads and moved into the darkness. One by one, they turned on their lights as they entered the forest, without stopping and without breaking stride. The five friends headed up the mountain, following the newly trodden path that was surprisingly evident. Adrenaline kept them all moving swiftly, even Troy. Bendi was nimble and quick, light on her feet. She seemed almost as at ease with the terrain as Selby, who did not so much as trip or stumble. The quiet, normally timid girl full of surprises and the self-proclaimed survivalist both moving as if they'd done this before. None of them thought about what they were doing. They just moved forward, up and over the ridge.

It was still too early for the lights to turn on, but Rebecca led the group to where one of the light contraptions sat in its lowered position. She wanted Bendi and Selby to at least get an idea of what they looked like, even if still lowered into the ground. They would almost certainly see the lights raised and on before the night was through, so they didn't spend long there before moving down to the level of the two entry points.

There was really no way of knowing if anyone was around, but they'd decided to go to the garage entry first to see if any vehicles happened to be parked outside. None were. No sign of any activity behind the garage door, and the road was quiet as well. This information did not tell them much. They would not know if anyone was inside for certain because they could not enter through the garage door. They'd have to go through the regular door.

Troy was going to keep watch at the garage door. Since they would be leaving him here as they made their way to the other entry, everyone got their 2-way radios in hand and switched them on. They checked their settings to ensure each was on the same channel with the volume set to level 3, loud enough to hear without carrying too far. Troy set up position behind one of the false trees at the top of a small rise a short distance from the garage. The garage door was in sight, but he would also be able to see headlights heading up the road sooner than if he were closer to the door.

"You set, Troy?" asked Selby. When he nodded in the affirmative, Selby continued, "When we get to the other entry, we'll get Bendi set up before we head in. If the door is locked, it will only take a moment to unlock it. Best guess, we should be inside in less than five, but if it takes a little more than that, don't worry. Unless you don't hear from us in ten minutes. Then maybe you can worry." He said this last lightly, jokingly.

"Let us know if you see or hear anything suspicious," Cassidi reminded him, unnecessarily.

"Sure thing," Troy reassured her, without a trace of the sarcasm her comment would have elicited just a few hours before. This exchange was an indication of the group's new sense of cohesiveness, as well as the urgency of their mission.

Rebecca, Cassidi, Selby, and Bendi left Troy. Not cowering, as he'd been the first time he'd been in nearly the same position, but, rather, with eyes peeled on the road leading away from the garage. "See you soon," said Rebecca with a smile, as Selby chucked him on the shoulder lightly before they all moved away towards the door entry.

At the door entry, they found it locked. Not that they really expected it to be unlocked at this time of night, even with the remote location. The fact that it was locked actually provided some comfort. It meant that it was possible no one was inside putting in overnight hours, since it seemed that during regular work hours the door was unlocked, as Rebecca, Cassidi, and Troy had seen on the first visit. Now, the gang, minus Troy, huddled around the door as Selby pulled out the key card and held it over the pad. There really was nothing to it. The card did its job with no more apparent delay than a normal key. Once that task was complete, they set Bendi up. She was hidden but had a good view of the door. They tested her use of the radio and found that she was far enough away that a person standing in front of the door could not hear her speaking, as long as she didn't talk above a whisper.

Cassidi led Rebecca and Selby inside the now unlocked door. They checked in with Troy, who reported that all was quiet from his post. "Any sign of life on the inside?" Troy asked into his radio.

"Not so far," Rebecca responded. "It was dark when we came inside, but the sensors on the entryway lights picked up our movement and turned on. We are going to have to be careful of that."

"Stick close to the walls," Troy offered. "At least you'll know someone else is there if you see lights on that you know you didn't trigger."

"Good point, Troy," Cassidi said into her radio.

"Thanks. Keep me posted," Troy said. "And be careful in there."

"Will do, will do," Selby chimed in. "You do the same. Don't fall asleep out there."

Troy gave a low laugh, "Not a chance."

"Are you still okay out there, Bendi?" Rebecca asked.

"Yes. It's quiet out here still."

"Okay. Good. Let's hope it stays that way," Rebecca replied. And with that, the radios fell silent for the moment.

Rebecca, Selby, and Cassidi stood in the lighted entry. The three of them discussed the plan to make their way to the restricted area and the lab, with Cassidi leading the way. They'd stick to the most direct route, hugging the walls in the hope that they would not trigger the lights. They briefly discussed doing a sweep of the place to see if anyone was there but tossed the idea out. They really had no idea how big this place was. But even with what they did know of it from Cassidi, they decided it would take too much time. None of them was in a hurry to spend more time inside than absolutely necessary. They would just have to make sure someone was posted at the lab door, keeping a watch and a listen for any sounds or movement that would indicate someone else was coming.

"What's the plan if we come to a hallway that's already lighted?" asked Cassidi. "The restricted area isn't too far from here, but it's still possible someone is inside."

"I say if we see lights, we get as close as we can to see who is there and what they're doing. Might give us almost as much info as snoopin' around in the dark," Selby suggested. "Sound okay to you, Becs?"

"No, it doesn't sound *okay*, but I think you're right. That's what we should do. I don't want to leave here without knowing more than we do now."

"Okay. Let's go, then," said Cassidi, taking the lead at the doorway heading into the rest of the complex.

Moving into the hallway, they were greeted with blackness. Cassidi turned on her headlamp. Rebecca and Selby left theirs off. Better to only worry about one person turning theirs off if they came upon an area that was lighted. Though the three of them had to worry about tripping the sensors on the lights themselves, the upside was that they would have warning of anyone else's presence ahead of them.

The biggest challenge would be in any of the rooms they were in. It was doubtful they'd be able to work without activating the lights. Once the lights were on, they would stay on, at least for a time. If someone *did* come down a hallway while they were in the lab or one of the other rooms, they would not be able to turn the lights off if that person decided to enter the room they occupied. Even if there were decent places to hide, whoever entered a lighted room would know someone had been there. Running didn't seem a viable option either. They would be trapped.

Rebecca, Cassidi, and Selby all pushed that thought away. They would deal with the situation if they had to. That's why Selby had his immobilizer and why the other two had their mini versions. No sense dwelling on it, right?

They made their way through the dark hallways. Footsteps and breathing the only sounds breaking the silence. The single beam from Cassidi's headlamp sliced through the darkness. Hallways broke off from one another or came to an end at a T juncture. Cassidi had to pause on a couple of occasions to orient herself, but it would only take a moment, and then she was moving on again. Rebecca found it impressive that after only a single visit, and one for which she had been heading in the opposite direction, Cassidi seemed to be quite sure of the way.

At each corner, Cassidi would switch off her headlamp before going around. This way, they would see if any lights were on down the hallway. Rounding one corner, they heard a click, as the hallway light turned on. They all jumped back at once. Hearts in throats. Eyes wide as they looked from one to the other. They were pinned against the wall, listening. No sounds. Cassidi slowly peered around the corner. The hallway was empty. She looked up. A sensor was placed such that they must have triggered it as they rounded the corner.

"It's a sensor. We hit it when we went around the corner. I think we need to get down low when we take any turns now, so this doesn't happen again," Cassidi reported. "Let's keep moving."

"No, wait," said Selby, "I think we should stay here until the light goes off. Time it. Time how long it takes for the light to automatically turn off. Might be helpful to know."

"Agreed," said Cassidi, noting the time on her watch, and leaning back against the wall to wait. Rebecca and Selby followed suit.

"Becs?"

The three in the hallway jumped. And then realized Bendi was breaking in on the radio.

"Yes? Everything okay out there?" Rebecca spoke into her 2-way.

"I don't know. I heard a branch snap and then what sounded like footsteps hurrying away through the trees."

"Did you see anything?" Rebecca asked.

"No. Nothing."

"Nothing happening over here," Troy reported from his post.

"It was probably just an animal," Rebecca said.

"Maybe. Probably. It just didn't sound like a four-legged creature, so I thought you should know," Bendi said. "Whatever it was moved away, and I haven't heard anything since. I waited to be sure."

"Great. That's good. You know how sounds can be distorted in the forest, especially at night," Rebecca said.

"Yes. I cannot think who else would possibly be in the woods in the middle of the night here, especially if Troy hasn't seen anything. But I wanted to let you know, since it seemed unusual to me."

"Thanks, Bendi. I'm glad you did. Definitely report again if you hear anything else that seems odd," Rebecca said. "You too, Troy."

"Absolutely," said Troy.

"I will," Bendi replied.

The radios went quiet again. Moments later, the hall light turned off. Cassidi looked at her watch, "Approximately three minutes."

"Okay. Three minutes. Not too bad. Might be good info to have in case we find ourselves in a sticky situation," said Selby. "We can keep movin' on now if you two are ready."

The remaining three hallways stayed dark. At each turn, Cassidi, Rebecca, and Selby dropped to the floor and took the corner on hands and knees to avoid the possibility of tripping any more light sensors. It worked. They now found themselves in front of the door identifying the next area as the restricted area. Selby unlocked the door and the three pushed on through. Cassidi took the lead again, stopping in front of a door after two turns down short passages.

"Okay. This is it. This is the lab I found," Cassidi said, indicating the sign identifying it as "Lab 03A." "The refrigeration room is down that first hallway, and the room where they took the people on the stretchers is further in. So. Should we start here?"

"Works for me," Rebecca responded as she pushed open the door. "Selby, you've got the door, right?"

"Yep. I'm on it, Becs. You two just do your thing."

All three stepped inside, but Selby stayed just inside the door, with it cracked enough to hear what was happening outside and to peer through the opening to keep an eye on the immediate hallway. He would also be able to see if any adjacent hallway lights came on. The lights inside of the lab lit up as soon as Rebecca had stepped inside. It was as they'd expected. Easier to search. Easier to get in trouble if trouble came looking for them.

CHAPTER 24

The lab had several computer stations. No one dared touch those. Computers were Troy's domain, but he wasn't in here. Not that he would have risked touching them either. There were microscopes and hooded work stations. Protective suits hanging in the corner. Cassidi went over to inspect one. It was a complete haz mat suit, but she had no reason to know this. Its intended use was clear, however.

"Look, Becs," she said, holding one out for Rebecca to see. "Whatever they're working on in here requires some pretty heavy-duty protection. This thing looks like it even protects you from the air you breathe. This is some serious stuff."

"Yeah, it sure is."

A small refrigerator contained sealed vials of a cloudy liquid. The label on the vials contained a combination of letters and numbers. Meaningless to the girls. Further investigation revealed an open notebook lying beside one of the computers. The page was open to a set of diagrams that looked like varying combinations of chemical components. Two of the diagrams had an "X" placed over them, one was circled, and two others had a "?" beside them. There was some writing in the margins. "Vitals stable, nine subjects. Too high a dose resulted in inability to recover in six subjects. No effect, zero subjects."

Cassidi gently turned to a few more pages, while Rebecca looked on. On each, there was a different set of diagrams, with similar notes indicating stable vitals, inability to recover, and no effect. The numbers varied across the pages. The notes were always jotted down next to a circled diagram. It appeared they'd found one of the scientist's notebooks for trials they were running on whatever they were working on in this lab.

Rebecca wandered over to a cart that held two plastic boxes with lids. The boxes weren't very large and, when she lifted one by the handle, she found it was not heavy. There was a light sound of glass tinkling inside. She set the box down gently, afraid to break something. As she did so, she noticed that the front of the box she was holding was labeled "Active" in red lettering. Rebecca examined the front of the second box. Same label.

"Cass," she whispered loud enough for her friend to hear from a few feet away, where she had stopped to look again at the refrigerator of sealed vials. "Come look at this."

"Active. Huh. What if that's the virus?" Cassidi asked.

"Yeah, that's what I was wondering, too. It would make sense with that notebook, with the notes about vitals," Rebecca said.

"I wonder if that would mean that an 'inability to recover' means the subject died. Subject being an actual person," Cassidi mused aloud.

"Hey. Girls. I can hear you whisperin'. How 'bout you filling me in on whatever it is you're discussin' over there?" Selby said from the doorway, without taking his eyes off the hallway outside.

"Oh. Sorry, Selby. Of course," Rebecca said as the girls made their way over to the door. Rebecca filled him in on what they had seen so far and told him of their speculations about the boxes labeled "Active" and the relationship to the notes in the notebook.

"It sure could be the virus. It could also be somethin' else. Though we know they brought people in here on stretchers, so that supports the hypothesis," Selby responded when Rebecca was finished.

"Yeah, it does. But the only thing that doesn't make sense about it is that the notes also talked about stable vitals. They're either testing on live people here, people who aren't sick—and where are they getting these people, if that's the case?—or maybe it's something else. I mean, we already know that everyone who has gotten the virus has died, so why would they keep testing it?" Rebecca said.

"You're right, Becs. That doesn't really make sense. But if it isn't the virus, what is it? Why are they bringing people in here on stretchers?" Cassidi asked.

"Maybe we should head on out, move on to the next stop," Selby chimed in. "Unless you have more to look at here?"

"I think we can move on. Doesn't seem like this lab is going to tell us much more. Not without understanding what the symbols in the diagrams mean." Rebecca said. "You ready to move on, Cass?"

"Ready. I wish I had my phone, though. I'd take some pics of those diagrams. Maybe Troy or Bendi would be able to make sense of them."

"Oh! I brought my pocket cam! Forgot all about it until you just said that, Cass. Thanks." Rebecca pulled off her pack, uncinched the top, and dug around for her camera. Finding it, she handed the bag to Cassidi and the two girls walked back over to the notebook to click off a few photos before rejoining Selby at the door.

Selby spoke into his 2-way, "Coast still clear out were you guys are, Troy and Bendi? We are getting ready to move from the lab to...where to, Becs?" Selby broke off, realizing they hadn't said where to next.

"I think, as much as I don't like the thought, I think we need to go to the hallway where Cass saw them take the stretchers next, see if we can find the room they disappeared into," Rebecca said. Cassidi shivered.

"Did ya hear that? The body room. We're moving on there. So, are we clear from where you guys are sittin'?" Selby said into the radio.

"You're clear from here," said Bendi. "I haven't heard anything else suspicious."

"Good to go from here, too," said Troy. "All's quiet and uneventful." Rebecca thought she heard a stifled yawn.

"Are you both holding up okay out there?" she asked, as a way of checking up on them, Troy especially.

"Doing good here," came Troy's reply. "It isn't exactly exciting, but I'm okay with that."

"Yes, I'm doing fine, too," Bendi said.

"Great. We're on the move," Selby said. He stepped aside and let Cassidi take the lead again.

Cassidi took them to the hallway where the men had disappeared into one of the rooms with the people on stretchers. Because she hadn't seen which door they went into, they were going to have to check all of the rooms and hope that they would know which one it was when they saw it. Though knowing it was the correct room would likely entail seeing these people still inside the room. How else would they know they were in the right place?

There were six doors down this hallway. Not too many. After coming up empty, with just a storage closet, two offices, and a restroom on one side, they dropped down to cross the hall to the other side to check the two rooms on that side. Upon opening the first door there, the lights all turned on, and they were confronted with a very long hallway with doors on both sides. A lot of doors. Unlike the other doors they had seen so far, these had small windows on the front. Rebecca went to the nearest one.

"I'd say this is it," she said, with a sound of disgust mixed with horror. The other two found their way to other windowed doors across from and beside the one where Rebecca stood. Inside each was a person hooked up to nodes attached to a monitor of some sort. They were strapped in, but it didn't appear as if they were conscious. Of course, it was in the middle of the night, so a normal person would be sleeping right now. This situation was anything but normal, and the people in these rooms all were lying on their backs, arms straight down to their sides, faces up.

"They almost don't look real," Cassidi commented. "The woman in here looks like a mannequin, except she is breathing. The look on her face looks...like nothing."

"Yeah, same here," Rebecca said.

"Yep, here, too," said Selby.

"Selby! You should be by the door," said Rebecca.

"Oh. Right," Selby responded as he jumped towards the door.

Just then, "Uh, guys. We've got company," came Troy's croaking whisper from across the 2-way radios.

Rebecca, Cassidi, and Selby froze, Selby with his hand on the door. They looked from one to the other and then around the well-lit hallway.

Cassidi was the first to raise her radio to speak, "Talk quick. What have we got?"

"Same white truck as last time, but no car. The car the guy Karl was driving isn't with the truck this time," Troy responded. "The truck just passed by me, and they are waiting for the garage to open. My guess is they're bringing in more people."

"We're in the place they took those people!" Cassidi exclaimed.

"Okay, Troy. Stay put, and don't talk after you see them go inside. We've got to hide," Selby said, recovering his composure.

"Right. Hide fast. The truck has just pulled in. Let me know when you guys are safe. I'm going silent now," said Troy.

"Where are we going to hide? They'll be coming here, and we know the lights will stay on for three minutes after we leave the room," Rebecca said.

"If they're bringing people again, it'll take them a few minutes to get them out of the truck and bring them here. Best guess is that it took more than five minutes, less than ten, by the time they got parked and to the point where they entered this room and I lost them the last time," Cassidi said. "We have enough time to leave. Backtrack towards the door. We can probably even be out before they reach here."

"Or..." said Selby.

"No, not 'or'! We've got to go!" said Cassidi.

"Or we could hide here. In one of the rooms. We might hear something," Selby said. "I wonder if there are empty rooms down the hall, where we could be closer to where they might put the new people."

Selby was already off down the hall before either of the two girls could protest. They could either leave, go back the way they came, or follow Selby. Rebecca could see what Cassidi wanted to do. She did, too, of course. But she couldn't leave

Selby here, and they came here for answers. This was one way they might get some. She took off after Selby, who was stopping at each window and looking in.

"You take one side, I'll take the other," Rebecca said to him as she joined him.

Cassidi glanced towards the door, then turned and ran after the other two.

CHAPTER 25

Rebecca was sharing a room with a woman who looked vaguely familiar. The three of them had split up, as there was not enough room for all of them to hide in the same location. They were near one another, with Cassidi across from her and Selby beside her. If anything happened to one of them, the other two would know. They had had to act quickly so that there was time for the hallway lights to shut off once they had vacated the space. It had taken only a few moments to make their way down the hall to the point where there were empty rooms. They positioned themselves next to these and hoped that the ventilation system would carry the voices through to where they were hiding. That is, if the men even came here this time.

Rebecca could hear her heart pounding in her ears. She was crouched under the table that held the vaguely familiar woman. It wasn't a great hiding place, but it was the only possible hiding place in the room. It was a low table with a covering over the top that didn't quite drop down all the way to the floor. If someone were to crouch down on the floor, they would be able to see her, sitting with her knees drawn up to her chest trying pull as much of her as away from the edges as possible. She was struggling to control her breathing. To quiet it.

There was a click in the hallway. Lights must have just shut off. Rebecca let out a small sigh. At least that wouldn't give them away. She strained her ears hard, listening for any sounds above those her heart and her own breath made. It was eerily quiet. Especially knowing how many people were behind the doors leading down this hallway. She didn't count. Didn't have time to. But it had to be at least 30. They had reached almost to the end of the hall before they'd come upon vacant rooms. She could see that the hallway came to a "T" and wondered if there were more rooms in the other two directions.

Voices. Nothing intelligible, just barely audible. Laughter. And then the door opened from the direction they had entered. Rebecca felt a little nauseous. It seemed unlikely they would enter her room if they were just bringing new people in. New "subjects." Then again, there was really no way she could know if that is what they were doing. Troy hadn't been able to see any more than the truck pulling into the garage. She was sure the door would have been closed behind them as it was the last time. What if they were here for another purpose this time?

But, no. She could now hear wheels on the floor as the men started to wheel in stretchers. It sounded like only two from the noises she could hear of one being rolled into the hallway, followed by a pause, and then the sounds of a second one being rolled through the door. And then she could hear the door falling closed. The men were still talking and laughing. She could hear two separate voices, so it seemed that they did not need the third individual. She wondered who didn't come. Was Troy's dad there again? Another good reason for Troy to have been posted outside and not in here with her and Cassidi. Lucky choice, since they had had no way of knowing that they would end up in their current situation. Didn't even really consider it as a possibility.

Rebecca shifted slightly, trying to get more comfortable before the men reached as far as the room she was hiding. She wanted no chance of making any sound they might hear outside. She hoped the other two were doing okay.

Especially Cassidi, who had already been in a tight spot here before. Her biggest concern with Selby was that he would do something insane trying to be a hero.

"Hold up. We're going right here," she heard a voice say just outside the door. Rebecca held her breath.

"You've got the female subject, right?" the second voice asked. Both voices were men.

"I have the female, so this side of the hall. Wanna help me out here, then we'll both get the male in the room across the hall."

"Sure. Be easier. Still get tangled up in all the wires trying to get them hooked up in the right places."

"Hehe. You'll get the hang of it. Boss wants the tests run first thing in the morning, so I want to be in and out quick. I need a little sleep if I'm gonna have to spend the whole day running tests on these two."

"What's his hurry? Seems like Karl is picking up the pace now, wanting everything done yesterday. It's like now he wants more. More subjects, more testing, more sending out. And he has no patience to wait for it. He used to want us to be more careful. Now he just seems to want more, no matter the cost. It isn't going to help his cause if the people in this city keep getting angrier and angrier."

"I think that's exactly why he's picking up the pace. He wants to move up the plans before there's chaos. Councilor

Manglebee is applying the pressure. Seems he feels like it's getting out of control here. Other cities too, from what I hear."

"Oh yeah? Where'd you hear…" the voice trailed off as the door closed behind them. She listened for a continuation of the conversation through the vents once they got through the door, but their voices were too muffled. She couldn't make out what they were saying.

Not much else to do but wait. Rebecca was too afraid to move until she knew the men were done and gone. She thought about what she'd heard in the snippet of conversation from the two men. Council *was* in on it. Or at least Head Councilor was. It now also seemed likely that whatever it was they were doing here, it had to do with the virus, and it was part of something bigger. A bigger plan. But what? It involved the government, at least at the highest level. And from what it sounded like, they were having trouble in other cities as well. Not just hers. Not just Montrose. They heard nothing about trouble anywhere else on the news reports. They were made to believe this virus outbreak was localized. Jonathan might have been right, though. They might not be dealing with an actual virus, or at least not one occurring and spreading naturally.

"…getting together to let off some steam next weekend. If we get the break we've been promised. Care to join us? Only rule is, no shop talk. We all need a *break* from this."

The two men were back in the hallway again. Rebecca perked up, hoping to hear more useful information.

"Yeah, yeah, sure. Sounds like fun. I, for one, will be glad for the no shop talk rule. Been eating, sleeping, and breathing shop lately."

"Great. We'll be ironing out the details this week. Now let's get this guy hooked up so we can get on out of here."

They wheeled the second individual into the room next to Cassidi. Rebecca wondered if Cassidi would have any better luck than she did in hearing conversation through the vents in the room she was hiding in. Didn't seem likely, but one could hope. Rebecca relaxed a little under the table. Now that the men weren't in the room right next to her, she felt she had a little breathing room for the period of time they were across the hall. She was relieved to hear that their plans were to finish quickly and get out of there. She wanted to talk to Cassidi and Selby. And Troy and Bendi. Looking at her watch, she saw that it was already almost 3:00 a.m. They needed to wrap things up here.

She finally heard the men opening the door across the hall. She stopped moving, holding her breath again. But now they were moving quickly, relieved of the weight of moving people and obviously ready to be finished with their tasks. They pushed the empty stretchers down the hall and out the door without saying anything else that would be useful to

Rebecca. The door closed behind them. The lights clicked off. But still they waited in their positions. It seemed no one wanted to risk moving too soon, in case one, or both, of them returned.

"Becs?" It was Troy. "Where are you guys? Are you okay?"

"Troy, yes. We're okay."

"Oh, thank god. I thought you guys would be coming out here while they were inside. When you didn't come, I got worried. They just pulled away. They're gone."

"Man, it's about time. I'm gettin' stiff as a board sitting under this table. It wasn't made for a guy my size to hide under," Selby chimed in from the room next to Rebecca's. "Comin' out now."

"I'm already out here. What's taking you two so long? I'm ready to *go*," said Cassidi.

Rebecca and Selby both joined Cassidi as she finished speaking.

"So, you are all okay? And the truck is gone?" Bendi, joining the conversation.

"Yes. Bendi, we are heading your way. I'm not sure what Troy and Cassidi heard, but I have some useful info."

"Just heard the juicy bits of conversation out in the hall. Definitely some useful stuff there. Did you hear more than that?" asked Selby.

"No. Just that. But it's something. I was hoping to look around more, but I don't think we have time," Rebecca said.

"I heard the same stuff you guys did," Cassidi said. "Really wish we had time now to go check out the refrigerators. At least those. But you're probably right, Becs. We should get going before the sun comes up."

"I'll head over to where Bendi is, too," said Troy. "We can head up from there."

"Good idea," Rebecca said. "See you both in a few." Rebecca turned to Selby and Cassidi. "So, you guys heard about Head Councilor? And the rest of it? When the guys were just outside our doors?"

"Oh, yeah. I can't believe it. Wait. I guess maybe I can. I think I really am not at all surprised. I should be. But I'm not," Cassidi said. "Jonathan was right, at least about BRO and Council being involved. Rrrrgh. I wish we had just a little more time in here!"

"I know, right? How many times have you guys been here? This is your…what?…third? fourth time?" Selby asked.

"It's our third. The first time we just observed from above. That's when we saw Remy and the woman, Bryn, talking outside. After it seemed Karl was reading Bryn the riot act. Second time is when Cass went inside last weekend. I'm not counting my first two times, when I went no further than the ridge," Rebecca responded.

"Becs, do you think these two guys were the same two we saw with Karl before? Karl was driving the car last time. I wonder why he wasn't there this time," Cassidi said.

"Really hard to tell. What do you think? You were the only one who was close enough to hear the voices last time."

"I think it was. I'm almost positive it was. Definitely the one guy, the one you called Zeus. His voice is pretty distinctive. But I'm pretty sure the other one was the same one."

Rebecca and Cassidi looked at each other. Troy's dad. Maybe. "Do we tell him?" asked Cassidi.

"Tell who, what?" asked Selby.

"Selby, if we tell you this, you can't say anything to anyone. Not even Bendi. She would have a hard time having this piece of information, and we don't know for sure if it's true or not. Right now, it's just speculation," said Rebecca.

"My lips are *sealed*," Selby promised. "I won't breathe a word of it to anyone."

"I think one of the guys is Troy's dad. One of the men sure looked like Troy. It sure looked like what I remember Troy's dad looking like, the few times I've met him," Cassidi said.

"*What?* You can't be serious," Selby said. Eyes wide under the headlamp, as the three of them stood pinned against a wall to keep from turning the lights back on. They still hadn't made a move from their position just outside the rooms they had been hiding in.

"I wish I were kidding," Cassidi responded. "It isn't something I want to believe. Like Becs said, we don't know for sure. So we really can't say anything to Troy or Bendi."

"No way, man. Not a word from me," Selby said.

"Okay, guys, we need to start making our way. I don't want those two to have to wait too long for us," Rebecca said.

"Oh, yeah. Right. Well, I'm ready," Cassidi said.

"Yes, yes. Let's get a move on," Selby agreed.

CHAPTER 26

The trip back through the maze of hallways was uneventful, and they made quick work of getting back out to where Bendi and Troy waited just outside the door. Bendi rushed up to Rebecca and hugged her, and then Cassidi. She stopped short of hugging Selby, giving him a shy smile, instead. Relief washed over Troy's face the moment he saw Rebecca come through the door. His smile included the two others as they came through.

"Those lights are on now," Troy remarked, glancing upwards.

Selby followed his gaze, "Whoa, you're right. They have a *really* strange quality about them. They act like they're bouncin' off of an object up there so that they are directed in a specific direction. But I don't see anything up there they can be reflected off of. So, I wonder how they're doin' that. And why."

"It looks like the light is hitting something, and then being diffused. It makes the light dimmer and less intense. More difficult to see," Bendi observed. "They have to serve some purpose, but what? They don't seem to be for the purpose of seeing."

"No, they don't," Selby said, still looking up. "They're more like lasers, except wavey, down low, but regular light up high. That color. Might be for camouflage, but maybe it's also being used because light at that end of the spectrum has more energy. Don't know why they'd do that…but might be somethin' to the color."

"How do you know this stuff?" asked Cassidi, in awe. Selby had turned into a bit of a mysterious figure now. There was so much about him that none of them knew. Cassidi found it intriguing.

"Have to for some of the…tools…my folks and I use. And some of it I learned about just because it's fascinatin' stuff," Selby responded. "Don't need to know it to learn the skills, but I like to know how things work."

"And the purple light technicalities?" Cassidi pressed further. "Need to, or want to?"

"Oh, that is definitely a need to know piece of information. Might do more harm than intended without understanding the physics of how our tools...our weapons...work."

"Weapons? You have weapons?" Bendi asked.

"Yes, indeed. Not something we ever want to have to use, but if our lives depended on it, we could. My parents had to use them before…"

"And you know how to use them?" asked Cassidi.

"I do. I've been in training from a very young age, so, yes, I can use them. Pretty good at it, too. At least in simulations."

"Can you train us?" Cassidi continued.

"Uh. No. No, I wouldn't be able to do that. Not now, at least. Takes a long time to learn the skills. And to handle them responsibly. Boy, did my folks drill that into my head. It's way too easy to do something stupid without even meaning to. Won't have that hangin' over my head. No way." Cassidi looked both disappointed and angry at his response. She let it drop, however. For now. But she wouldn't leave it dropped.

Knowing how to use more than just the close-range tasers would make her feel a lot safer with what they were doing. She had no idea what was next, but this wasn't over.

They had made some big discoveries tonight. Discoveries that indicated that what they'd learned was just the tip of the iceberg. No. They weren't done yet, so she wouldn't leave the topic of training alone for long.

"While I find this new side of you intriguing and all, and I wouldn't mind learning what you know, I think we can save this for a later conversation," Troy interjected. "The clock is still running and I, for one, would like to know what it was you guys found out in there."

"Yeah, we need to fill you two in. What we found out wasn't much, but it's big," Rebecca said. "Let's get away from this place first, though. I know those two guys left, but I don't feel comfortable just hanging out here in the open."

With that, the group headed into the trees and up to the ridge. It was a good place to stop to talk. It was far from the entrances, so no risk of being caught should anyone happen to return. And while the slope coming up this side of the mountain was nowhere near as difficult as the front side, it was still good to pause for a breather before heading down. Rebecca filled Troy and Bendi in on what she, Selby, and Cassidi had heard and seen inside. She told them about their findings in the lab and the conversation the two men had in the hallway. Again, without mentioning that they thought one of them might be Troy's dad.

"Can I see the photos you took?" asked Troy. Rebecca nodded, taking her pack off her back and retrieving the camera. She turned on the display and swiped through to the first of the images on the display so that he could see them in order. Bendi moved around so that she could look at them over Troy's shoulder.

"Do they make any sense to either of you?" Rebecca asked.

"Yes. It looks like a diagram for DNA structures. It looks like they are testing different structures, making little changes and seeing what happens when those changes are made," Bendi responded.

"Well, it looks like Selby isn't the only one full of surprises," Cassidi commented.

"Can they change biological structures like that?" asked Rebecca.

"Sure, they can. They've been making synthetic biological organisms for years now," Bendi said.

Bendi was always so quiet. She was relatively new to the group and never really said much about her family. They all knew her family was involved in government because they were all on the educational and training tract for policy and governance. Rebecca tried to recall if Bendi ever said what department her parents worked for or what she would be doing for her work assignment. She thought she recalled something about the food sector.

"Bendi, do your parents work in the Food Safety & Accessibility Division?" Rebecca asked.

"Yes. They do. Why?"

"Do you know this because it's part of your training program?"

"No. Well, not directly, at any rate. There is a subdivision that deals with testing synthetic food for safety and nutritional composition. This isn't the area my parents work in, but it is the area I am interested in. They don't have the climate under control yet, so it is important that we continue to be able to feed everyone, to be able to create safe and nutritious food to supplement our natural crops. These diagrams aren't for food, but I recognize that they are showing DNA components. I can't tell you what it is for or what it all means. Only that it looks similar to what I have seen in synthetic food testing."

"Anyone else have any mind-blowing knowledge or secrets they want to share?" Cassidi said with only a hint of sarcasm. She really did want to know. "Here I thought we all knew everything there was to know about one another…"

"I'm a deep well of mystery," Troy responded. "No one can know the depths of this great mind."

"Ugh," Cassidi said, rolling her eyes.

"Okay, guys, let's get back on track here. It's after 4:30 and we still have to get down this mountain and back home," Rebecca intervened before the conversation got too far off track. "We now know that BRO is working on some sort of synthetic biological organism. It appears they are testing human subjects. From the notes, then, it sounds like some of the subjects don't survive what they are doing to them. This makes it sound to me like it easily could be the virus. Do you guys agree?"

Nods all around.

"And Council is in on it. Don't forget that part," Selby said.

"Right. At least Manglebee is. It also seems like this is much bigger than just Montrose. We don't know how big or in what way, but from what those men were saying, it is bigger," Rebecca added.

"They are planning something big, no doubt," Selby agreed. "I'm thinking we might not have a lot of time to get to the bottom of this. Whatever they are planning, it sounds like they want to do it soon. So, what are we gonna do with this information?"

"What *can* we do with it?" asked Troy. "We can't go to Council. We don't know enough to stop them because we don't even know yet what exactly they are doing! We have been down here three times now. Each time we get a little more information, but it is never enough to get the big picture."

"We are running out of time and options. We need to think big now. No more small-time stuff," Selby looked around at each of them in turn. It was dark out still. Not much of the full moon filtered through the forest. But their headlamps were still on, lowered around their necks so that they did not blind one another while talking. In the glow of the light, Selby looked a little menacing as he spoke. Rebecca saw Bendi shudder. But she didn't disagree.

The group stood silent, realization settling in. Five friends up against a government. They had all already put themselves in risky situations, but it wasn't enough. Selby was right. They had to think big. All of their parents worked in government. Rebecca had a disturbing thought: they had seen someone who might be Troy's dad, but *all* of their parents worked in government. How many of them knew about this? How many of them were involved? She felt nauseous. She also felt like she had to keep this thought to herself. She could not suggest that possibility to this group of friends. The idea was too much to think about right now.

"I wonder where BRO is getting their 'subjects,'" Cassidi said. "Maybe one of us can get on the inside if we can figure out how to become a subject."

"Not a good idea. At all," Troy said.

"Well, wait a minute. It might not be a bad idea," Selby said.

"Thanks, Selby," Cassidi gave him a smile. He was kind of becoming a hero of sorts to Cassidi. And then she shot daggers at Troy. He shrugged his shoulders in reply.

"I don't know, Cass. If we do something like that, how do we keep the person in there safe? And how does it help us? Those people weren't even conscious. It was more than just being asleep. We don't know what these tests are that they're running either. You saw in the notes how many of their tests didn't work, and it sounds like the person dies when the test doesn't work," Rebecca couldn't see for the life of her how this would be helpful. Yes, it would get someone on the inside, but that's it. And it could result in a friend dying if things went wrong.

"All of that is true, Becs. But let's not throw this idea out completely. I say we think about it. We try to come up with a way to get inside, even if people are there, to get more intel. We can't keep doing these small-scale attempts. No offense to what you guys have been doin'. After tonight, though, I think we can't keep goin' in and then being chased out so easily. We need a way to stay inside until we get what we need," Selby said.

"I know you're right. I just can't see how it would work. I can't see it now, anyways," Rebecca said. "But I agree that we need to think about it more. We really do need a way to spend enough time inside to get better information. I don't know what we do with it yet, once we get it."

"One thing at a time, Becs. Let's not get too far ahead of ourselves. We need to know what we're dealin' with before we know what we can do with that information. Good planning goes a long way. My folks have taught me that. And it's true," Selby said.

Troy stifled a yawn, "I can agree that we need to find a way to get in there. I'm just not sure being a test subject is a good idea. Maybe there is another way. I say we all go home now and sleep on it. I don't think we'll solve it up here, tonight. Or, actually, this morning. The sun will be up over the ridge soon."

"Yeah, I agree. Let's all go home and sleep on it. It's Saturday. Can we all meet up tomorrow? See what we come up with?" Rebecca asked the group.

"I can meet up in the afternoon, after lunch. Sunday morning is a simulation morning for me. But I'm good to go after lunch. Listen, I can bring my folks in on this whenever we want. Keep that in mind. They have a lot of skills," Selby said.

"Thanks, Selby. We can keep that in mind. Right now, I'd rather not." Rebecca knew Selby's parents would most likely be safe, given what she now knew about them, but she still didn't want to take that chance. They still worked for government, just like her parents, and the rest of her friends' parents. It was too big a risk right now.

"Is everyone else good for, say, 1:30. My house. Study group. That'll be the excuse," Rebecca continued.

"Works for me," Cassidi said.

"I'm in," Troy chimed in.

"Yes. I can make it then," said Bendi.

"Great. Let's get down this mountain and get home to our beds. Get as much sleep as you can. Then see what you can come up with. We'll share our ideas at my house on Sunday. 1:30."

The group parted ways just as the sun was rising over the ridge. Lucky for them, it was a Saturday. They all managed to crawl into bed undetected. Also lucky for them, they were teenagers. No one expected them to be awake before noon on a Saturday.

CHAPTER 27

Rebecca awoke with a start. She'd been dreaming again. She lay in a puddle of sweat. Out of breath. Heart racing. What was she just dreaming? Her mind struggled to recall. Funny how quickly a dream can become elusive once you wake up. It was something about being in that place. She was a subject. There were people jabbing needles in her. She couldn't move or speak. Couldn't scream. She sat up and looked around her room, getting her bearings again. Looking at her watch, she realized she had only been asleep for four hours. Not nearly long enough.

She flopped back down on her bed and threw her arm over her eyes. Sleep. She wanted more sleep. Needed it.

Instead, her mind filled with thoughts that refused to leave her alone. Manglebee was up to something. That much was clear. And it involved testing on people from her city. People were dying at a rapid pace, and it was looking more and more like these deaths were part of a larger plan. It was not a virus.

Rebecca wondered how far all of this reached. No one thought Council was really up front about much of anything. They told you what they wanted you to believe. They tracked people, dictated what they would do with their lives, limited their knowledge of what was happening in other regions. They made people disappear if they got too far out of line. Were those disappearances connected to what was happening now? Rebecca sat up again. Wait! Is *that* who they were doing the testing on? The people they disappeared? That would make sense. But, from the tests they saw in the notebook, that would be a *lot* of people. Could be, though. But *why*? Killing so many citizens seemed to be going too far, even for Council.

All of this speculation was making her head spin. Sleep deprivation wasn't helping either. With a groan, she flopped back down again. She made a mental note to talk to the others about the possibility that maybe they were using those they disappeared as the test subjects. She wasn't sure that that piece of information helped them at all, but she still wanted to see what they thought about it. She tried to think about what they could do to get inside, but her head was starting to throb. She desperately needed more sleep. She picked up her phone and fed music to her speakers, closed her eyes, and willed her mind to pay attention to the music and nothing else. In moments, Rebecca was back to sleep. A fitful sleep, but still sleep.

****

Rebecca awoke at 2:00 in the afternoon, groggy, but feeling better than she had when she first woke up. Her headache was gone, and she felt like she might be able to string more than two cohesive thoughts together. After she ate, she thought, as her stomach rumbled loudly. She couldn't remember when she had last eaten. Sometime on Friday. Did she eat dinner last night? Her stomach said probably not, so she rolled out of bed, and headed downstairs.

Her parents were home. Her mom was in the living room watching the Council News. An update on the virus. Talking Head was saying that the virus was reaching epidemic proportions. The city's quarantine had not kept it contained, and it was spreading to other areas in the region. Rebecca's mom stared at the screen with unseeing eyes. She wondered how much of this her mom was hearing. Rebecca herself was disgusted. Of course, they had no information on *how* it was spreading or what it exactly this virus was. Of course not. Because *they* were responsible.

Rebecca had heard enough. She made a beeline to the kitchen. Her mom hadn't even noticed Rebecca enter the room, and Rebecca hadn't announced her presence. She glanced back at her mom once more, as she passed through the door into the kitchen. She couldn't imagine her mom knew anything about this. Surely, she wouldn't be involved in her own son's death. It was beyond Rebecca's ability to imagine that that could be true. Rebecca then realized that her parents could know about what Manglebee was up to without being directly involved in Jonathan's death. That made her feel a little better. Not much, but a little.

"Rebecca? Is that you?" Her dad's voice drifted out of the office, a room located off the living room. It was mostly her dad's space. He worked from home much more than her mom. Rebecca guessed that's what he was doing now. It was expected of him, but now it was also a way to stay busy, so he didn't have to think too much.

"Yeah, Dad. It's me. Just getting something to eat."

"Ah, okay. Maybe you can finish off that pasta in there. Hate to throw it away."

"Sure, Dad."

"You doing okay, Rebecca?" Her dad was making an attempt again to check in on her. *What do you know, Dad?* She shook off the question as quickly as it arose. Her parents were devastated by Jonathan's death. They couldn't be involved, she told herself again, firmly. She felt sorry for them.

Poking her head around the corner and giving her dad what she hoped was a reassuring smile, she said, "Yeah, Dad. I'm doing okay. School is busy. That helps."

"Good. Good." He attempted a smile in return. It did not extend to his eyes. "Rebecca, you can talk to me anytime you need. You know that, don't you?"

"I do know that. Thanks, Dad." He gave her a nod, and a long look, checking to see if he should say more. He decided not to, and nodded again, absently, turning back to his computer.

"Oh, one more thing," he said looking up from his computer again, just as Rebecca started to move away. She turned back to him. "Your mom and I are going to be gone for the day again tomorrow. You're okay fending for yourself, aren't you? We'll be back late evening."

"Yeah, sure. No problem."

"Good. Good." He turned back again to his work.

Rebecca went back into the kitchen, wondering what it was her parents were doing again disappearing for an entire day. She retrieved the pasta from the refrigerator. Taking the lid off and looking inside, she decided it looked fine to eat cold. She grabbed a fork from the drawer and wandered back into the living room, intending to head back up to her room with her food. However, she noticed that the news was finished and there was now a movie on. Her mom was still staring at the screen with that vacant look.

Rebecca felt the edges of her heart, the tightening, squeezing sensation that happened whenever she thought of Jonathan, and now, seeing her mother, she felt it again. She moved to the couch and sat down, pasta bowl in her lap, and leaned into her mother. Her mother leaned back, resting her head on Rebecca's shoulder, but still staring at the screen.

They sat that way for a long time. Rebecca ate her pasta and let the movie distract her. Her mother seemed to relax a little. After a bit, they shifted positions, but the closeness remained. It had been a long time since they'd felt this close, and Rebecca enjoyed it while she could. They said nothing. And that was okay. It was exactly what they both needed just then.

****

When the movie was finished, Rebecca took her bowl into the kitchen and placed it in the dishwasher, then headed back up to her room. It was early evening, but already she felt like she could go to sleep again. She sat on the edge of her bed. Exhausted. Overwhelmingly exhausted. She didn't think that she could come up with any sort of plan tonight. Not as tired as she was. And, quite frankly, she really just wanted a night of *not* thinking about it. She didn't choose any of this. It wasn't like her to get involved in anything that would cause trouble.

She picked up a pillow and heaved it at the wall. She did it again with her second pillow. And her night clothes. Top first, then pants. She looked for something else nearby to throw, but everything else was breakable. At that moment, she felt breakable as well. But she also felt *angry*. Angry at Jonathan for dying. Angry at her parents because they seemed to need her reassurance rather than giving her theirs. Angry at BRO and Council. Angry at the loss of her childhood. She hadn't been totally innocent. She knew that life was a game you had to play to get along in this world, but now she knew it was so much worse than that. She knew it was a game she could no longer play. And she was angry about that. She wasn't ready for the responsibility that was now hers, but she had no choice. She had to make herself ready.

But not tonight. Tonight, she would rebel against her new role. Instead of thinking the thoughts she didn't want to think, instead of trying to plan for a mission that could cost them someone's life, she opted for avoidance. Just for tonight. She could think again in the morning. The gang wouldn't be there until after lunch. She picked up her pillows and night clothes from the floor, placing her pillows back on her bed and changing into her sleep shirt and pants. Rebecca climbed into bed and spent the evening watching mindless videos on her phone.

She fell asleep early, phone falling on her chest and staying there.

CHAPTER 28

A hand covered her mouth, pressing hard so that she couldn't scream. Rebecca thought it was another dream, until she opened her eyes to find the hand still there, and a second hand pinning her down to the bed. She tried to thrash, to break free, but she was no match for the figure looming above her. It was pitch dark in her room. She couldn't see who it was. She forced herself to relax, hoping it would make the intruder relax. He did, but as soon as she made a move to escape, he had her again; this time he held her down even tighter.

"Rebecca. Stop. I do *not* want to hurt you, but I cannot have you screaming or alerting anyone. I cannot have you running out of this room to your parents."

Rebecca thought she detected a movement across the room. A second person. She knew she had no chance. Oddly, she felt herself calm down. She felt her rational mind awaken from its sleep. *Think. Don't make any sudden movements. He said he doesn't want to hurt you, so don't fight.* She tried to see who it was. She knew, of course, it had to be someone from either Council or BRO. Her eyes were adjusting to the dark, but not enough to see details. There was something vaguely familiar about the figure above her, however…

As if reading her thoughts, the voice said, "You and your friends were at the BRO facilities last night. We know you were there, and now we intend to find out why."

That voice…she knew it, didn't she?

"Now. This is how this is going to work. If you play nice, so will we. For now. For obvious reasons, we cannot stay here for our little chat. So, we will blindfold you. But you have a choice. You can cooperate and walk out of here on your own two feet, or we can give you a little something to knock you out, and we will carry you out of here."

That last bit caused her to panic. She tried to shake her head no, but the grip on her was too tight. The intruder seemed to catch what she was trying to do, however. "Okay, I think you are choosing the first option. If so, nod yes." He released his hold a little so that she could move her head. She nodded yes.

"Okay. Good choice."

"Bring the blindfold over," he said to the darkness on the other side of the room. So, there *was* at least one other person in the room.

"I'm going to let you sit up. My partner here will then place the blindfold around you. When we are finished, we will walk you down the stairs and outside to where we have a vehicle parked. I am only warning you this once: *do not* try anything. You will quickly regret it. Understood?"

She nodded yes again.

With that, he let her sit up, as the second individual crossed the room. He had the blindfold over her eyes before she could see any more than the movement of a shadow in the dark. The hand at her elbow indicated it was time to stand up and move. Rebecca complied.

Her mind was racing. Her parents would be gone for the day, certainly leaving before she would normally awaken on a Sunday, so they would never suspect anything was up. The gang wasn't going to get here until 1:30 in the afternoon. She had no idea what time it was now, but she assumed 1:30 was a long way off. Long enough for these two to make her into their next subject. Or worse. Or maybe…

We were looking for a way to get on the inside. Maybe this is it. Maybe if I can keep my cool, I can get the intel we need. If I'm not here when they get here, they'll guess what happened. I know they will. They'll come looking for me. All I need to do is stay calm, see what I can get from these two, and play along until the gang comes to get me. Selby will know what to do.

Her captor led her down the stairs and out the front door, with his "partner" following closely behind. Their vehicle was, as he'd said, just outside. In this area of the city, houses were widely dispersed. Neighbors were not sitting right on top of each other because each government house had property around it. He helped her into the back seat. His partner climbing in the door on the opposite side, sitting next to her. Making sure she did not try anything. She couldn't escape once the doors were closed, not from the back. She heard the back doors lock automatically. Only a person on the outside could open them. What they were more worried about was her trying to take off her blindfold and attempting to harm them. It would be a foolish move, of course, but that didn't mean she wouldn't try. Going to BRO was foolish, and she had done that. So, as a precaution, the partner would sit next to her in the back seat.

To Rebecca, the drive felt long. She guessed they were heading away from the city because of the lack of turns they were making and because, after a short time, they picked up speed. They had to be outside of the city boundaries. Where could they be? The only things outside of the city were the agricultural regions and the parks, and the few other occupied city units within Region 3. Beyond that was the Borderlands, closer to Montrose than Montrose was to another city unit. The areas surrounding each region that were out of bounds for citizens. They were meant to provide a barrier between regions, to keep citizens contained. Rebecca had no idea how large the Borderlands surrounding her region was.

The vehicle finally slowed. A final turn. A stop. The driver got out. She heard the sound of a garage door opening, except that this one seemed to be operated manually, as she didn't hear a motor, just a scraping and a creaking. Strange. The driver got back in the vehicle and pulled it forward. He stopped again and got out to close the door behind them. He also turned on a light. Rebecca could see the hint of the light through the edges of her blindfold. The door on her side opened, and a hand was again at her elbow.

She let him guide her out of the car. They were inside, but it was still chilly. Rebecca was wearing just her sleep clothes. The hand stayed at her elbow and guided her through two more doors. Still chilly. Did they not have any heat in this place? Rebecca's teeth started chattering.

"Get her a blanket, would you?" A new voice. Female. Moments later, the weight of warmth draped around her shoulders, and she pulled the corners close, waiting for her muscles to relax and her teeth to still. A blanket. Okay, so they were at least somewhat thoughtful. Apparently not into torturing her just now. *That's a relief.*

"Hello, Rebecca. We need you to leave your blindfold on. Got it?" Rebecca nodded. "Seems you have been doing some digging into some dangerous territory. You know that, don't you?" It was the woman again. Rebecca nodded once more. She didn't yet trust her voice.

"You entered dangerous territory as soon as you crossed over that mountain. I am not sure how you and your friends did it without being detected by SMALS and called in. But you're going to tell us." This time, the male spoke. The only one who had spoken before.

"Rebecca, we will need you to tell us what it is you and your friends are up to. But, take your time. We will know if you aren't telling truth. So be sure when you start talking, you are willing to divulge what you were doing and how you did it. Honestly. All of it."

Rebecca swallowed hard. Her mind raced. What should she tell them? How much could she say that would satisfy them without telling them everything. She would not give away Troy or Selby's secrets. This was her doing. She would somehow have to convince them that she was the one responsible for all of it. That her friends were just along for the ride. If anyone was going to take the fall for this, it would be her. Her palms were sweating. She wiped them on her pants, then grabbed the corners of the blanket tight again.

She risked a question, first. "Who are you? Are you with Council, or BRO?"

"That is not something you have a right to know. You are the one providing us with the information. Not the other way around." The male voice. Impatient and barely contained.

Well, that didn't work.

Rebecca decided to start with Jonathan. For one, it would buy her time. It *was* part of the story, but there was no real risk in telling it. No risk to anyone other than herself, that is. Rebecca cleared her throat and wiped her palms again.

"My brother," she began, "Jonathan. He died. From the virus."

"Yes, we know," said the woman, in a gentler, softer voice. "We are sorry you had to experience that."

This reaction took Rebecca by surprise. She felt the stinging behind her eyelids, the tears threatening to emerge. She had not at all expected empathy, and it caught her off guard. She squeezed her eyes tight. She would not show weakness, not to these people.

"Yeah, well, he was the reason I went inside BRO."

"I'm not sure I follow. Why would your brother's death lead you to trespass onto the ranch and into the BRO facilities?" said the female voice. Rebecca wondered if she was the one in charge. She hoped she was because the woman seemed to be less inclined to lose her patience. She was almost kind. Which was odd.

"When my brother got sick, he knew he was going to die, just like everyone else. At first, we thought he could fight it. The first morning I found out about it, I promised him I wouldn't tell our parents right away, just in case he got better. He was never one to get sick, so we thought he would be different. But he wasn't. I could see it as soon as I got home from school that day. I told my parents, and by the next morning, he was bad. He knew for sure he would not make it. I knew he would not make it. So, a couple of days before he died, when we were in his room alone, Jonathan told me that he was suspicious of this virus. He told me he didn't think it was a virus at all."

"He told you this after he got sick? After the first couple of days? How did he manage that?" the male voice said, then sucked in his breath as if he did not mean to say what he did.

"What my colleague here *means*," said the woman, with a tone of admonishment directed towards the man, "is that, from what we understand, the virus completely incapacitates its victims very quickly. How was it your brother was able to carry on conversations with you? Are you sure he wasn't hallucinating?"

"I thought maybe he was when he first started talking to me about it. I mean, I knew that was a symptom, and his fever was high. But Jonathan never actually hallucinated during his illness. He tossed and turned a lot in his sleep. It seemed like he was having bad dreams. When he was awake, he didn't hallucinate, but he didn't seem *there* either. His eyes wouldn't focus on anything. I'd be right above him, looking into his eyes, but it never seemed he was seeing me there. It never seemed like he saw anything, actually. His eyes looked…empty…"

Rebecca paused. This was the first time she had told the story in so much detail. She hadn't been able to say this much to Cassidi. It had still been to soon. Her emotions too raw. The words wouldn't come then. They didn't come easy now, but she could say them. In part because enough time had passed that the pain was retreating to someplace deeper inside of her. Someplace where she could protect it and keep it hidden. And in part because she had to say it. Jonathan's story had to be told here. The woman seemed empathetic. Telling Jonathan's story might help Rebecca. If so, then Rebecca might be able to get closer to living up to what Jonathan asked of her. So, she added another layer of protection, steeled her heart, and continued with the telling.

"When Jonathan started telling me about the things he had been doing, about what he thought about the virus, his eyes were clear. He was *there*. He was looking at me when he talked to me. He was not hallucinating. The illness was bad for Jonathan, but it didn't seem as bad as it was for other people I heard about. Jonathan got clear three different times during those last days."

There was quiet in the space. Rebecca got the feeling that the others were at least a little surprised about Jonathan. She could almost feel them looking at her with a measure of disbelief. The woman broke the silence, "What, exactly, did he tell you during these…clear…moments?"

Rebecca filled them in. She told them about the lights and about the notes he had taken and placed in the box. She told them how he had left her with the task of finding out what the virus was. She told them about seeing the lights for the first time herself, and her first trip up to the ridge. She did not tell them about Daniel finding her there. It didn't seem necessary and she didn't want to get him in trouble. She wished she could leave Cassidi, Selby, Troy, and Bendi out of the story as well, but that was obviously impossible. They already knew. She could only hope to minimize the role they played. She also did not tell them about her fear of heights. Another detail she thought unimportant.

When it came time to talk about her friends, she gave them as few details as possible. Her friends were already involved, and there was no way to leave out their understanding of Jonathan's suspicions. Aside from Troy, the others had joined the efforts willingly. Even Troy had, eventually. He could have declined, and he didn't. So, Rebecca told them the basics for how her friends came to be involved.

Rebecca also told them about the trip up with Cassidi and Troy when they discovered the entrance to the facility, but she skipped over the second trip over, when Cassidi had gone inside the facility the first time. They didn't seem to know about that particular outing, so she left it out.

"How did you avoid SMALS?" the woman asked.

"I found a way to confuse the trackers, to scramble the GPS system so that it looked like we were at home still. And we left our phones behind as well."

The man chuckled. "Clever girl," he said.

"Yes. Impressive," the woman said. "What did you see in the facility?"

Here is where Rebecca had to think things through. She would not give away Selby's secrets, so she couldn't tell them about the gear he had brought along. She also was not willing to let them know about what they had learned in the lab. Not entirely. In the end, she said that they had gone in through the front entry, had found a lab and seen vials with an unknown substance it in, as well as the boxes on the cart, but that they didn't know what any of it meant. She said that they were beginning to explore more when they heard voices, so they hid until the coast was clear, and then got out as quickly as they could.

Rebecca heard the woman let out a long breath. "Is there anything else you should tell us?" Rebecca shook her head, wiping her palms again under the blanket. "There's a glass of water next to you, on your right, if you need a drink." Not in a position to trust her captors, Rebecca made no move for the glass, though she was incredibly thirsty.

"Okay. If there is nothing else, you'll excuse us for a moment," she said. Then, "Watch her. Make sure she does not take off that blindfold. If she's thirsty, help her with the glass. We will return shortly."

CHAPTER 29

After what seemed an eternity, sitting in the dark with a silent presence watching over her, she heard a door open. She felt the shift in the air as the man and the woman walked past her. Rebecca sat up straighter, as the pit of her stomach dropped down lower. It was not until this very moment that she realized that no matter how much time had passed, no one would ever come for her. Oh, her friends would look. If she were not home when they arrived at 1:30—which was how long from now? She wondered—they would certainly set out on a rescue attempt. But they would be looking in the wrong place.

With mounting fear, she understood that her friends would never, ever, know where to begin looking. *She* didn't even know where she was. She only knew that there was no way she was in the facility. They drove too far, and this place had an entirely different feel about it. That much was easy to tell, even with a blindfold on. Her own safety was one thing, but the gang could put themselves in danger with absolutely no chance of success. This, more than anything else so far, brought a sense of dread and absolute terror. Both of which she knew she could not show. She would not give them any more of an upper hand than they already had.

"Well, Rebecca. It's quite an interesting tale you tell. We are impressed by your ability to evade SMALS, but we don't think you are telling us everything." The woman spoke, and Rebecca held her breath, not moving a muscle. She would let them speak, and only say more if they demanded it of her.

And then…

"Maybe this will help. Take off her blindfold," she directed. Rebecca turned her head from left to right, unsure if she actually heard correctly, and not trusting the situation in the least. What were they going to do now?

Take off her blindfold, apparently. As one of the other two in the room walked to her chair, reached behind her, and pulled the blindfold up and over her head, freeing her vision to discover…

Daniel?

Daniel?

She blinked hard. There were lights on in the room, but maybe having the blindfold on for so long was causing her eyes to play tricks on her. She opened them again. Yes. Daniel. And he was *not* giving her his charming smile. Had she really felt comfortable around him the last time they met? What was he *doing* here? He stepped aside to reveal the owners of the other two voices. Remy. And Bryn. The two people she had seen outside of BRO after the woman, Bryn, argued with Karl. This could *not* be good. How? How did they find out?

Rebecca opened her mouth to ask that very question, but no words came out. Remy chuckled for the second time, "I can see we have surprised you as much as you surprised us."

"We have decided that you are too much of a liability to leave out there acting of your own accord. You have just enough information to be a threat to the success of our operations, let alone risking your own life and that of your friends. Better your risk is actually beneficial, rather than blindly dangerous." Rebecca still could not grasp Bryn's intent. What did they plan to do with her now?

"How...how did you know we were there?" she asked, wanting, still, to buy time while she tried to think of a way out of this.

"Daniel, you want to share with your little friend here what you saw?" Remy said, more directive than question.

"First, you were on our property that day Dad and I spotted you when doing our perimeter checks—" he began.

Bryn interrupted, "Which you neglected to tell us. First indication you were leaving out potentially important details. Sorry, Daniel. Continue."

"I didn't entirely believe your story but gave you the benefit of the doubt because I am sure at least part of it was correct. I knew you had just lost your brother, and I felt bad for you. You also didn't seem to be the type of person to cause trouble. But something just didn't sit right with me. When I saw you at school, you looked more and more…worn out. Instead of getting better, you seemed to be getting worse.

"And then I saw you and your friends huddled together in the park, packs on the table, but sitting on the grass obviously not wanting anyone to know what you were up to. I watched you. I followed you. When you all met for the second time in the park, I was camped out behind the bushes. I didn't hear much. You guys were good there. You were pretty quiet. It was a bit boring, actually," and there was his first smile. Rebecca found herself smiling back without meaning to. She pulled her lips back into a straight line.

Daniel continued, "I didn't hear much, but I did hear something about Friday. Friday. That was one long day. I had no idea when you were going to be doing whatever it was you were doing. I kept my eyes on you the entire school day, but you seemed to be doing exactly what you should be doing at school. So, I followed you home. I waited. Nothing. I sat there for hours, hidden in the bushes along the side of your house. Not happy to find myself sitting in bushes again. Had nothing real to eat, but I couldn't risk leaving.

"Finally, I saw a light go on, in what I assumed was your bedroom, late at night. Whatever I had been waiting for was about to happen. When your light went off, I waited near the front of the house, but saw nothing, so I went to the back. Saw you crossing the field, heading back to your barn. I followed you guys. *Not* easy to do without a light. Good thing the hardest part was on my turf. I know those grounds like the back of my hand, and you guys were heading up a path that should not have been cleared, yet it was."

Remy broke in this time, "Yet another indicator that you haven't been completely up front with us as we'd asked. Daniel said it was obvious this wasn't your first time going up this way, that it seemed like you had already made a trail before this trip." Rebecca stared, eyes forward. Not daring to react. How had she not known Daniel was around? She could not believe he had been following them. She was done for.

Daniel picked up the story again. "I saw two of your friends posted outside. I saw you and two others use an access card to somehow open the door. I saw you had radios to talk to one another. I watched to see if you would come back out right away, but when you didn't, I left to go tell Remy."

Rebecca suddenly remembered something. She spoke to Daniel, "You reported us to your brother, but I *saw* you on one of my earlier trips. Yeah, you're right. I'd been there before. More than once. And that first time, I saw *you* spying on the facility. You were hiding, obviously not wanting anyone to see you there." She didn't know why this was important, except that she felt no need to protect Daniel now and telling his brother and Bryn about him might deflect some of the attention away from her. Not that that would do any good in the long run, but she couldn't think of anything else to do. She also was genuinely curious. If he was in on all of this, what was he doing hiding out, spying?

Daniel was taken aback. He recovered quickly, however. "Nice, Rebecca," he said without sarcasm. "I never knew I was seen."

Remy took over the conversation, "Daniel saw you guys break into the facility using equipment not readily available to citizens. Not even those whose parents work in government. He did the right thing in coming to talk to me. Anyone else, other than Bryn here—which he would have had no way of knowing—would not have been a good choice. Lucky for him, and for all of you, that I am his brother. He came to me to warn me about you guys breaking into the facility. Seems Daniel here was also questioning what was happening inside BRO, hence, the spying on a facility he was not even supposed to know about. Him coming to me to tell me about you breaking in was the first I knew that my kid brother had also been poking around where he didn't belong."

"Your actions, Rebecca, have put a lot of people in danger. If you had been caught, you would have undone a lot of the work we have already done. You put Daniel in danger, your friends, the two of us, and others. You've left us with few options," Bryn said.

"BRO's operations are not what they seem, as I am sure you've realized," said Remy. "My family, other than me, has remained in the dark about what is really happening inside this secret facility, but your actions caused me to have to bring my kid brother into a situation I had hoped to protect him from. To be fair, it is not entirely your fault, seeing as he was already spying on us." A stern look, disapproving, for Daniel, and then Remy's attention was back on Rebecca.

"Bryn and I are part of a group of citizens, coming from every region of Anecor, working to stop Council. We are members of a resistance organization. We have been working with the organization for the last year to bring down Council."

"A year?" asked Rebecca. "They've been planning this…whatever it is they're doing here…for the past year?"

"Yes. Longer actually. BRO is a piece of the puzzle. A big piece. BRO has a legit arm of the organization that is working on bovine research, just as the name says. That is why they are located on the ranch. Their normal operations are located in facilities outside of that small valley, closer to the house. I went to work for BRO after graduation, about two years ago. I had no idea about this secret sector of the organization. Council has co-opted BRO in order to carry out a devious plan to further control the population. Karl brought me into the secret arm after the first few months with BRO because of my work in genetics. At first, I thought they were doing something to help, to benefit society. Bryn set me straight on that one. It was then I joined the resistance. We hope that we can prevent them from implementing their full plan, though we are still in the process of finding out exactly what that is."

"But in the meantime, you are *killing* people. My brother is dead! Countless others are dead and dying. You obviously aren't doing a very good job," Rebecca shot at them. If they were part of a resistance, why were they participating in killing so many people?

"There is so much more to this story than you know, Rebecca. You might be better served to hold your accusations until you have a better understanding," Bryn warned. "I can understand why you are upset. But your anger is misplaced."

Rebecca tried to calm herself. "Fill me in, then."

Bryn smiled a tired smile, "At this point, we intend to. It seems your participation in this group is the only good way forward for all of us. I hope you can convince your friends of the same. You have all made yourselves a part of this, whether you like it or not. However, before we continue, we need some more information from you. Like, where did you get all the equipment you were using and what method did you use to trick the trackers?"

"I can't tell you," Rebecca said. "Not until my friends agree to be a part of this. They will be at my house at 1:30 this afternoon. We were going to discuss what to do next. So, if I'm not there, they will come looking for me. At BRO."

The implications of what she said came quickly to the other three in the room. All three looked at their watches. Bryn ran her hand through her hair. Remy paced in short strips back and forth across the concrete floor. Daniel crossed his arms and gave Rebecca a hard look. She held his look and returned it, until both looked away.

"Where were you guys going to discuss this?" Bryn asked, considering their next move.

"My house. It isn't unusual for my friends and I to gather over the weekends. We just leave our phones downstairs now. And since Jonathan died, my parents sorta keep to themselves a lot. We wouldn't have been disturbed. But, today, even less of a chance. They're gone all day. Don't expect them back until late evening."

"Looks like we're all going to Rebecca's house to play," Daniel said.

"I suggest we leave now, if we hope to reach her house before her friends decide to be heroes," Remy said. "Should we blindfold her again, Bryn?"

"No. At this point, it serves no purpose. Rebecca, if you and your friends don't join us, we will not be able to let you continue on your way. I know you want to stop what is happening in Montrose. So, do we. But it is much, much bigger than Montrose. We really cannot leave you and your friends to continue your work on your own. I'm sorry."

"What will you do to any of us who don't join you?" Rebecca asked.

"I'm afraid that wouldn't be up to us. Remy and I are not in charge. We would not be the ones to decide what happens if you don't join us," Bryn responded.

"Then who does?"

"We are not at liberty to say at this point," Bryn said, as she started heading across the room. "Let's go. It seems we are in a bit of a hurry now."

Rebecca stood and followed Bryn across the large room she was just now taking note of. It was sparsely furnished. There were a number of computer stations and other electronic equipment Rebecca couldn't make out. A couple of padded chairs in addition to desk chairs. A cot along the wall. There was a makeshift kitchen, as well. There was a doorway on the opposite side of the one Bryn was heading towards now. That must have been where she and Remy went to talk when they left her waiting with Daniel keeping an eye on her.

"What is this place?" Rebecca asked as she caught up with Bryn, Remy and Daniel right on her heels.

"Used to be some sort of office, we think. Before The Reckoning. Now we use it as our pod's headquarters," Remy responded.

Remy opened the garage door while Bryn and Rebecca climbed in the back seat. Daniel ducked outside and waited for Remy to climb in and pull the truck out of the garage. He closed the door and hopped in the passenger front seat. Rebecca looked around at the buildings that surrounded headquarters. They were all vacant. Many of them crumbling to the ground, evidence of extensive fire damage, and nature starting to take over again. Even the headquarters building was not entirely intact. A large section off the back was a pile of rubble. Vines were crawling up the sides of the standing walls.

"I had no idea anything like this existed," Rebecca commented. "Are we in the Borderlands?"

"Yes," came Remy's reply, as they sped away from the ruins of a world that existed just a few short years before Rebecca was born and towards her house in Montrose, where her friends were due to meet her in an hour.

CHAPTER 30

Remy drove frighteningly fast. They were on a small road, not very well maintained, and they bounced over deep, rough potholes that jarred their insides. Rebecca wondered how Remy had avoided them on the trip out. He certainly was taking no care to now. As she watched the scenery fly by, Rebecca's head filled with questions. This new turn of events was quite a shock. They had help now. That was good. This resistance group could get into the Borderlands without being detected. They had vehicles they could use. Or at least one. She wondered how they got this truck. Government-level workers had vehicles, and there were job related vehicles, used only by workers on the job. Non-government level citizens could check out a vehicle for recreational purposes, but those were just as highly monitored as the work vehicles. Yet, Remy was driving a vehicle for his own use and into an area designated out of bounds, without being detected.

Transportation was another way Council exerted its control over the population, only allowing travel to designated areas, for specified amounts of time, and in limited numbers. If a family wanted to go camping beyond the transit zone in their own Quadrant, they had to find out when vehicles were available, and which outer camping areas had openings when. In this way, Council prevented the likelihood of large numbers of citizens congregating away from the eyes of the city. The likelihood of a rebel group being able to establish themselves in the wild was slim, Rebecca thought. So, how did these guys do it?

Rebecca was realizing that she was thinking along lines she never would have considered until just now. The idea of a rebellion or resistance would never have entered her mind before today. She had no reason to conceive of such a thing, even with her growing understanding of the sinister motives of Council—her knowledge of which was apparently only scratching the surface. The degree to which Council seemed to control society for their own power was mind boggling. And Rebecca was sure she was only beginning to see just how far it went, and just how far Council would go to keep their power.

They turned down the road that would take them to Rebecca's house. "Where's a good place to put the truck? Someplace it isn't likely to be seen by a neighbor passing by?" Remy asked.

"Go around back. The drive will lead back to the barn. You can pull in there."

"A barn?"

"Yeah, we have horses. It isn't big, but big enough the truck can slip just inside the double doors. I'll have to hop out to get the doors open."

Remy drove up the drive and to the back by the barn. Daniel got out to open Rebecca's door. She slid out of the seat and walked to the code panel, punched in the code, and the doors swung open. She gestured to Remy to pull in and waited for him and Bryn to join her and Daniel at the door. After punching in the code again, the doors swung closed and the four walked quickly to the back door. Rebecca led them in and to the dining area.

"We can talk in here. When my friends arrive," she said, indicating the chairs around a table, "which will be any moment now."

They sat around the table in an uncomfortable silence. Bryn pulled out her phone and exchanged messages with someone. "How are you using your phone without being tracked?" Rebecca asked, looking at the unusual phone Bryn was using the first time they had seen her.

"These aren't our normal phones, as you can see," Bryn responded, finishing a message and tucking her phone away. "They aren't Council-issued. So, Council can't track them."

Before Rebecca could ask more, they were alerted to the arrival of the gang. "Wait here. I'll go get them."

Rebecca went to the front door. All of her friends were there. Right on time. Rebecca took a moment to marvel at that highly unusual occurrence. They all filtered in, dropping their packs, phones tucked safely inside, in the entry way.

"Since my parents aren't here, we can talk in the dining area. More room there."

They followed Rebecca in. Cassidi stopped dead in her tracks when she saw the three individuals sitting at the table. Troy ran into the back of her. "Cass, what are y—" Troy stopped, too.

"Hey, man, what's the holdup?" Selby asked. There was some shuffling around as slowly everyone filtered into the dining room. "Whoa," Selby said, realizing what caused the traffic jam. He looked to Rebecca. They all looked to Rebecca.

"Becs?" Cassidi said.

"Everyone, this is Remy, Bryn, and Daniel. They are part of a resistance organization working to take down

Council. After they kidnapped me and took me to their headquarters in the dark of night and blindfolded, we found out we are on the same side. We have to work with them."

"A resistance? To take down Council? Well aaaalright…'Nough said…count me in," said Selby, striding over to shake each of their hands in turn and taking a seat at the table. "So where do we start?" The three at the table couldn't help but smile. Selby had that effect on people.

The other three were not so quick to accept what they had just heard. "They *kidnapped* you?" asked Cassidi.

"Yeah. Turns out Daniel caught wind of our plan and saw us go into BRO. So, Bryn," she said turning from Cassidi to address Bryn sitting at the table, "would you mind filling these guys in on what you've told me so far?"

Bryn considered a moment how much she should tell them before getting more information from them about the technology they had and their motives. "Okay, I suppose we can do it this way. Bring you all up to speed. But I want to tell you ahead of time the same thing I told Rebecca here. As Rebecca said in her, uh, introduction, you do not have much choice here. Our organization simply cannot allow you all to continue on without joining up with us. It is far too dangerous, and you have too much information. We can't trust you to act independently, and we can't trust you to let things alone now, no matter what you say."

Troy looked stricken as he stumbled into the nearest empty seat. Bendi's face did not betray anything other than calm. Cassidi was, predictably, annoyed at being told she had no choice, at being told what she *had* to do. "What if we don't agree to join you?" Cassidi asked.

Bryn laughed, "Rebecca asked exactly the same question." Her laughter ended abruptly; her smile vanished, "If you do not agree to join us, the leadership will determine your fate. Remy and I will not be able to do anything to intervene. You must understand, this is so much bigger than the five of you. So much more than what you see here in Montrose. Now, let's get you up to speed with what Rebecca knows. Then we have a couple of questions for you, before we provide any more information. Questions Rebecca wouldn't answer before the rest of you were involved."

Bryn and Remy proceeded to tell the newcomers everything they had already told Rebecca. About BRO, the little bit about Council's plan, and about how Remy came to find out about this plan. Selby had his arms folded in front of him on the table, leaning into the conversation as much as possible, intent on not missing a word. The others sat in stunned disbelief.

"So, your parents, are they in on it?" Cassidi asked Remy and Daniel.

"No. They only know about the cattle research. The front operation for the rest of this. The secret facilities are located in an area of the ranch that isn't used for anything. The valley there isn't part of the cattle functions of the ranch, so my parents don't ever go out that way. Not anymore. We are a research ranch, which is why BRO is there. The cover part of BRO, at any rate." Remy was the one to respond.

"Okay, Remy, let's stop there," Bryn said. "If you guys are going to be a part of this, we need the answers to a couple of questions. But, first, is there anyone who is opting not to join us?"

For a moment, Troy looked like he was about to back down. "Troy, please don't. You heard what they said. And now we at least have some help." At Rebecca's comment, Troy seemed to resign himself to this new situation, as he leaned back in his chair sulking. None of the others made a move to decline participation in the resistance. They were all obviously uneasy, however.

"Okay, then. We essentially want to know two things. First, what did you do to evade the trackers? We know about leaving the phones behind. That part isn't important. We want to know what you did to take care of the internal trackers. And second, Daniel saw that you had radios for communication and an access card that somehow gained you entry into the facility.

Where did you get these items and what other technology do you have?"

"That was all me," Selby said, proudly, but also to protect Troy, who would have had to admit to knowing information on his Dad's computer. While Selby had safeguarded his own family's background for years, keeping it all from anyone outside, he offered up his access to this technology here, without revealing how he got ahold of it.

"I won't tell you who my connections are, but I got the technology that got us into BRO and provided us with a little bit of safety."

"Please elaborate…I'm sorry, I don't know your name," Bryn said.

"Selby. My name's Selby. I was able to get us 2-way radios. Good ones that let us communicate between us three inside and Troy and Bendi outside. Heeeeey, I bet that was you, Daniel, that Bendi heard step on a branch, breakin' it, and then running off into the woods…sloppy, man…sloppy. We were sure it was probably an animal, though, so I guess you got away with it."

"I'm sure it was my brother, here," said Remy. "We'll have to work on your stealth," he continued, raising a single eyebrow. "He's new to this, too. You'll all be trained. Go on, Selby."

"Hehe. Yeah, so, we had the 2-way radios, like I said. I also got a card that's programmed to decode any electronic door. Just hold it up like you do any access card and, presto, you're in. Programming's beyond my skills, but I bet ol' Troy here could figure it out if he had time. He's good like that."

"We might have to put you to that test, Troy. If you think you could figure out how that card works, without damaging it, and then replicate it, we could learn a lot more a lot faster." Troy fidgeted at Remy's words, but did not protest. He also did not say whether he thought he could accomplish what they wanted.

"Selby, you mentioned protection. What did you have for protection?" Bryn asked.

"Just some tasers. Direct-contact immobilizers, but amped up to provide a brief time of total incapacitation. And I had a full-scale immobilizer. Didn't trust this lot with one of those without training."

"You've been…trained?" Bryn was watching him closely, and Selby suddenly realized he might have said too much.

With no way to completely backtrack, he continued, "Yeah, I was trained on this. My connection wanted to make sure I knew how to handle it if I was going to be using it. That's all I'm saying about that. Listen, I know you probably want to know more, but don't ask. I won't give away my contact without their consent. Won't tell you why they have these things. Just know that they don't know exactly why I'm using them, so the mission I was on with these guys was safe."

"Okay, we'll leave it be for now," Bryn relented. "Now, how about the technology for avoiding the trackers. We are very curious as to how you got away with it, and we want to be certain that what you did actually took care of covering up your movements."

"Oh, no worries there. It definitely took care of it. I have a scrambler. It's a device that I can sync up to ten trackers with. Once a tracker is synced up, it will scramble the GPS system. And the best part of that is that it does so without SMALS being able to detect that a tracker has been disabled."

"Nice. I'll want to have a look at that soon," Bryn said. "Well, Selby, it looks like you're going to be quite useful to our operations. Thank you for the information." Selby beamed.

"Now," Bryn continued, "I have been given clearance to fill you all in on what we know so far. After that, we will have to make arrangements to bring all of you in to headquarters to meet the rest of our pod. You'll also need to be given safe phones that you will *only* use to communicate with pod members. And then we will have to set you up with training sessions. That will be trickier for the time being since all of you still have to go to school. We'll figure something out. For now, make yourselves comfortable and listen closely."

CHAPTER 31

Everyone settled back into their chairs, eyes on Bryn, waiting to hear what she had to say. Even Troy looked curious. "I suppose we first need to give you all a bit of a history lesson," Bryn said. Every last one of them, including Daniel, groaned.

"I know. You think you already know the story because we've all heard the same thing from the time we entered school until the time we graduated. And, I'm afraid to say, it doesn't end there. We all get sick of the information overload about how great Anecor is now because of the hard decisions Manglebee made, etcetera, etcetera. But I'm sure you all also know, or at least suspect, that this isn't entirely the truth. In order to understand where Council is headed with this, and perhaps their motives, some context is helpful."

Bryn went on to explain. Some of what Council taught was based on the truth but spun to make them look good. Apparently, tensions had been rising across the country for a decade or more prior to The Reckoning. The world was seeing an increase in technological innovation at the same time that economic disparity was also on the rise. The rich were getting richer and the poor were getting poorer. The gap between the two getting wider and wider, with no more middle ground. A small, wealthy class was tightening the reins on global control, but everyone else was getting restless and angry.

During this time, AI was spreading as a means to increase production without having to pay workers. This only made matters worse. There were fewer jobs and nothing in place to ensure the well-being of all the workers who now had nothing. Food was getting increasingly expensive as a changing climate resulted in crop failures due to disease outbreaks and catastrophic weather events. These catastrophic weather events, along with increasing and devastating wildfires, displaced a lot of people as well. During this time, everyone still owned cars, but more and more people couldn't afford to drive them. Even those with jobs found that they had to find other ways to work more often than not because gas prices got to be too high for most to afford.

All of these factors converged to create a great deal of uncertainty and chaos. Enter Manglebee. He came out of nowhere, promising to fix the system. Promising to create a balanced society if the people of the United States elected him as president. He made people believe again with his smooth-talking ways. He had a way with words that made people think that he was going to look out for them, that no longer would the wealthy oligarchs control the country. He pulled the masses in, spinning his web of lies.

It didn't matter to the citizens of the country that they knew little about this new man on the stage. They liked that. They thought it meant he was not like the others. They believed he understood their plight. It didn't matter that he could not provide any details for how he would accomplish the lofty promises he made. The country elected him. He won by an unprecedented landslide. But it wouldn't take long for citizens to realize the magnitude of their error.

Manglebee took advantage of the citizens in this country in a vulnerable situation. He only wanted power and control. He wanted wealth. As soon as he was elected, he ousted most of those already sitting seats in the government, only keeping the people who helped him obtain power and who would remain loyal. He got rid of the court system, with the exception of the highest court, which he stacked with judges who would always rule in his favor. This is the court system still in place. It was, and still is, called the Supreme Court. When he moved to abolish elections, the Court backed him. When he ditched the Constitution in favor of the Vision, the Court, of course, ruled in his favor. This Vision, which he and his 12 advisors wrote, allowed him to restructure the government and this country's society.

Manglebee continued to try to sell the people his Vision. He used the media to repeatedly replay events showing violence, poverty, and destruction. He would then promote his Vision as the means to fix it all. He would say that these events were all the result of a great imbalance in society and that he would restore this balance. Manglebee blamed citizens for the state of the country and the environment, but said that, with proper direction, citizens had an opportunity to be a part of the solution.

But citizens were angry. This is not what they had voted for. As more and more of their rights were stripped, they did the only thing left they knew to do. They took to the streets. Rioting and violence rose. There were widespread strikes, with those who still had jobs refusing to go to work. Citizens who could manage to get there, in whatever ways were available to them, made their way to the Capital, which, at that time, was in a place called Washington D.C. They protested. They damaged government property. Of course, Manglebee was not even there to witness these events. He had retreated to a safe place at the first signs of wide-spread dissent.

When his ongoing messaging didn't work, he opted for other means to heel the population. First, he cut off food supplies. He cut off the last of the fuel supplies. And he brought out his army in full force. Though the numbers weren't particularly large, since many bailed and joined those on the streets, the army still had the heavy artillery. Manglebee put that advantage to use. Tanks rolled through the streets taking out anyone gathered in groups. Tear gas and nerve agents were used on crowds. Grenades launched. Known leaders were made an example to their followers. The citizens of the United States were brought to their knees. We had had a Civil War in this country before, but what happened during The Reckoning was not Civil War. It was not citizens against citizens, two warring belief systems dividing a population. It was one man and those who would do his bidding against the citizens of this country.

With the military doing Manglebee's dirty work, the people didn't have a chance. Still they fought, in large numbers. At this point, they had nothing to lose but their lives. Unfortunately, many, many people lost those too. The count of citizens who died under Manglebee's directive has never been released, but the population was significantly reduced. Enough so that Manglebee could reorganize the land and society into its current structure and shift people around in both space and jobs to keep society functioning and citizens under tight control. Council-issued phones, internal trackers, and SMALS provided added insurance.

But it's difficult to keep everyone under control at all times. Impossible, really. So, there were those who tried to rally the cry again, to get people to rise up again. Unfortunately, the deep wounds were still too raw. There hadn't been enough time passed for large numbers to take to the streets again. Too many remembered what it was like. Too many were too tired to struggle any longer, too fearful of repeating history. They wanted some sense of security. Those who did try to rise up, they're the ones who were disappeared. They were either killed or taken to one of the large prison compounds located in the Borderlands. Neither Bryn nor Remy knew exactly how many compounds there were. These were under the tightest security, of course, with well-guarded perimeters surrounding them, even in the Borderlands. There were at least ten of these compounds from the intel that had been gathered thus far.

"Our organization, Colossus, is different. The leaders remember what The Reckoning was like as well. Unlike all of us in this room, the leaders of this movement were around before The Reckoning. They understand what we lost during that time." Bryn was saying, "And unlike those we hear about from Council News, the ones who are disappeared, they know that the best way is to do our work quietly, covertly. Colossus, as an organization, recruits its members very carefully. The goal is to work in the shadows to take down Council and Head Councilor Manglebee. We use our skills and knowledge to operate as close to the inside lines as we can get.

"In Colossus, members have an understanding that we will not make any big moves until we have a chance at succeeding. There is too much at stake to allow ourselves to be careless. We do not want another Reckoning like the one this country went through just over twenty years ago," she continued. "Rebecca, this is why we operate the way we do. If we move too soon, we risk another Reckoning. Our goal is to cripple Council first, and then take them down. Undoing the structure Manglebee has created is not done overnight. It takes time. After two years, we *are* making progress. The best thing that you guys can do for your brother, Rebecca, is to work with us. You all obviously have some skills we could use, or you would not have been able to get as far as you did without detection. No, you don't really have a choice, but your full participation and cooperation will be your greatest weapon to carry out Jonathan's request of you."

"We hope that in sharing this information with you, you will be able to trust us. Just as we have to trust you guys," Remy interjected. "You will be our youngest members. This goes for you, too, Daniel. Taking responsibility for your well-being is not an easy choice for Colossus. This is not a game. What we are doing is dangerous. Any one of us is at risk of getting caught. If that happens, it is unlikely that individual survives, and quite possible the whole organization goes down as well. We have had some close calls already. Too close. For your safety, and for the safety of other members, we have to have your complete cooperation, your trust, and your willingness to share your skills and knowledge to help us take down Council and Head Councilor Manglebee."

"So, just like that, with words that sound, frankly, like the propaganda tactics Council uses, we are supposed to trust you?" said Cassidi, for whom trust was never easy.

"We are not trying to sell you on anything. We do, however, hope that you see the benefit of cooperation as well as the risk to Colossus for taking you in. Don't forget, we have to trust you all as well. We normally screen our members carefully. The unusual circumstances under which we have brought you in goes against our normal process. If we did not know some of your history, if Daniel did not know something of you from school, and if you had refused to share any information with us, things would have looked much different for you," Bryn said.

"Cass, these guys make some good points. They do have to trust us as well. Think about it. We wanted to get to the bottom of this virus. This group has more information than we do. They are already on the inside of BRO. I think we could help each other," Rebecca said. "We all know that Council doesn't have our best interests in mind in how they operate. Even for all of us, who are on the government track, it is easy to see how Council works to keep control. And now we know why."

"Hey, this is great. We get the chance to be a part of somethin' big. I mean *big*. How can you say no to that, Cass? Troy? Not me, I'll do whatever I can to help," Selby said.

"I will, too. If what you say is true, the work we are assigned to do after university only helps Manglebee continue to cause so much harm to people, and it sounds like it will be worse than we even know. If what you say is true," Bendi spoke up for the first time. "I will do what I can to keep that from happening."

"Okay. Okay. I can see I'm out numbered, and I'm not going to be left out. So. Okay," Cassidi sighed in an exaggerated fashion, "I'm all in. But this is only for you, Becs. And Jonathan."

"Are you going to tell us more about what is happening inside BRO? This history lesson is fantastic," Troy said, dripping sarcasm, "but how about some real information about what is happening *now*?"

"Troy," said Rebecca, "Please. Stop being so…well, so confrontational. I don't think you are helping." Troy was taken aback at Rebecca's direct comment. He knew he had gone too far.

"Sorry, Becs. It just feels like these guys are coming in and taking over, and you all are acting like it is no big deal to go along with them when we really have no clue as to whether or not they are telling us the truth about any of this. For all we know, they could be working for Council."

"If that were the case, I don't think I would be here right now, Troy. I am going to trust them. I feel like I have good reason *to* trust them. They could have killed me out there today, Troy, but they didn't. I'm very much still here. And they are offering us a way to continue what we have started, but with help," Rebecca said.

Troy turned white, Rebecca's words obviously sinking in. He had been so worried about losing control of the situation that he hadn't actually considered the fact that Remy and Bryn really could have killed Rebecca, and there would have been no way any of them would have even known about it. She would have just been—*gone*. He swallowed hard, twice, before nodding his head in consent. "Okay. I'll commit. You will have my full cooperation," he said, looking at Rebecca, rather than Bryn or Remy.

CHAPTER 32

While the gang's participation seemed agreed upon prior to Bryn beginning to provide them with information, the tension was still palpable, the agreement forced and tenuous. Now, there seemed to be a shift, a movement, however small, towards unity, and everyone in the room relaxed a little.

"Daniel tells me that all of your parents work for government. We need to be clear, here. Our goal is to bring down Council and reform a government that truly represents citizens. If we succeed, everything will change. For everyone." Remy said with a pointed look around the table.

"We cannot guarantee," said Bryn, "that your lives will be as…comfortable…when we are done. For you, because of your participation in Colossus, that is a given. Because we also cannot guarantee success. However, we need you to realize what this might mean for your parents and any siblings. But, as far as we know now, the direct involvement in Council's schemes is limited to the highest levels of Council and the very select few outsiders necessary to achieve their goal. We don't know the identity of all of the players here in Montrose, or anywhere for that matter, but we are getting closer."

There was a sense of uneasiness around the room from the newcomers. Except Selby. He had been trained for survival his whole life, so this piece of information did not faze him. Rebecca immediately thought of Troy's dad. She hesitated a glance in Cassidi's direction. Yes, Cassidi had thought of the same thing. Now, however, was not the time to bring it up. At some point, they would have to tell Bryn and Remy, but they would wait on that. Wait until they had more information. Wait until they understood things better. After all, they were not positive the person they saw was Troy's dad.

"Just how big is Colossus? Bringin' down Council is huge!" Remy and Bryn laughed at Selby's question.

"We've grown a lot over the past year. We have at least two pods in every region, and up to five in places like Region 1 and Region 6," Bryn said. "You've hit upon one of the reasons for our name: Colossus. We all know our task is big.

Huge, as you say. But we know it's worth it. It is necessary," Bryn responded.

"What is it you do for BRO?" asked Bendi. "How did the two of you become part of what BRO and Council are doing?"

"The simple answer is that we were brought on as scientists," Bryn looked at the faces around the table and knew that she was not going to get away with just the simple answer.

Blowing air through her cheeks, she continued, "I'll try to sum this up for you quickly. I imagine we don't have all night, and we have to determine before we leave when we can get you all out to headquarters. It has to be soon.

"So. I specialize in human infectious diseases. You all know Remy's family works the ranch and the purpose of the ranch is in research. Remy happens to be brilliant with genetics. While he has obviously studied bovine genetics because of his assumed job assignment, he has an excellent grasp of human genetics as well."

"It was a hobby of mine throughout school," Remy interjected. "I had to study bovine genetics, but I was highly interested in human genetics. There was value in understanding human genetics along with bovine genetics because cows are a food source for many, so I was allowed to pursue my hobby."

"Little did he know how Council, and BRO, would end up using this hobby, and talent, of his," Bryn said. "I was brought in a few months before Remy. At that time, I was not part of Colossus. Karl knew my father, who also obviously worked in the field of medicine, and so he knew of my skills in immunology. It was Karl who pulled strings to get me into BRO. At the time, I was partnered with Manuel, who was a human geneticist. We were told we were working on understanding the connections between our genes and the impact of infectious disease, namely viruses, on humans. We were told we were part of a bigger project to understand how diseases in cows can be transmitted to people and then how to prevent that transmission."

"So, you thought you were helping people? Doing something good?" asked Rebecca.

"Exactly," said Bryn. "Manuel was part of Colossus, but I did not know this until he was disappeared, and I was contacted by our pod's leaders. I joined up immediately. Then Remy here was brought into BRO as Manuel's replacement."

"I was told the same thing as Bryn was originally. But rather than leaving me in the dark, Bryn fairly quickly brought me up to speed on the real goals of BRO and the connections to Manglebee and the upper levels of Council. I was brought into Colossus almost from the start of working in this secret arm of BRO."

"And Karl, he isn't part of Colossus, right?" asked Selby.

"Right," Remy replied.

"If you guys have been working on this for a year, and people only started getting sick a few months ago...at the end of the summer...what happened? How do you explain *that?*" Troy asked, thinking he might be catching Bryn and Remy in a lie. "Obviously, this virus is being released on purpose. BRO is killing people *on purpose*."

"Yes, you are correct; BRO is doing this on purpose, but that is not their official story. Not what they tell low-level scientists like Remy and me." Bryn's lips formed into a tight line. "We were told there was an accident. That this virus was released from the lab accidentally, and now it is up to us to stop it. But it's a wild goose chase. Essentially, they have us working on something they don't intend to use as they say. They are asking us to figure out how this virus is attacking the human system so that they can stop it. But that is not true. They are really using our research to figure out how to perfect targeted attacks. Colossus, however, believes that we might be able to eventually use the work Remy and I are doing as a way to at least reduce the impacts of the virus until we can put an end to Manglebee's plan."

"Like the rest of society," Remy added, "BRO is highly structured. There are three levels within this secretive arm of the company. The three levels are not allowed to interact and do not know what the other two levels are working on. We are not supposed to question this structure. But because of the virus's release, they had to let us in on another division's operations. There was no other way for them to explain the supposed outbreak and our now limited involvement in this part of the program."

"Why don't they give the same story to the people in Montrose?" Rebecca had assumed long before now that there was something the news reports weren't saying. Now she understood what that was, but it seemed to her that the story they told Remy and Bryn could have been provided as a cover story to the city as well.

"Oh, no, Becs. They couldn't do that," Selby said. "People would panic if they thought a simple little accident could do so much damage. Not to mention how that would make BRO look. No *way* Council wants anyone to question BRO. Am I right? Or am I right?" This last was directed at Remy and Bryn.

"Very sharp, Selby," Bryn said. "You *are* right. We were ordered not to say a word of this outside the walls of BRO for the very reasons you just stated."

"You mentioned 'targeted attacks'," Bendi cut in. "What do you mean by this?"

"The goal isn't to just release this virus into the world to attack everyone. This is why it's important that the virus does not spread the way we are used to seeing. It isn't contagious. With a synthetic virus, they can control this component. They use a combination of technology, human genetic structures, and this synthetic virus to control who catches the virus."

Troy whistled, impressed at the possibilities in spite of himself. "How are they doing this?" The way to win Troy over was to feed his endless curiosity and his need to know at *least* as much as everyone else. He preferred to know more. Rebecca smiled at his question.

"We don't know all of the specifics yet because, again, much of the information is kept from us and, up until now," Bryn glanced at Selby, "we haven't been able to break into the highest levels of the system. We have been able to determine some of the mechanisms, if not all of the details."

"They have used the information we have given them on human genetics and infectious diseases to create a virus that can kill, but not spread. They have created something that is fast acting, with a 100% death rate. No natural immunity. No treatment. Even though this is the task they have put Bryn and me on, they continue to come up with excuses not to test our results. There will be no treatment before they release the virus on a larger scale. Karl will make sure of that."

"How are they targeting only certain people?" asked Rebecca. If they were targeting specific people, it means that Jonathan did not just randomly catch the virus. For some reason, they wanted him gone. He had believed someone was onto him, that he was being watched, not by SMALS, but by real humans. Perhaps he was right.

"That's wrapped up in the technology they are using," said Remy. "From what we have gathered, they are using mini robots, designed to mimic the way bees function in their hives. These robotic insects are fed the virus. They are then programmed to deliver it to certain individuals. We *think* they are using the internal trackers for this purpose. The robots inject the virus and return to the facilities when their task is complete."

"Must be a pretty small…uh…bite, if people don't know they've been bitten. Otherwise, seems someone would have made a connection already." Cassidi commented.

"I must say, I'm really impressed with the five of you," Bryn said. "You are asking really good questions and making excellent observations. Hard to believe you're so young, really."

"We're not a naïve bunch of kids, you know," Troy bristled. "We're all highly ranked in our levels."

Cassidi sank a little lower in her chair, Troy's comment a reminder of her fear of not living up to the expectations for her assumed assignment, of not being as smart as everyone else at the table. Forgetting the fact that Bryn's comment was a direct response to her own observation about the detectability of the injections.

"I'm sure you are," Bryn smiled.

"Yep. You guys lucked out gettin' ahold of us on your team," Selby added.

"Back to your observation, Cassidi." Bryn brought the conversation back on topic again. "We think the injection site must be small. In addition, these aren't actual insects. They are injecting a virus into your system and not the type of toxins we are used to from insects, the ones that cause the reactions on our skin when we are bitten."

"The lights you see, those lights act as the homing system, the white flashes are the robotic insects." Remy continued with what they knew of the robots so far. "The energy of the lights ensures that the robots make it back to the hive when their job is done. The robots 'live' in these containers. We haven't confirmed this yet, but we think that they are programmed to target specific people each time they go out. They withdraw a specific amount of the virus determined based on the individual they are targeting. When the 'hive' opens at 2:00 a.m., they leave the hive to deliver the virus, and then return before the hive shuts down again at 4:00 a.m."

Ah, that's what the lights are for, thought Troy. Ingenious. Aside from Bryn and Remy, and Troy, everyone else's eyes at the table widened upon hearing, finally, the answer to the mystery of the lights. Even Daniel. Apparently, he had not yet heard this part. Rebecca had been watching Daniel from time to time. He was exceptionally quiet, while the rest of them asked questions or made comments during the explanations. She wondered if he had been filled in on all of this already. If he had, apparently, they had left out the part about the lights, as he seemed just as surprised by it as they were. Rebecca pulled her eyes away from him, just as he caught her watching him, their eyes momentarily locking. Her face reddened, and she hoped no one else caught the exchange. She didn't dare look around to check.

CHAPTER 33

Daniel caught Rebecca's eye, and she quickly looked away. He wasn't certain yet what she thought about all this. He didn't know what *he* thought about all this. Before just over a week ago, he knew of her existence, but they had never interacted. He had a hard time believing that the girl he saw in the halls at school, the girl whose parents both were Tier 3 government workers, was wrapped up in this…this…mess. He couldn't believe he was either. And Remy. This entire turn of events was a bit overwhelming.

****

Daniel had wondered what had been going on with Remy for a while now. He had often seemed preoccupied, but when Daniel tried to approach him about it, he just said work was getting to him. That he was just working too hard because there was so much to do. Remy was taking over the field operations for BRO, or so the story went. It's what he told his parents and Daniel when he got moved over to the secret arm of BRO. Their dad was involved in oversight of the ranch, and therefore coordinated with BRO on the cattle research operations, though BRO brought in its own scientists to assist.

Remy was gone a lot. He said that BRO was sending him off to other ranches and to Division meetings about the progress of BRO's work. Their parents seemed proud of Remy's new role, but Daniel thought it seemed like he was working too hard and gone too much. He felt like Remy was holding something back. Remy looked more than just tired and overworked. He often looked troubled.

On a morning when Remy was occupied in a conversation with their dad about the ranch, Daniel had snuck into Remy's room and went digging around in his stuff. He found a bag he hadn't seen before, and inside was information on the work Remy was doing for the secret arm of BRO. He didn't really understand fully what it was he was reading, but he knew enough to know that he wasn't looking at bovine research. After flipping through more pages, he found a schedule that indicated a meeting between Remy and two people he had never met, Bryn and Karl, at the Dale Valley facility.

The Dale Valley facility. There was no Dale Valley facility. Dale Valley wasn't used for anything. It was just a small valley full of trees. The only thing it was ever used for anymore, and only rarely, was the occasional hike on unmaintained remnants of trails. The family used to hike there more as a family, when the boys were little, but now, their parents never went there. He would have doubted Remy ever did either anymore, until now anyways, and Daniel hadn't actually been out there in over a year.

On the day that Rebecca, Cassidi, and Troy saw Daniel in the trees, he had just discovered the facility himself. He had taken off that morning, much as the other three had, to go see what he could find out. He had discovered the dirt track that they used to drive into the facility and had followed it to the entrance. At that time, he didn't know Remy was inside. He saw Remy when the other three did: when he came outside to talk to Bryn. He, of course, was also unable to hear their conversation.

Finding the facility, and seeing Remy there, was a complete shock to Daniel. It was obviously meant to be a secret, but it was entirely unclear to him why. He had been trying to figure out a way to approach his brother about what he now knew, but he couldn't quite figure out how to do it. If he told Remy about snooping around in his room, Remy would kill him.

He was still trying to figure it out on the day he followed the five friends, shockingly, over the ridge and right to the secret facility. Now he was even more confused. And then, as he looked on in utter astonishment, Selby used an access card to unlock the door and three of them disappeared inside. He looked on, hidden in the trees just above the door. Not too far from where Rebecca, Cassidi, and Troy had been when they spotted him down below the first time. Daniel, of course, did not know this.

When Rebecca, Cassidi, and Troy went inside, Daniel weighed his options. They were few. When the three didn't come back out right away, he saw his options dwindle down to one. He had to tell Remy. Which would mean he probably had to tell Remy he already knew about the place because otherwise, Remy would not necessarily have been the person Daniel would have gone to with this matter. He would have gone to their father instead. So, while Daniel knew he would have to confront Remy with what he had already discovered, he also knew he had no other choice. Whatever was going on in there had to be important enough that they had to hide the facility where it wouldn't be discovered. It also had to be something important enough that a girl like Rebecca would be willing to break into it in the middle of the night. He had no idea what that could possibly be, but he would find out.

Daniel ran back home as quickly as he could and wasted no time waking up Remy to tell him what he had seen. And what he already knew. Except that he got no words out before Remy cut him off.

Remy grabbed his arm and pulled him close. His look was not kind. "*Not here*," Remy said in a hardly audible, but angry voice.

Remy threw on shoes and socks, grabbed a coat, and the two of them went outside, away from the house.

"Now. Talk."

Daniel spilled everything. Including his discovery of the papers. He made sure to tell him he only did so because the change in his brother had him worried. Didn't seem to help much. Remy was livid. After pacing for a good five minutes, he pulled out his Colossus phone and called Bryn. Fortunately, she answered, in spite of the hour. Remy walked away from Daniel, where he could talk to Bryn without being overheard. Daniel was too scared to even try to eavesdrop. When he finished talking to Bryn, he strode back over to Daniel.

"You're coming with me, right now." They climbed into a ranch vehicle that Daniel hadn't even known was still running. He thought this one was out of commission and turned to his brother in surprise once both doors were closed. Remy didn't even look his way and didn't offer an explanation. Daniel wasn't about to ask. It could wait.

They drove in silence, in the dark, to headquarters, where Bryn was already waiting. Once inside, Daniel was made to repeat what he discovered and what he saw to Bryn, who he was meeting for the first time. He had assumed Remy already filled her in, but maybe she had wanted to hear it directly from him, too. After Daniel finished talking, Bryn stayed silent for what seemed to Daniel like an eternity. He had no idea what to expect. Still no clue as to what was going on and why the three of them were meeting in this cold room in an abandoned and only partially standing building.

Bryn had then peppered Daniel with questions about Rebecca and the others. Questions about what the group was like at school. What did Daniel know of their families? Who else did they hang around with? She also wanted to know everything about Daniel's interaction with Rebecca the first time they met up on the mountain. He had told her everything already, but she asked again. Because Daniel was not in the same social tier as the others, he couldn't provide Bryn with a lot of in-depth information, but he did the best he could to give her as much as possible.

"We have to bring Rebecca in. She seems to be the one leading this group of kids. And we have to do it soon, before they can do any real damage," Bryn spoke to Remy.

"Agreed. Tonight?"

"Yes. We will go in the early morning hours, when everyone is sure to be asleep. And we will have to hope that we can find a way in." Bryn said.

"What will you do with Rebecca?" asked Daniel.

"Question her. Find out from her what she and her friends are up to. What happens after that depends on her responses," Bryn responded.

"You won't...hurt her, will you?"

"That depends on her responses," Bryn said again. Upon seeing Daniel's reaction, she added, "We hope not to. We really hope not to. In the end, it will be up to those higher up than the two of us."

"Bryn, I think it's time we fill Daniel in a bit, before he starts getting the wrong idea about us," Remy said, realizing how bad their cryptic conversation had to sound to Daniel's ears. He wanted Daniel to sweat a bit. He wanted him to get an idea about how serious all of this was, but now it was time to tell him.

When Remy had called Bryn, they had argued over what to do with Daniel, now that he had discovered the hidden facilities. Bryn had wanted to find a way around telling Daniel.

Remy thought that was a bad idea. He knew his brother. His brother would continue digging until he had more answers. They could not avoid telling him. Fortunately, those who made the decisions agreed with Remy. They further instructed Bryn and Remy to bring Daniel into the fold of Colossus. Their reasoning was that it was better to include him in their operations than to let him in on the secret and then just leave it at that. Once he knew about Colossus, keeping him out of the operations was more dangerous than including him. He was Remy's brother. Any other alternatives were out of the question.

****

Bryn and Remy had proceeded to fill Daniel in on Colossus and inform him of the decision to include him in the organization. There was never a doubt that Daniel would agree. Of course, he would. They also sketched out some of the most important information about BRO but left out many of the finer details they were now providing the entire group.

In return, as his first contribution to Colossus's mission, he was to first fill them in on as much as he could recall of Rebecca's house so that they could find a way in. He was instructed to accompany Remy that night to extract Rebecca from her home and bring her to headquarters. And now he sat at the table, hearing for the first time many of the details about The Reckoning and the specifics on BRO's operations.

CHAPTER 34

"Question," said Selby.

"Go ahead," Remy responded.

"A *lot* of people have died since last summer, but if we're talkin' a hive of robotic insects here, being sent out every single night, then it seems to me that even in a city the size of Montrose, most of the population would be dead already!"

"True. It seems that not all of the robots are delivering the virus every night. Some of them are part of experiments testing range and the effects of obstacles, like mountains and buildings, on the ability of the robots to find their way back to the hive," Remy explained.

"But, why are they doing all this?" asked Bendi. "What is the goal?"

"Montrose," said Bryn, "is the testing grounds for a larger plan to squash a growing restlessness across Anecor. It seems that Head Councilor Manglebee is becoming very uncomfortable with the increasing incidents of rebellious acts in defiance of Council's rules and Manglebee's Vision. They can no longer keep up with it through disappearances, so they are moving to a more drastic measure. It seems they not only want to rid Anecor of known instigators, but also of potential trouble-makers. All in one shot. Cull, or *thin,* the heard, so to speak."

"Is it really that bad?" Rebecca asked, shocked to think that there could be so much discord in the rest of the country and the people of Montrose were oblivious to it. Not only that, the people in her city were being used as test subjects for a devastating plan to kill off a large number of citizens across the country again, just to satisfy Manglebee's need to maintain power and control. It sickened her to think about. Jonathan was just a test subject to Karl and Manglebee.

"Oh, yes, it is really that bad," said Remy. "Now you know what it is we are up against, and why it's so important we act quickly, but secretively. To make matters worse, it seems Manglebee is starting to get impatient. He isn't going to want to wait much longer to implement his plan at full scale."

"How do you guys know all this?" asked Cassidi.

"You guys will learn much more about this in the days and weeks to come," Bryn reminded the group. "But Colossus has a number of operatives across the country. You will meet other members of our pod soon. We have to work covertly, and in a way that is most likely to preserve the secrecy of our organization, but we have been able to piece together bits of information over time. We are missing some of the details, but we think we are getting a good idea of the overall picture of what we are dealing with."

"I think," Bryn said, checking her phone, "we are going to need to wrap this up soon. Remy and I have to go fill in our pod leaders, who are on their way to headquarters now, and lay out a plan for what to do with the six of you to get you trained. I'm sure Rebecca will also want us out of here well before her parents might be home." Rebecca gave a small smile in agreement.

"Another quick question…" Selby said, "so when my friends Becs, Cass, and Troy here saw you and Karl in some kinda heated argument outside, why was that?"

"When Karl and I were arguing?" Bryn was confused.

"Yeah," said Rebecca, realizing she hadn't actually filled them in on the details of previous visits. "Cass, Troy, and I. I mentioned I'd made more than the one trip to BRO. The first time the three of us saw you, you had stepped outside with

Karl. You were having an argument, telling Karl he had gone too far. Then Karl went inside, and a little while later, we saw you and Remy talking outside."

"Oh, yes. That." Bryn said. "I was confronting Karl, probably overstepping the line more than I should have. I was confronting him over why they weren't testing anti-virals yet with so many people dying, and he was putting me off again. Which I had fully expected. The real purpose of the exchange, however, was to distract Karl so that Remy could gather information from a new lead. That was when we found out that Manglebee is getting impatient to act."

"So, if they aren't testing your anti-virals and they are already releasing the synthetic virus, what are they doing with the bodies they bring into BRO on stretchers?" Cassidi asked.

Remy and Bryn sat up straight in their chairs with looks of surprise. "Bodies? What bodies?" asked Bryn.

"The bodies they're bringing into the restricted area. The ones they're running tests on," Cassidi responded.

"Tests?" asked Remy, leaning so far forward over the table he was almost on top of it. "What kind of tests?"

"No clue," Rebecca said. "You guys don't know about this?"

"No," Bryn said. "We don't. Congratulations…it looks like you've just identified our new assignment. And welcome to Colossus."

The Undoing story has just begun! Rebecca's journey will continue in the second book, The Breaking, upon its release.

Hello Readers!

I am grateful to you for taking the time to read the first book in The Undoing Trilogy. I hope you enjoyed reading it and will continue to follow Rebecca's story for the next two books. If you enjoyed the book, I would greatly appreciate it if you would *leave a review on Amazon*. As a new and independent author, reviews are the best way to help others discover *The Undoing Trilogy*. Your review does not have to be long! Even a couple of sentences is helpful.

Feel free to contact me at desserae.k.shepston@gmail.com!

Thank you,

Desserae K Shepston

Gratitudes

The completion of this book would not have been possible without the support and votes of confidence I continue to receive from friends and family.

I would especially like to thank Gail, Shay, and Kelly for reading drafts of this book. Their feedback and suggestions made it a much better story. I am truly grateful.

About the Author

Desserae K Shepston is writer, traveler, and adventure seeker. She has an affinity for YA novels, especially science fiction-dystopian. In 2018, she left the stationary life and career behind for a life on the road in a 1993 RV, traveling North America with her best friend and four cats, and living her passion for travel and an outdoor life. She wrote her first book, *Travel Cats: tips for beginning an rv journey with your feline family,* after working through the kinks of RV living with cats herself. Also look for her children's book, *The Adventures of Gatsby the Travel Cat in Mesa Verde* due to be released at the end of February 2019. Desserae has lived in Chicago; Garmisch, Germany; Austin; and now, everywhere North America.

CPSIA information can be obtained
at www.ICGtesting.com
Printed in the USA
LVHW090502040319
609380LV00001B/201/P